JACK WILLIAMSON

One of the pioneers of science fiction, winner of the Hugo Award for his autobiography, WONDER'S CHILD: *My Life In Science Fiction*, Jack Williamson has been writing great fiction for over fifty years. Numbered in his *oeuvre* are such classics as *The Humanoids*, *The Legion of Space*, *Seetee Ship*, as well as some memorable collaborations with Frederik Pohl, including the *Starchild* trilogy. Throughout his career, Williamson has been noted for his scientific extrapolation. He has also written some of the classic fantasies, including *Darker Than You Think* and *Golden Blood*. His newest novel, FIRECHILD, will be published in a Bluejay edition in 1986. He lives in Portales, New Mexico.

ILENE MEYER

A relative newcomer to the field of science fiction and fantasy, Ms. Meyer has been a professional gallery artist for over ten years. Her work has been exhibited also at science fiction conventions, where it has garnered awards. She has painted SF and fantasy covers for a number of publishers in the last two years, and is currently doing illustrative work in a number of different fields. She makes her home in the Seattle, Washington area.

BLUEJAY ILLUSTRATED EDITIONS

This distinguished and carefully produced series includes science fiction and fantasy classics by some of the greats in the field, including L. Sprague de Camp, Norman Spinrad, Theodore Sturgeon, Jack Williamson among others, with original illustration by such outstanding artists as David G. Klein, Tim Kirk, Rowena Morrill, and others. All are printed on acid-free paper and bound in handsome trade paperback editions.

*Books by Jack Williamson
from Bluejay Books*

DARKER THAN YOU THINK,
Illustrated by David G. Klein

FIRECHILD (1986)

THE LEGION OF TIME, Illustrated by Ilene Meyer

WONDER'S CHILD: MY LIFE IN SCIENCE FICTION
(Autobiography)

THE LEGION
OF TIME

JACK WILLIAMSON

Illustrated by Ilene Meyer

BLUEJAY BOOKS INC.

Contents

THE LEGION OF TIME

Chapter 1

APPOINTMENT AT
THE RIVER

THE BEGINNING OF IT, FOR DENNIS LANNING—THE VERY beginning of his life—was on a hushed April evening of 1927. Then eighteen, Lanning was slender and almost delicately featured, with straw-yellow hair which usually stood on end. He usually wore a diffident smile; but his gray eyes could light with a fighting glint, and his wiry body held a quick and unsuspected strength.

In that beginning was the same fantastic contrast that ran through the whole adventure: the mingling of everyday reality with the stark Inexplicable.

Lanning, the last term, shared a Cambridge apartment with three other Harvard seniors, all a year or two older. Wilmot McLan, the mathematician, was a lean grave man, already absorbed in his work. Lao Meng Shan, proud but soft-spoken son of a mandarin of Szechwan, was eagerly drinking in the wonders of modern engineering. Good friends and swell fellows, both. But the one who stood closest to Lanning was Barry Halloran.

1

Gigantic red-haired All American tackle, Barry was first and last a fighter. Some stern bright spirit of eternal rebellion he and Lanning shared together. That spring the sky was still an exciting frontier, and they were taking flying lessons at the East Boston airport.

All three were out, however, on this drowsy Sunday evening. The house was still, and Lanning sat alone in his room, reading a thin little gray-bound book. It was Wilmot McLan's first scientific work, just published at his own expense. *Reality and Change*, he had called it, and this copy was inscribed, "To Denny, from Wil—a stitch in time."

Its mathematics was a new language to Lanning. He leaned back in his chair, with tired eyes closed, trying to form some clear picture from the mist of abstruse symbols. McLan had quoted the famous words of Minkowski: "Space in itself and time in itself sink to mere shadows, and only a kind of union of the two retains an independent existence." If time, then, were simply another extension of the universe, was tomorrow as real as yesterday? If one could leap forward—

"Denny Lanning!"

A voice had spoken his name. Dropping the book, he sat upright in the chair. He blinked and swallowed; a quick little shudder ran up and down his spine. The door was still closed, and there had been no other sound. But a woman was standing before him on the rug.

A girl . . . beautiful!

A plain white robe swept long to her feet. Her hair was a shining mahogany-red, confined in a circle of something blue and brilliant. The composure of her perfect face seemed almost stern; but, behind it, Lanning felt—agony.

Before her, in two small hands, she held an object about the size and shape of a football but shimmering with deep inner splendors, like some incredible diamond.

Her grave eyes were on Lanning. They were wide, violet. Something in their depths—a haunting dread, a piercing, hopeless longing—stabbed him with pity for her. Then amazement came back, and he stumbled to his feet.

"Hello!" he gasped. "Yes, I'm Denny Lanning. But who are you?" His glance went to the locked door behind her. "And how'd you get inside?"

A faint smile touched the white cameo of her face.

"I am Lethonee." Her voice had an unfamiliar rhythm, a lilt that was almost song. "And I am not really in your room, but in my own city, Jonbar. It is only in your mind that we meet, through this." Her eyes dropped to the immense jewel. "And only your study of time enabled me to reach you now."

Open-mouthed, Lanning was drinking in the slim clean youth of her, the glory of her hair, her calm deep loveliness that was like an inner light.

"Lethonee—" he murmured, relishing the sound. "Lethonee—"

Dream or not, she was beautiful.

A quick little smile, pleased and tender, flickered across her troubled face.

"I have come a long way to find you, Denny Lanning," she said. "I have crossed a gulf more terrible than death to beg for your help."

A queer, trembling eagerness had seized him. Incredulity struggled with a breathless hope. A throbbing ache was in his throat, so that he couldn't speak. He walked uncertainly to her, and tried to touch the slim bare arms that held the shining object. His quivering fingers found nothing but air.

"I'll help you, Lethonee," he gulped at last. "But how?"

Her silver voice sank to an awed, urgent whisper. From the startling whiteness of her face, the great violet eyes seemed to look far beyond the room.

"Because destiny has chosen you, Denny Lanning. The fate of the human race is on your shoulders. My own life is in your hand, and the doom of Jonbar."

"Eh!" Lanning muttered. "How's that?" He rubbed his forehead bewilderedly. "Where's Jonbar?"

His wondering dread increased, when the girl said:

"Look into the time crystal and I can show you Jonbar."

She lifted the huge jewel. Her eyes dropped to it. And colored rays shattered from it, blindingly. It exploded into a prismatic glare. The fire-mist slowly cleared, and he saw— Jonbar!

The loftly, graceful pylons of it would have dwarfed the skyscrapers of Manhattan. Of shimmering, silvery metal, they were set immensely far apart, among green parklands and broad, many-leveled roadways. Great white ships, teardrop-shaped, slipped through the air above them.

"That is my Jonbar, where I am," the girl said softly. "Now let me show you the city that may be—New Jonbar—lying far-off in the mists of futurity."

Bright flame veiled the city, and vanished again. And Lanning saw another more wondrous metropolis. The green hills along the horizon were the same. But the towers were taller, farther apart. They shone with clean soft colors, against the wooded parks. The city was one artistic whole; and its beauty caught his breath.

"New Jonbar!"the girl was breathing, reverently. "Its people are the *dynon*."

There were fewer ships in the air. But Lanning now saw tiny figures, clad it seemed in robes of pure bright flame, launching themselves from lofty roofs and terraces, soaring above the parks in perfect, wingless freedom.

"They fly through adaptation to the *dynat*," she whispered. "A power that makes them almost immortal. God-like! They are the perfect race to come."

Prismatic flame hid the vision. The girl lowered the crystal in her hands. Lanning stepped back. He blinked at the reading lamp, his books, the chair behind him. From that old, comforting reality, he looked back to the white wonder of the girl.

"Lethonee—" He paused to catch his breath. "Tell me, are you real?"

"As real as Jonbar is." Her voice was hushed and solemn. "You hold our destiny, to give us life or death. That is a truth already fixed in the frame of space and time."

"What—" Lanning gulped. "What can I do?"

Dread was a shadow in her eyes.

"I don't know, yet. The deed is dim in the flux of time. But you may strike for Jonbar—if you will. To win or to perish. I came to warn you of those who will seek to destroy you—and, through you, all my world."

The rhythm of her voice was almost a chant, a prophecy of evil.

"There is the dark, resistless power of the *gyrane*; and black Glarath, the priest of its horror. There is Sorainya, with her hordes of fighter slaves."

Lethonee had become almost stern. Sadness darkened her eyes, yet they flashed with unquenchable hatred.

"She is the greatest peril." Her voice lifted, like a battle-chant. "Sorainya, the woman of war. She is the evil flower of Gyronchi. And she must be destroyed."

Her voice fell, and Lethonee looked at Lanning, over the giant crystal, her white face filled with a tender and almost childish concern.

"Or else," she finished, "she will destroy you, Denny."

Lanning looked at her a long time. At last, hoarse with a sudden emotion, he said: "Whatever is going to happen, I'm willing to help—if I can. Because of you. But what—what am I to do?"

"Beware of Sorainya!" Those words were bugle notes, but then her voice dropped appealingly. "Denny, make me one promise. Promise you won't fly tomorrow."

"But I'm going to!" Lanning protested. "Max—he's the instructor—says Barry and I can solo tomorrow, if the weather's right. I couldn't miss it."

"You must," said Lethonee.

Lanning met her violet eyes. A surge of unfamiliar feeling

swept away some barrier between them. He looked into her very heart—and found it beautiful.

"I promise," he whispered. "I won't fly."

"Thank you, Denny." She smiled and touched his hand. "Now I must go."

"No!" Alarm took Lanning's breath. "I don't know half enough. Where you are, really. Or how to find you again. You can't go!"

"But I must." A shadow fell on her face. "For Sorainya could follow me here. And if she finds that the crisis turns indeed on you, she will strive to take you—or even destroy you. I know Sorainya!"

"But—" Lanning gulped. "Will I see you again?"

"Your hand is on the wheel of time," she said, "and not mine."

"Wait!" gasped Lanning. "I—"

But the fire of a million sunlit prisms had burst again from the jewel in her hands. Lanning was momentarily dazzled, blinded. And then he was alone in the room, speaking to vacant air.

Dream—or reality? The question racked him. Could she have been an actual person, come across the gulf of time from the remote possible future? Or was he crazy? Dazed, he picked up the little gray book, and reread a paragraph of Wil McLan's:

"To an external observer, gifted with four-dimensional senses, our quadraxial universe must appear complete, fixed, and forever unchanging. The sweep of time is no more than the hand of a subjective watch; it is no more than the intangible ray of consciousness, illuminating human experience. In any absolute sense, the events of yesterday and tomorrow are alike eternal, immutable as the structure of space itself."

But the haunted loveliness of Lethonee rose against the page. How did that fit with her tale of worlds that might be, striving for existence?

He flung aside the book, helped himself to a generous slug of Barry Halloran's Irish whisky, and walked blindly down through Harvard Square. It was late when at last he came in to bed, and then he slept with a dream of Lethonee.

He wanted to tell Barry, next morning; for they had been closer than brothers. But he thought the big redhead would only laugh—as he himself might have laughed if another had told him the thing. And he didn't want laughter at that dream, not even from Barry.

Half sick with a confusion of wonder and doubt, of hopeless hope for another glimpse of Lethonee and bitter dread that she had been all illusion, Lanning tried to read a textbook and found himself aimlessly walking the room.

"Buck up, kid!" Barry boomed at him. "I never thought you'd be shaky—Max says you've got the nerves of a hawk. I'm the one that should be turning green around the gills. Come out of it, and let's catch some sparrows."

Lanning stood up, uncertainly—and then the phone rang. He had made his own expenses, that year, covering university activities for a Boston paper; and this was his editor. It was an assignment that could have been evaded. But, listening, he saw the tragic eyes of Lethonee.

"Okay, Chief," he said. "On the job." He hung up and looked at Barry. "Sorry, old man. But business first. Tell Max I'll be out tomorrow. And happy landings, guy."

"Tough luck, kid."

The big tackle grinned, and crushed his hand, and ambled out.

Lanning read in his own paper, four hours later, that Barry Halloran was dead. The training plane had gone out of control, two thousand feet over Boston harbor, and plunged down into the Charles River channel. Grappling hooks had brought part of the battered wreckage up out of the mud, but the body had not been recovered.

Lanning shut his eyes against the black headlines, reeling. He was sick with a dread that was almost terror, numbed with a black regret. For Lethonee had saved his own life, he knew—but at the cost of Barry Halloran's.

Chapter 2

THE CORRIDOR OF TIME

LANNING FELT NO GRATITUDE FOR THE WARNING THAT HAD saved his life, but rather a sick regret, an aching sense of guilt for Barry's death. Yet he could feel no actual resentment toward Lethonee—the tragedy seemed a terrible proof of her reality. In her grave and troubled beauty, surely, there had been no evil.

A kind of excitement buoyed up Lanning for a few days, and made his grief endurable. There was his hope that she would come back—her memory was a haunting pain of loneliness, that would not die. Even her enigmatic warning, and his vague expectancy of unknown perils lent a certain spice to existence.

But life went on, after the funeral preached for Barry's unrecovered body, as if Lethonee had never come. Lao Meng Shan turned to China, eager to put his new science at her service. Wil McLan was off to Europe, on a fellowship in theoretical physics.

And Lanning presently embarked for Nicaragua, where American marines were straightening out the Sacasa-Chamorro fracas, on his first foreign press assignment. Barry's

8

uncle had offered him an advertising job. But a burning unrest filled him, born of the conflicts within him, of doubt and hope, wonder and grief, dread and bitter longing. He saw no way ahead, save to break old ties, to forget.

It was on the little fruit steamer, bound for Corinto, that he first saw—Sorainya! And knew, indeed, that he had not dreamed, that he would never forget, nor ever escape the strange web of destiny flung across space and time to snare him.

Velvet night had fallen on the tropical Pacific. The watch had just changed and now the decks were deserted. Lanning, the only passenger, was leaning on the foredeck rail, watching the milky phosphorescence that winged endlessly from the prow.

But his mind saw, instead, Lethonee's jewel of time, and her slim haunting form behind it. And it startled him strangely when a ringing golden voice, in pealing mockery of her own, called:

"Denny Lanning!"

His heart leaped and paused. He looked up eagerly, and hope gave way to awed wonderment. For, flying beside the rail, was a long golden shell, shaped like an immense shallow platter. Silken cushions made a couch of it, and lying amid them was a woman.

Sorainya—woman of war!

Lethonee's warning came back. For it was a warrior queen in the shell, clad in a gleaming crimson tunic of woven mail that swelled with her womanly curves. A long thin sword, in a jeweled sheath, lay beside her. She had put aside a black-plumed, crimson helmet, and thick masses of golden hair streamed down across her strong bare arms.

The white tapered fingers, scarlet-nailed, touched some control on the low rim of her strange craft, and it floated nearer the rail. Upraised on the pillows and one smooth elbow, the woman looked up at Lanning, smiling. Her eyes were long and brilliantly greenish. Across the white beauty of her face, her mocking lips were a long scarlet wound, voluptuous, and malicious.

Flower of evil—Lethonee's words again. Lanning stood gripping the rail, and a trembling weakness shook him. As if in a dream, swift, unbidden desire overcame his incredulity. He strove desperately to be its master.

"You are Sorainya?" He held his tone grave and low. "I had a warning to expect you."

She sat up suddenly amid the cushions, as if a whip had flicked her. The green eyes narrowed, and her body was tense and splendid in the gleaming mail. Her red mouth became a thin line of scorn.

"Lethonee!" She spat the name. "So that slut of Jonbar has found you?"

Lanning flushed with anger, and his fingers drew hard on the rail. He remembered the cold glint of an answering hate in the eyes of Lethonee, and her stern statement, "Sorainya must be destroyed."

"So you are angry, Denny Lanning?" Her laugh was a mocking chime. "Angry, because of a shadow? For Lethonee is but a phantom, seeking with lies and tricks to live—at the cost of other lives. Perhaps you have discovered that?"

Lanning shuddered, and wet his lips.

"It's true," he whispered. "She caused Barry's death."

The scorn had fallen like a mask from Sorainya's face. Now she tossed her splendid head, and pushed back the tumbled glory of her hair. The sea-green eyes danced an invitation, and she smiled.

"Lethonee is no more than a spectre of possibility." Her tone was a suave caress. "She is less than a single speck of dust, less than a shadow on the wall. Let's forget her, Denny Lanning! Shall we?"

Lanning gulped, and a tremor shook him.

"But I am real, Denny." Her bare arms opened, beckoning. "And I have come for you, to take you with me back to

Gyronchi. That is a mighty empire, more splendid than the pallid dream of Jonbar. And I am its mistress."

She stood up with one flowing movement, tall and regal in the scarlet mail. Her bare arms reached out, to help Lanning to the golden shell. Her cool green eyes were shining with intoxicating promise.

"Come, Denny Lanning. To rule with me in Gyronchi."

Lanning's hands gripped the rail until his knuckles cracked. His heart was pounding, and he drew a long shuddering breath.

"Why?" His voice rapped harsh and cold. "Of all men, why have you come for me."

The shell drifted closer, and Sorainya smiled.

"I have searched all space and time for you, Denny Lanning. For we are the twain of destiny. Fate has given us the keys to power. Together on the golden throne of Gyronchi, we can never fail. Come!"

Lanning caught a sobbing breath.

"All right, beautiful," he gasped. "I don't know the game. But—you're on."

He climbed upon the rail, in the starlight, and reached out his hand to take Sorainya's.

"Denny—wait!" spoke an urgent voice beside him.

Lanning drew back instinctively, and saw Lethonee. A ghostly figure in her straight white robe, she was standing by the rail, holding the great jewel of time between her hands. Her face was drawn, desperate.

"Remember, Denny!" her warning rang out. "Sorainya would destroy you."

Sorainya stood stark upright upon the shell, her tense defiant body splendid in the scarlet armor. Slitted, her greenish eyes flamed with tigerish fury. Strong teeth flashed white in a snarl of hate. She hissed an unfamiliar word, and spat at Lethonee.

Lethonee trembled, and caught a sobbing breath. Her face had drained to a deadly white, and her violet eyes were flaming. One word rang from her lips: "Go!"

But Sorainya turned to Lanning again, and a slow smile drew across the blackness of her hate. Her long bare arms opened again.

"Come with me, Denny," she whispered. "And let that lying ghost go back to her dead city of dream."

"Look, Denny!" Lethonee bit her pale lip, as if to control her wrath. "Where Sorainya would have you leap."

She pointed down at the black tropic sea. And Lanning saw there the glittering phosphorescent trail that followed a shark's swift fin. The shock of cold dread had chilled him, and he climbed stiffly back from the rail. For he had touched, or tried to touch, Sorainya's extended hand. And his fingers had found nothing at all!

Shuddering, he looked at the slim white girl by the rail. He saw the gleam of tears in her eyes, and the pain that lay burning beneath the proud composure of her face.

"Forgive me, Lethonee!" he whispered. "I am sorry—very sorry."

"You were going, Denny!" Her voice was stricken. "Going—to her."

The golden shell had floated against the rail. A warrior queen, regal, erect, Sorainya stood buckling on the golden sword. Her long green eyes flamed balefully.

"Lanning," the bugle of her voice pealed cold, "it is written on the tablets of time that we are to be enemies, or— one. And Gyronchi, defended by my fighting slaves, by Glarath and the *gyrane*, has no fear of you. But Jonbar is defenseless. Remember!"

One sturdy foot, scarlet-buskinned, touched something at the rim of the yellow shell. And instantly, like a projected image from a screen, she was gone.

Lanning turned slowly back toward Lethonee. Her face, beneath the band of blue that held her red-glinting hair, was white and stiff with tragedy.

"Please," he whispered. "Forgive me."

No smile lit her solemn face.

"Sorainya is beautiful," her voice came small and flat. "But if you ever yield to her, Denny, it is the end of Jonbar—and of me."

Lanning shook his head, dazed with a cold bewilderment. "But why?" he demanded. "I don't understand."

The wide violet eyes of Lethonee looked at him for a long time. Once her lip stiffened, quivered, as if she were about to cry. But her voice, when at last she spoke, was grave and quiet.

"I'll try to tell you, Denny." Her face was illuminated, like a shrine, by the shimmer of the jewel in her hands. "The world is a long corridor, from the beginning of existence to the end. Events are groups in a sculptured frieze that runs endlessly along the walls. And time is a lantern carried steadily through the hall, to illuminate the groups one by one. It is the light of awareness, the subjective reality of consciousness.

"Again and again the corridor branches, for it is the museum of all that is possible. The bearer of the lantern may take one turning, or another. And always, many halls that might have been illuminated with reality are left forever in the dark.

"My world of Jonbar is one such possible way. It leads through splendid halls, bright vistas that have no limit. Gyronchi is another. But it is a barren track, through narrowing, ugly passages, that comes to a dead and useless end."

The wide solemn eye of Lethonee looked at him, over the slumberous flame of the jewel. Lanning tensed and caught his breath, as if a light cold hand, from nowhere, had touched his shoulder.

"You, Denny Lanning," she went on, "are destined, for a little time, to carry the lantern. Yours is the choice of reality. Neither I nor Sorainya can come to you, bodily—unless perhaps at the moment of your death. But, through a partial mastery of time, we can each call to you, begging you to carry the lamp into our different halls. Denny—"

The silver voice caught with emotion.

"Denny, think well before you choose. For your choice will bring life to one possible world. And it will leave another in the darkness, never to be born."

A choking lump had risen in Lanning's throat. He looked at Lethonee, slim and immaculate and lovely in the jewel's clear light.

"Have no doubt—never again," he whispered huskily. "Because I love you, Lethonee. Just tell me what I must do. And tell me if I can ever come to you."

Her fine head shook, in the blue halo.

"Your life has not yet run to the moment of your choice," she said slowly. "And the event is vague and ambiguous in the mist of possibility."

Lanning tried again to touch her arm—in vain.

"Just remember me, Denny," she was breathing. "Remember what I have told you. For Sorainya still has her beauty, and Glarath the *gyrane's* power. Beware of Gyronchi. And the hour will come. Farewell."

Her eyes dropped to the jewel, and her fingers caressed its bright facets. Splintering diamond lances burst from it, and swallowed her in fire. She was gone.

Shaken with a curious weakness, suddenly aware of complete exhaustion, Lanning caught the rail. His eyes fell to the water, and he saw the glitter of the shark's black fin, still cruising after the ship.

Chapter 3

THE KEY TO GYRONCHI

HIS LIFE WAS A DUSKY CORRIDOR, AND THE PRESENT, A LAMP that he carried along it. Dennis Lanning never forgot Lethonee's figure of speech. Eagerly he looked forward to discovering her again, at some dark turning. But he walked down the hall of years, and looked in vain.

Nor could he forget Sorainya. Despite revulsion from all the ruthless evil he had sensed in her, despite Lethonee's warning, he found himself sometimes dreaming of the warrior queen in the splendor of her crimson mail. Found himself even dwelling upon the mysterious menace of Gyronchi, an eagerness mingled with his dread.

The hall he walked was a corridor of war. An old hatred of injustice set him always against the right of might. War correspondent, flying instructor, pilot, miliatry adviser, he found forlorn causes on four continents.

He fought with words when he could find no better weapons. Once, waiting for Viennese doctors to persuade an obscure African amoeba to abandon his digestive tract, he wrote a utopian novel, *The Road of Dawn,* to picture the world that ought to be.

16

Again, in the military prison of a dictator whose war preparations he had exposed, he wrote a historical autobiography in the current style among journalists, in which he tried to show that the world was nearing a decisive conflict between democratic civilization and despotic absolutism.

In all those years, he had no glimpse of Lethonee. But once, on the field with the native army in Ethiopia, he woke in his tent to hear her grave warning voice still ringing in his ears:

"Denny, get up and leave your tent."

He dressed hastily, and walked out through the camp in the thin bitter wind of dawn. The tent, a few minutes later, was struck by an Italian bomb.

Sorainya came, once.

It was a night in Madrid, the next year, where he had gone to join the Loyalist defense. He was sitting alone beside a little table in his hotel room, cleaning and loading his automatic. A queer little shudder passed over him, as if his malaria had come back from the Chaco and the Jungle War. He looked up, and saw that long shallow shell of yellow metal floating above the carpet.

Sorainya, in the same shining scarlet mail, looking as if he had seen her five minutes ago, instead of nine years, was lounging on her silken cushions. A bare arm flung back the golden wealth of her hair, and her greenish eyes smiled up at him with a taunting insolence.

"Well, Denny Lanning." Her voice was a husky, lingering drawl, and her long eyes studied him with a bold curiosity. "The ghost of Jonbar has guided you safely through the years. But has she brought you happiness?"

Lanning had grown rigid in his chair. He flushed, swallowed. The sudden white dazzle of her smile caught his breath.

"I am still the mistress of Gyronchi." Her voice was a caress. "And still the keys of fate are in our hands, if we but choose to turn them."

Her white and indolent arm indicated a space on the silken couch beside her.

"I have come again, Denny, to take you back with me to the throne of Gyronchi. I can give you half a mighty empire—myself, and all of it. What about it, Denny?"

Lanning tried to control his beath.

"Don't forget, Sorainya," he muttered. "I saw the shark."

She tossed back her head, and her hair fell like a yellow torrent across the colored cushions. And the lure of her smile set a pain to throbbing in his throat.

"The shark would have killed you, Denny. But you should know that death alone can bring you to me—and to the strong new life the *gyrane* gives. For our lives were cast far apart in the stream of time. And not all the power of the *gyrane* can lift you out of the time-stream, living—for then the whole current must be deflected. But the stream has little grasp upon a few dead pounds of clay. I can carry that to Glarath, to be returned to life."

She came, with a gliding pantherine movement, to her knees on the cushions. Both hands pushed the flowing gold of her hair behind her red-mailed shoulders. And her bare arms reached out, in wide invitation.

"Denny, will you come with me tonight?" urged the golden drawl. "The way is in your hand."

Trembling, hot with desire, Lanning looked down at his hand. The automatic had slipped in his unconscious fingers, until its muzzle was pointed at his heart. His finger was near the trigger. One little pressure—it would be so like an accident.

Her indolent voice was seductive music:

"Gyronchi is waiting for us, Denny. A world to rule—"

The white and gold and crimson of her beauty was a stabbing pain in his heart. His pulse was hammering. His finger curled around the cool steel of the trigger. But sanity

remained in one corner of his mind, and out of it spoke a voice
like the quiet voice of Lethonee:

"Remember, Denny Lanning! You carry a light for the
world to come."

Carefully, he made his quivering fingers snap on the safety,
and he laid the gun down beside him on the little table. His
voice a breathless rasp, he said:

"Try again, Sorainya!"

The green eyes glittered, and her red lips snarled with rage.

"I warned you, Denny Lanning!" All the indolence gone,
her voice crackled brittle and sharp. "Take the side of that
phantom of Jonbar, and you shall perish with her. I sought
your strength. But Gyronchi can win without it."

With a tigerish savagery, she whipped out the long golden
needle of her sword.

"When we meet again, guard yourself!"

A savage foot stamped down, and she was gone.

Those two anachronistic women set many a problem that
Lanning could not solve. If they were actual visitors from
conflicting possible worlds of futurity, he had no evidence of it
save his own tortured memory. Many a weary night, pondering
the haunting riddle, he wondered if he were going mad.

But a package that presently came to him in Spain contained
another thin little book from Wilmot McLan, now the holder
of many degrees and professor of astrophysics at a western
university. Inscribed on the flyleaf, "To Denny, from Wil—a
second stitch in time, to repair my last," the volume was
entitled: *Probability and Determination.*

One underlined introductory paragraph Lanning searched
desperately for a relevant meaning:

"The future has been held to be as real as the past, the only
directional indicator being the constant correlating entropy and
probability. But the new quantum mechanics, destroying the
absolute function of cause and effect, must likewise annihilate
that contention. There is no determination in small scale

events, and consequently the 'certainties' of the microscopic world are at best merely statistical. Probability, in the unfolding future, must be substituted for determination. The elementary particles of the old physics may be retained, in the new continuum of five dimensions. But any consideration of this hyper-space-time continuum must take note of a conflicting infinitude of possible worlds, only one of which, at the intersection of their geodesics with the advancing plane of the present, can ever claim physical reality. It is this new outlook of which we atempt a mathematical examination."

Conflicting . . . possible worlds!

Those words haunted Lanning. Here, at last, was light. Here, in his old friend, was a possible confidant: the one man who might understand, who might tell him whether Lethonee and Sorainya were miraculous visitors out of time, or— insanity.

At once he wrote McLan, outlining his story and requesting an opinion. Delayed, doubtless by the military censors, the letter at last came back from America, stamped: Removed— Left no Address. An inquiry to the university authorities informed him that McLan had resigned to undertake private research. His whereabouts were unknown.

And Lanning groped his way alone, through the dark hall of wars and years to 1937. Lao Meng Shan's cable found him at Lausanne, recuperating from the war in Spain, the splinter of a German shell still aching in his knee. He was writing another book.

Turned philosopher, he was trying to analyze the trends of the world: to pick out the influences of good and evil, the resolution of whose conflicting forces, so he believed, would either establish the new technological civilization or hurl the race back into a savage twilight.

"Denny, my old American friend," the cable ran, "humanity needs you here. Will you fly to China?"

Direct action had always been the only anodyne for

Lanning's tortured mind. And the newspapers, that day, stirred his blood with accounts of hundreds of women and children killed by unexpected air raids. Ignoring the stiffening pain in his knee, he laid aside the ancient problem of good and evil, flew to Cairo, and caught a fast steamer east.

Chapter 4

THE SHIP OF THE DEAD

WINGED DOOM WAS A WHISPER IN THE SKY. SIRENS MOANED warning of the *pei chee*—the "flying engines." Frightened Shanghai had been blacked out, but already yellow bursts of ruin and death had flared above Chapei in the north and eastward along the Whangpoo docks, where the first Japanese bombs were falling.

Limping on his game left leg, where Krupp steel still made an excellent barometer of impending weather, Lanning stumbled across the Lunghwa field, south of the sprawling city, to the battered antique of a plane soaring in the line. The cool of midnight cleared the sleep from his head, and he shuddered to the drumming in the sky.

Lao Meng Shan, now his gunner, was already beside the machine, dolefully shaking his watch. Solemnly, in his careful English, he shouted above the roaring motors:

"Our commanders are too confident. My watch stopped when the first bomb struck. That is a very bad omen."

Lanning never laughed at superstition—few fliers do. But his lean face smiled in the darkness.

"Once, Shan," he shouted in reply, "an ancient warrior

named Joshua stopped the sun until his battle was won. Maybe that's the omen. Let's go."

Adjusting his helmet, the Chinese shrugged.

"I think it means that we shall not come down alive. If it is written, however, that we must die for China—"

He clambered deliberately into the rear cockpit.

Lanning tried the controls, signaled the ground crew, and gunned the motor. The time-proven machine lifted toward the thrumming in the sky. The fact that most of the defending aircraft had been bombed into the ground on the day before, he thought grimly, was a more conclusive omen than the watch.

Darkness was a blanket on the city, northward, hiding cowering millions. Troop lorries and fire trucks shrieked through the streets. Anti-aircraft batteries were hammering vainly. Probing searchlights flared against the white puffs of exploding shells, uselessly seeking the raiders.

Spiraling for altitude, Lanning narrowed gray eyes to search a thin cloud-wisp above. He winced to a yellow flare beneath. For his mind saw the toppling wreckage of a splendid modern city ruined, and heard shrieks and groans and wailing cries for aid. He could amost smell the sharp odor of searing human flesh. His thin body tensed, and he fired a burst to warm the guns.

They were level with the cloud when it burned white, abruptly, in the glare of a searchlight. A dark bomber was slipping out of it, swaying between the gray mushrooms of shells. Lanning tipped the ancient plane into a power dive. Shan waved cheerfully. Their machine guns clattered. The bomber swerved, and defending guns flickered red. But Lanning held his sights on it, grimly. Black smoke erupted from it suddenly, and it toppled earthward.

One . . .

He was pulling up the battered ship, gingerly, when a roving searchlight caught and held them. Black, ominous holes peppered the wings. Glass shattered from the instruments before him. A sudden numbness paralyzed his shoulder.

The betraying light went on. But gasoline reeked in his nostrils, and a quick banner of yellow flame rippled backward. Twisting in the cockpit, he saw behind them the second enemy, diving out of the cloud, still firing.

And he saw the dark blood that stained Shan's drawn face. They were done for. But Shan grinned stiffly, raised a crimson hand to gesture. Lanning flung the creaking ship through a reckless Immelmann turn. The attacker was caught dead ahead.

A red sledge of agony smashed all feeling from Lanning's right leg. But he held straight for the other ship, guns hammering. It dived. With flaming gasoline a roaring curtain beside him, Lanning clung grimly to its tail. The tiny puppets of its crew jerked and slumped. Then it, too, began to burn.

Two . . .

But an explosion buffeted Lanning's head. Metal fragments seared past. Hot oil spattered his seared face. The motor stopped, and a new torturing tongue of yellow licked back.

Strangling, Lanning sideslipped, so that the wind stream would carry away the heat and suffocating fumes. He looked back at Shan. The crimson face of the little Oriental was now a dreadful mask. With a queer, solemn little grin, he held up something in a dripping hand—his watch.

A cold shudder went down Lanning's spine. He had never laughed at superstition. And now this evidence that human intuition could perceive the future seemed as shocking, suddenly, as the close approach of death. A stark incredulity had frozen Shan's grin, and he pointed stiffly. Lanning's eyes followed the crimson-streaming arm. And a cold hand stopped his heart. For something was flashing down beside them.

A queer-looking ship—or the dim gray ghost of a ship. It was wingless, flat-decked—like no ship the sky had ever seen. Its slim hull was like a submarine's, except that its ends were two massive disks of metal, which now shone greenishly.

A singular crew lined the rail, along the open deck. At first they seemed spectral and incredible as the ship. Several were strange in odd trim tunics of silver-gray and green. But there were a few in familiar military uniforms: a French colonel, an Austrian lieutenant, a tall lank captain of the Royal Air Force. Lanning's mouth fell open, and a sudden agony of joy wrenched his sick body.

For he saw Barry Halloran!

Unchanged since that fatal April day of ten years ago, even wearing the same baggy cords and football sweater, the gigantic tackle towered above the rest. He saw Lanning, and grinned, and waved an eager greeting.

The ghostly craft swept closer, dropping beside the burning plane. Suddenly, somehow, it turned more real. Lanning's pain was drowned in wonderment, and he ceased to breathe. He saw a thin white-haired man—a queer familiar figure—busy beneath the small crystal dome that capped a round metal turret, amidships. A tube like the muzzle of a crystal gun thrust out of the turret. A broad, blinding yellow ray funneled from it, caught the plane, drew.

Lanning felt a momentary wrenching pull. The plane and his body resisted that surge of mysterious force. Red mighty hands of agony twisted his hurt body. Then something yielded. And the ship became completely real, close beside the flaming plane.

Agony wrapped Lanning again, as his fingers slipped useless from the stick. He coughed and strangled, slipping down into a sea of suffocating darkness. Searing torture consumed him. Then he was being drawn over the rail of the stranger, out of that hurtling furnace.

Ghost ship no longer, it was still incredible. Quick, tender hands were laying them on stretchers. But Lanning was staring up at big, red-headed Barry Halloran, magically unchanged by ten years of time.

"Sure, old man, it's me!" boomed the once familiar voice. "Just take things easy. These guys will fix you up as good as new—or better. And then we'll have a talk. Guess I'm way behind the times."

A phantasmal ship, manned with a crew of the dead. Lanning had not been superstitious; not even, in the conventional sense, religious. His faith had been a belief in the high destiny of man. He had expected death to blot him out, individually; the race alone was eternal. This Stygian craft ship was, therefore, utterly unexpected—but it looked decidedly interesting.

"Barry!" he whispered. "Glad—see you—"

A wave of shadow dimmed his eyes. Blood was welling from his shoulder, hot and sticky against his body. A dull throbbing came from his shattered leg. Dimly, he knew that the men in gray and green were picking up the stretcher. But his awareness flickered out.

Chapter 5

THE SHATTERED MAN

WHEN DENNIS LANNING BEGAN TO BE FULLY CONSCIOUS again, it seemed that he had always been in that small, green-walled room. His old restless, rootless life seemed dream-like, somehow remote beyond reality—all save somehow the visitations of Lethonee and Sorainya.

Dimly he remembered an operating room: blinding lights; bustling men in white masks; the glitter and clink of surgical instruments; Barry Halloran standing by with a grin of encouragement; the first whiff of some strange anaesthetic.

Shan was lying in the opposite bed, quietly asleep. And Lanning, in some forgotten interval, had met the two others in the ward. They were Silvano Cresto, Spanish ace shot down in the Moroccan war; and Willy Rand, U.S.N. missing when the ill-fated airship *Akron* was destroyed at sea. The latter was now propped up on his pillows, inhaling through a cigarette. He grinned.

"Smoke?"

"Thanks." Lanning caught the tossed white cylinder, in spite of a dull twinge from his bandaged shoulder. He asked, "What's up?"

Willie Rand exhaled white vapor. "Dunno."

"What is this—ship? Where're we going?"

"Her name's the *Chronion*." Rand blew a great silver ring. "Cap'n Wil McLan. We're bound, they say, for a place called Jonbar—wherever that is!"

Wonder stiffened Lanning. Wil McLan! His old roommate, who had been the student of time. Jonbar! Lethonee's city, that she had showed him, far-off in some dim futurity.

"But why?" he gasped. "I don't understand!"

"Nor me. All I know, messmate, I turned loose when the wreckage of the *Akron* was rolling over on me, and tried to dive clear. Something smashed into me, and I woke up on this bed. Maybe a week ago—"

"A week!" Lanning stared. "But the *Akron*—that was back in 'thirty-three!"

Rand lit another cigarette from the first.

"Time don't make no difference here. The last man on your bed was the Austrian, Erick von Arneth. He came from the Isonzo front, in 1915. The one in the Chink's bed was the Frenchman, Jean Querard. He was blown up in 1940, fighting to save Paris."

"Forty!" Lanning whispered softly. Was tomorrow, then, already real? Lethonee—and Sorainya!

A brisk man in gray and green hastened into the ward, gently removed the cigarettes and replaced them with odd-looking thermometers. Lanning took the instrument out of his mouth.

"Where's Barry?" he demanded. "I want to see Barry Halloran. And Wil McLan!"

"Not now, sir." The rhythmic accent was curiously familiar—it was like Lethonee's! "It's time for your last IV. You'll be able to get up when you wake. Now just lie back, sir, and give me your arm."

He put back the thermometer. Another man rolled in a wheeled instrument table. Deft hands bared and swabbed

Lanning's arm. He felt the sting of a hypodermic. And quiet sleep came over him.

When at last he woke, it was to a new, delicious sense of health and fitness. The bandages were gone. His shoulder, his shattered leg, felt well and whole again. Even the German steel no longer ached in his knee.

Shan, he saw, was gone from the opposite bed. In it lay a big man, swathed in bandages, regarding him with dark, stolid Slavic eyes. A silent orderly came in, thrust a dozen little glowing needles into the Russian's bandages, and laid Lanning's old uniform, cleaned and neatly repaired, beside his bed.

"Boris Barinin," the orderly informed him. "Soviet rocket-flyer. We picked him up near the pole in 'forty-seven. Smashed, starved, frozen. Ripe for us. You may go, sir. Captain McLan will see you."

Lanning put on the uniform, elated with his new sense of health, and eagerly climbed to the deck of the *Chronion*. It was seventy feet long, between the polished faces of the great metal disks, and broken only with the turret amidships. Some mechanism throbbed softly below.

The ship must be moving. But where?

Looking about for a glimpse of the sun or any landmark, Lanning could see only a curiously flickering blue haze. He went to peer down over the rail. Still there was nothing. The *Chronion* hung in a featureless blue chasm.

The danacing shimmer in that azure mist was oddly disturbing. Sometimes, he thought, he could almost see the outline of some far mountain, the glint of waves, the shapes of trees or buildings—incongruous impressions, queerly flat, two-dimensional, piled one upon another. It was like a movie screen, he thought, upon which the frames were being thrown a thousand times too fast, so that the projected image became a dancing blur.

"Denny, old man!"

It was a glad shout, and Barry Halloran came to him with an

eager step. Lanning gripped his hand, seized his big shoulder. It was good to feel his hard muscles, to see this reckless freckled grin.

"You're looking fit, Barry. Not a day older!"

The blue eyes were wide with awe.

"Funny business, Denny. It's ten days since they picked me up, trying to swim away from that smashed crate in the Charles, with both legs broken. But I gather you've lived ten years!"

"What's ahead of us, Barry?" Lanning asked huskily. "What's it all about?"

The big tackle scratched the unkempt tangle of his red hair.

"Dunno, Denny. Wil has promised us some kind of a scrap to save this place they call Jonbar. But what the odds are, or who we're going to fight, or how come—I don't know."

"I'm going to find out," Lanning told him. "Where's Wil McLan?"

"On his bridge. I'll show you the way."

They met four men in the gray and green, just coming on the deck, carrying two rolled stretchers. Following them was the little group of fighting men in their various uniforms. Lao Meng Shan grinned happily to see Lanning, and introduced the others.

The Spaniard, Cresto. Willie Rand. The lank British flyer, Courtney-Pharr. Hard-faced Erich von Arneth. Dapper little Jean Querard. And Emil Schorn, a duel-scarred, herculean Prussian, who had been taken from a burning Zeppelin in 1917.

"Where we go?" Cresto shrugged, white teeth flashing through his dark brown grin. "*Quien sabe?* Anyhow, *amigos*, this is better than hell! *Verdad?*" He laughed.

"We are fighting men," rumbled Emil Schorn, grimly smiling. "We go to fight. *Ach*, that is enough."

"Quite a gang, eh?" Barry Halloran led Lanning on, to a small metal door in the turret. Inside, another man in gray and green waited alertly behind a bulky thing like a cannon with a barrel of glass. "You'll find Wil up under the dome."

Lanning climbed metal steps. Standing behind a bright wheel, under the flawless shell of crystal, he came upon a slight, strange little man—or the shattered wreck of a man. His breath sucked in, to the shock of sympathetic pain. For the stranger was hideous with the manifold print of unspeakable agony.

The hands—restlessly fumbling with an odd little tube of bright-worn silver that hung by a thin chain about his neck— were yellow, bloodless claws, trembling, twisted with pain. His whole thin body was grotesquely stooped and gnarled, as if every bone had been broken on some torture wheel.

But it was the haggard, livid face, crosshatched with a white net of ridged scars, that chilled Lanning with its horror. Beneath a tangled abundance of loose white hair, it was a stiff, pain-graven mask. Dark, deep-sunken, the eyes were somber wells of agony—and hate.

Strangely, those dreadful orbs lit with recognition.

"Denny!" It was an eager whisper, but strangely dry, voiceless.

The little man limped quickly to meet him, thrust out a trembling hand that was thin and twisted and broken, hideous with scars. His breath was a swift, whistling gasping. Lanning tried to put down the puzzled dread that shook him. He took that frail dry claw of a hand, and tried to smile.

"Wil?" he whispered. "You are Wil McLan?"

He choked back the other, fearful question: *What has happened to you, Wil?*

"Yes, Denny," hissed that voiceless voice. "But I've lived forty years more than you have—ten of them in Sorainya's torture vaults."

Lanning started to that name. And the old man stiffened as he spoke it, with hate glaring again in his hollow eyes—the unquenchable hate, Lanning thought, that must have kept his shattered body alive.

"I'm old, Denny," the dry rasping ran on. "I was fifty-three when the *Chronion* was launched at last on the time stream, in 1960. The ten years in Gyronchi—" The seamed face went white, the whisper sank. "They were a thousand!

"The last four years, in Jonbar, I've been preparing for our campaign." The shattered body came erect with a tense and desperate energy. "Old!" he rasped again. "But not too old to best Gyronchi!"

A sudden eager hope had risen in Lanning, above all his wonder and dread.

"Jonbar?" he whispered. "Then—then have you seen a girl named Lethonee?"

Desperately, he searched that scarred and tortured face. A painful pulse was throbbing in his throat. The tension of his hope was agony. Was it possible—possible that the "gulf more terrible than death" could now be crossed?

The broken man nodded, slowly. The stern strength of hate seemed to ebb out of him, and the bleak grimness of his face was lit with a stiff little smile.

"Yes, Denny," his whisper came softly. "Indeed I know Lethonee. It is she who set me free from the dungeons of Sorainya. It is for her, and her whole world, that we must fight. Or Gyronchi will—erase them."

Lanning caught his breath. Trembling, his fingers touched Wil McLan's twisted shoulder.

"Tell me, Wil," he begged. "This is all a riddle—a crazy, horrible riddle! Where is Jonbar? Can I ever really reach Lethonee? And, Sorainya—" Dread choked him. "What did she do to you?"

"I'll tell you, Denny—presently."

McLan's hollow eyes flashed to the knobs and levers and complicated dials of an instrument board. Moving with a swift precision that amazed Lanning, his gnarled fingers touched the knobs and levers, spun a polished wheel. He whispered some order into a tube, peered ahead through the crystal dome. An alert, surprising strength moved his shattered frame.

"Presently," his hoarse whisper came aside to Lanning. "As soon as this task is done. Watch, if you like."

Standing wonderingly behind him, Lanning stared out through the crystalline curve of the dome. The blue, enveloping haze flickered more violently. Bent over a creeping dial, McLan tapped a key. And the blue was gone.

The *Chronion* was flying low, over a gray, wave-tossed sea. It was late on a gloomy afternoon, and thick mists veiled the horizon. The little craft shuddered, abruptly, to the crash of mighty guns.

Lanning looked questioningly at Wil McLan. A twisted arm pointed, silently. And Lanning saw the long gray shapes of battle cruisers loom suddenly out of the haze, rocking as they erupted smoke and flame.

McLan tapped the keyboard beyond the wheel, and the *Chronion* slipped forward again. The turret revolved beneath them, and the crystal gun thrust out. Below, the stretcher crews moved alertly to the rail.

Peering through the fog of battle at the reeling ships, Lanning distinguished the Union Jack, and then, on another vessel, the German imperial standard. Suddenly, breathless with incredulous awe, he fitted this chaotic scene into what he knew of naval history.

"The *Defense* and the *Warrior!*" he gasped. "Attacking the *Weisbaden!* Is this—Jutland?"

Wil McLan glanced down at the dial.

"Yes. This is May 31, 1916. We await the sinking of the *Defense*."

Through the haze of acrid smoke, the *Chronion* slipped nearer the attacking British vessels. Suddenly, then, the German cruiser fleet loomed out of the mist, seeking with a hurricane of fire to cover the stricken *Weisbaden*. Two terrific salvoes rocked the doomed flagship *Defense*, and it was lost in a sheet of flame.

The intermingled battle cruisers of both fleets were still plunging through the clouds of battle, belching smoke and death, as Wil McLan brought the *Chronion* down where the *Defense* had vanished. Shattered wreckage littered the sea, rushing into a great whirlpool where the flagship had sunk.

A long helix burned incandescent in the crystal gun, and a broad yellow ray poured out into the drifting smoke. His sweater stripped off, Barry Halloran jumped overboard, carrying a rope. He was dragged back, through the ray, towing a limp survivor. Dripping blood and brine, the rescued sailor was laid on a stretcher, rushed below.

Courtney-Pharr was poised to dive, when the steel prow of the disabled *Warspite* plunged suddenly out of the blinding smoke. He stumbled fearfully back. Lanning caught his breath. It had run them down!

But Wil McLan tapped a key, spun the shining wheel. Green radiance lit the great terminal disks. And the battling fleets were swept away into blue flickering twilight. The broken old man sighed with weary relief, and rubbed tiny beads of sweat from his scarred forehead.

"Well, Denny," he whispered. "One more man to fight for Jonbar."

"Now!" demanded Lanning, breathless. "Can you explain?"

Chapter 6

THE WINDOW INTO TIME

LEANING AGAINST THE INSTRUMENT PANEL, WIL MCLAN pushed back the snow-white shock of his hair. Then, as he still paused, his twisted fingers began tracing the white scars that seamed his face.

"Please forgive my voice, Denny," his hoarse whisper came at last. "But once in the dungeon, when I was nearly dead with thirst and begging for anything to drink, Sorainya had molten metal poured down my throat. Not even Lethonee's doctors can grow new vocal cords. Sorainya'll pay for that!"

Hate had flared in the sunken eyes again, and drawn the gnarled body taut. The old man tried to compose himself. He unclenched his hands, and his twisted face tried to smile, and he whispered deliberately:

"Time was always a challenge to me. When we lived in a simple continuum of four dimensions, with time the fourth, its conquest appeared deceptively simple—through some application, perhaps, of the classical Newtonian dynamics.

"But Max Planck came along with the quantum theory, de Broglie and Schroedinger with their wave mechanics, Heisen-

36

berg with his matrix mechanics. Every new discovery seemed
to complicate the structure of the universe—and the problem
of time.

"With the substitution of waves of probability for concrete
particles, the world lines of objects are no longer the fixed and
simple paths they once were. Geodesics have an infinite
proliferation of possible branches, at the whim of subatomic
indeterminism.

"Still, of course, in large masses, the statistical results of
the new physics are not much different from those given by the
classical laws. But there is a fundamental difference. The
apparent reality of the universe is the same—but it rests upon a
quicksand of possible change.

"Certainty is abolished. Let a man stand on a concrete floor.
It is no longer certain that he will not fall through it. For he is
sustained only by the continual reaction of atomic forces, and
they are governed by probability alone.

"It is merely a very excellent statistical probability that
keeps the man from radiating heat until his body is frozen
solid, or absorbing it until he bursts into flame, or flying
upward into space in defiance of Newtonian gravitation, or
dissolving into a cloud of molecular particles.

"Mere probability is all we have left. And my first actual
invention was a geodesic tracer, designed for probability
analysis. It was a semi-mathematical instrument, essentially a
refinement of the old harmonic analyzer. Tracing the possible
world lines of material particles through time, it opened a
window to futurity."

The hoarse whisper paused, and old Wil McLan limped to
the side of the dome. His scarred trembling hands lifted a
black velvet cover from a rectangular block of some clear
crystal mounted on the top of a metal cabinet.

"Here is the chronoscope," he said. "A sort of window into
time. It creates special fields, that bend radiation into the time-
axis. We get a stereoscopic image in the crystal screen—

there's a selective fluorescence to the beat frequencies projected from below."

The old man snapped a switch, manipulated dials at the end of the crystal block. It lit with a cloudy green. The green cleared, and a low cry escaped Lanning's lips. Within the crystal, microscopically clear, he saw a new world in miniature.

A broad silver river cut a fertile green plain dotted with villages. Beyond the river rose two hills. One was crowned with a tremendous citadel. Its mighty walls gleamed like the strange red metal of Sorainya's mail. Above the frowning towers were flowing banners of yellow and crimson and black. A wide gate opened, as he watched, in the foot of the hill. An armored troop poured out.

"Watch the marchers," rasped McLan.

Lanning bent closer to the crystal block. It seemed suddenly that he was looking through a window, into an actual world. He found the soldiers again, and uttered a muffled cry.

"They aren't men!" he gasped. "They're—insects!"

"Half ant," whispered the shattered man. "Half human. Sorainya's biologists have made some diabolical experiments. Those monsters are her warriors, bred to terrorize her slaves. That's her castle, where I was jailed. But look at the other hill."

Lanning found it, topped with a temple of ebon black. The building was vast, but squat and low, faced with endless colonnades of thick square columns. From the center of it rose a beam of *blackness*, of darkness thick and tangible, that widened into the sky like the angry funnel of some unimaginable tornado.

"The temple of the *gyrane*," husked Wil McLan, "where Glarath rules." He was adjusting the dials again. "But watch!"

A village of flimsy huts swam closer. The marching column of gigantic anthropoid ants was swiftly surrounding it, driving the villagers—a fair-skinned sturdy-looking folk, although ragged and starved—before them from the fields.

"This cruel thing happened while I was in prison," the old man rasped. "The offense of the people was that they had not paid their taxes to Sorainya and their tithes to the *gyrane*. The reason they had no grain to pay them, is that Sorainya and her lords, hunting a convict for sport, had trampled and destroyed the fields."

Armed with heavy golden axes and short thick guns of crimson metal, as well as their own frightful mandibles, the six-limbed fighters made a monstrous ring about the frightened village. And now an armored vehicle came lumbering down from the red citadel, and through the line of giants. A hot white beam flickered out of it, and miserable buildings exploded into flame. The wind carried a wall of fire across the village.

An entirely human figure, in black-plumed scarlet armor, sprang from the tank to join the great black half-human ants. A thin yellow sword played swiftly, cutting down men and women and children as they fled from the flames, until the slaughter was done. Then the human figure turned back from the new desolation, flung up the crimsoned sword in triumph, and slipped off the helmet. A flood of yellow hair fell down across the scarlet mail. Lanning's breath sucked in, and a bright pain stabbed his heart.

"Why, that—" he gasped. "That's Sorainya!"

"Sorainya," whispered Wil McLan. "The lovely queen of Gyronchi."

He snapped a switch, and Sorainya dissolved, with her black warriors, into the pellucid transparency of the crystal block. His hollow eyes lifted slowly to Lanning, and in them was his slumberous hate. His gnarled hands knotted and relaxed, and lifted once more to fondle the little worn bright cylinder of silver that hung from him throat.

"It happened," the hoarse voiceless gasp went on, "that Gyronchi was the first future world, out of those possible, that the chronoscope revealed. Happened that I found Sorainya, splendid in her armor, fencing with one of her human ants.

"You can see that she is—well, attractive. At first the range of the instrument was limited to her youth, where scenes of such barbarity are less frequent. Remember, Denny, I was thirty years younger when I first saw her back in 1945. Her glorious beauty, the military pomp of her empire—I was swept away.

"Neglecting all the other possible worlds, I followed her, for months—years. I didn't know, then, all the harm the temporal searchbeam was doing." His white head bowed; for a moment he was speechless. "But no process whatever can reveal the state of an electron without changing that state. The quanta of my scanning ray were absorbed by the atoms that refracted them. The result was an increase in the probability factor of Gyronchi—that is the root of all the tragedy."

The scarred face made a grimace of pain.

"The blame is mine. For, before I was aware of it, the absorption had cut down the probability of all other possible worlds, so that Gyronchi was the only one the limited power of my instrument could reach. That blinded me to the crime that I was doing.

"But I'm afraid you can't understand my passion for Sorainya."

Lanning's hoarse and breathless whisper was an echo of his own: "I can."

The sunken eyes flamed again, and McLan fondled the silver tube.

"I watched her, with the chronoscope," the rasping words ran. "Sometimes I was driven to despair by her remoteness in time and probability—and sometimes to desperate effort. For I had resolved to conquer time, and join her in Gyronchi.

"In 1952, after seven years of effort, I was able to communicate. By increasing the power and focal definition of the temporal radiation, I was able to project a speaking image of myself to Sorainya's fortress."

Agony stiffened McLan's scarred face. His lean jaw set. His breath came in rasping gusts, and it was half a minute before he could speak again.

"And so I made suit to Sorainya. At first she seemed puzzled and alarmed. But, after I had made several bodiless visits to her apartments, her attitude changed suddenly—perhaps she had got advice from Glarath."

His clenched hands cracked.

"She smiled," the old man rasped. "She welcomed me and asked me to return. And she began to ask about my discoveries—saying that perhaps the priests of the *gyrane*, being themselves able scientists, could solve my remaining problems. If I could come to Gyronchi, she promised, I might share her throne."

Lanning bit his lip and caught a gasping breath. Memory of Sorainya's visits mocked him. But he did not interrupt.

"A mistrust of the priests, fortunately," McLan went on, "kept me from divulging very much. But Sorainya's encouragements redoubled my efforts. There is a terrific resistance to the displacement of any body in time. For the geodesics are anchored in the future, as well as in the past. The removal of a living person, which might warp all futurity, is impossible. And even to dislodge inert matter requires tremendous power.

"Nothing less than atomic energy, I soon perceived, could even begin to overcome the resistance. I set out, therefore, with the searching ray of the chronoscope, to study the atomic science of the future. But there I met a curious difficulty.

"For the instrument, which, after all, can only trace out probabilities, sometimes queerly blurred the fine detail of script or printing. Lōs Alamos and the Kremlin were equally open to the searching beam. I studied the works of many future scientists—of John Barr and Ivor Gyros and many more. But essential words always faded.

"There is a law of sequence and progression, I found at last, operating along a fifth rather than the temporal dimension, which imposes inexorable limits. It is that progression which actually creates reality out of possibility. And it is that higher law which prohibits all the trite absurdities met with in the old speculation about travel in time, such as the adventurer in time who returns to kill himself. The familiar logic of cause and effect is not abolished, but simply advanced to a higher dimension.

"With the search beam, I was able to look through the curtains of military secrecy. I studied uranium and hydrogen bombs, and found them useless to me. The first crude atomic heat engines, that ran on fission energy, were no better.

"It was only through independent research into atomic probability that I learned how to cause and control the fusion of ordinary hydrogen into heavier elements. I built the first hydrogen converter in 1958. It developed eight thousand horsepower, and I could carry it in one hand. But listen!"

He paused, to let Lanning hear the soft thrumming that vibrated through the deck. A weary triumph lit his emaciated features.

"The power of three hundred Niagaras!" he whispered. "From only a spoonful of water. Energy enough to break the wall of time! And I found a lever—the very absorption of the temporal ray, that had troubled me so much, is due to a resisting field, against which our drive reacts. For two years I worked desperately on the *Chronion*. Designed only for travel in time—not for a fighting machine—it was finished in June, 1960.

"At once, from my lonely laboratory in the Colorado Rockies, I set out for Gyronchi." The rasping whisper turned raw with bitterness. "I was a fool. I hoped to reach Sorainya and share her diamond throne."

A spasm of agony racked the white, tortured face.

Chapter 7

COMMANDER OF THE LEGION

THE RASPING WHISPER PAUSED. OLD WIL MCLAN LIMPED swiftly about the dome, reading dials and gauges. His gnarled scarred hands deftly set controls, and moved the shining wheel. Aware of the soft steady thrum of the converter beneath, Lanning realized that the *Chronion* was moving again, through the blue flickering chasm. Through time?

"I went alone," Wil McLan looked back to him, with hollow, haunted eyes. "For the *Chronion*, with all her millions of horsepower, could not have drawn a crew of sound men from their places in time. Even alone, I had difficulty. An overloaded field coil burned out. The laboratory caught fire, and I was badly injured. The very accident, however, so weakened my future geodesics that the time-drive could pull me out. At the very instant the burning building collapsed, we broke free into the time stream."

The dark, smouldering eyes stared away into the shimmering abyss beyond the crystal dome.

"You have seen Gyronchi, in the chronoscope." The old man shuddered. "And one look at my body can tell you

43

enough of what reception I had from Sorainya, when at last I came to her red citadel."

The lean, white-wealed face went hard again with agony and hate. Great tears burst suddenly from the sunken eyes. The broken, bloodless claws of hands came up again, unconsciously, to the bright silver tube. Lanning looked quickly away, until McLan went on:

"Excuse my self-pity, Denny. And I shall spare you the humiliating details of Sorainya's treachery. The instant she had lured me off the ship, her monsters seized me. She mocked me for daring to desire the queen of Gyronchi, and offered me my life for the secrets of the time ship.

"When I wouldn't talk, she threw me into her dungeons, and turned the *Chronion* over to the priests of the *gyrane*." The whisper had become a thin, dry sobbing. "For ten years, in her torture vaults, Sorainya tried to extract my secrets, while her priests studied the ship."

The sobbing ceased. The dreadful eyes went shut. The seamed, livid face of Wil McLan, terrible with its web of white scars, became a mask of death. His twisted body quivered, and his breath was a hurried gasping. Lanning looked away again, until at last the old man whispered:

"It was Lethonee who set me free; I think you know her."

A little tremor of eagerness and dread ran over Dennis Lanning. He tried to speak, made only a little gulping sound, and waited silently.

"She came to me in Sorainya's dungeons," said Wil McLan. "White and beautiful, holding her time crystal—that's another geodesic tracer, somewhat like my chronoscope.

"Lethonee forgave all the harm my experiments had done Jonbar. She planned my escape. She searched time for the hour when the disposition of the guarding giants would make it possible. She examined the locks, and brought me measurements, for the keys, which I carved, there in the cell, from the bones of a previous occupant.

"When the chosen night came, she guided me out of the

dungeons, through the quarters of Sorainya's sleeping soldiers—the queen had them roasted alive when she found that I
was gone. Lethonee picked out a safe way for me down the
cliff, and across Gyronchi to the black temple.

"Glarath and his priests had taken the *Chronion* there.
Apparently they had dismantled and studied the drive. Perhaps
they had not understood it completely, however, for they had
not ventured on any time trips of their own. But with what they
learned, and power from the *gyrane*, they had made a golden
shell——"

Lanning caught his breath.

"I've seen that!" he gasped. "Carrying Sorainya!"

"Her projected image," said Wil McLan. "But Lethonee
guided me to the temple," he resumed his whispered narrative. "The alarm spread. The fighting things roused the
priests. With seconds to spare, I got aboard the *Chronion*,
started the converters, and escaped into time. I returned to the
early twentieth century. And then at last, guided by Lethonee
down the fainter geodesics of her possible world, I came to
Jonbar."

"Jonbar—" Lanning interrupted again, with a quick gesture
at the crystal block of the chronoscope. "Can we see Jonbar,
in that? And—Lethonee?"

Very gravely, Wil McLan shook his white, haggard head.

"Presently, we shall try," he whispered. "But the probability factor of Jonbar has become so small that I can reach it only
with the utmost power of the scanning beam, and then the
images are very poor. For Jonbar is at the brink of doom."

His broken fingers touched the thin white cylinder that hung
from his throat.

"But there is still one chance." A stern light flashed in his
hollowed eyes. "Jonbar hasn't given up. It was Lethonee's
father, an archeologist digging in the Rockies where my
laboratory used to be, who found there the charred books and
age-rusted mechanisms from which he rediscovered the secret
of time.

"He made the time crystal. With it, Lethonee soon discovered the menace born of my unwitting tampering with probability. And she brought me to Jonbar to aid the defence. That is why I have been gathering up you and your men, Denny."

Lanning was staring at him, frowning.

"I don't understand," he muttered. "What can we do?"

"These two possible worlds, each armed with the secret of time, are fighting for survival." A fierce glint burned in the old man's eyes. "Either Jonbar or Gyronchi—either Lethonee or Sorainya—may exist. But not both. The battle is on, all along the front of time. The outcome will be fixed by that higher progression, in the fifth dimension."

"But you can see the future," broke in Lanning. "Can't you tell?"

"The chronoscope reveals no certainties," said McLan. "Only probabilities—which it changes even as it reveals them." His white head shook. "I know, though, that the balance of probability is far in favor of Sorainya."

Desperately, Lanning had clutched at his thin shoulder.

"But we can help?" he demanded. "What is our part?"

"No direct geodesics link Jonbar and Gyronchi," explained McLan. "Therefore they have no common reality. They are contradictory. They can explore each other's trains of probability. But there can be no physical contact, because the existence of each is a denial of the other. Their forces, therefore, can never come directly to grips.

"Our contemporary world, however, joined by direct geodesics with all possible futurities, has a common existence with both Lethonee and Sorainya. That's how you get into the picture, Denny."

"Huh?" Lanning leaned forward desperately. "They both talked of destiny. You can tell me what they meant?"

The blue haunted eyes looked at him steadily, from beneath that startling shock of snowy hair.

"You are in the key position, Denny," breathed McLan.

"Fate has made you the champion of Jonbar. Your triumph alone can save it. If you fail, it is lost."

"And that's why they came to me?"

"Sorainya has sought to cause your death." The old man nodded. "To carry you to Gyronchi, where your aid would insure her victory. And Lethonee took it upon herself to watch over you, until the moment we could pull you aboard the *Chronion*."

"Death . . ." Lanning whispered the echo. "Then we are—dead?"

"I came back to find you and a band of your contemporaries, to serve Jonbar. Since it is impossible to draw a sound, living man from his place in time—to do so might wrap the whole continuum—we had to wait until the moment when each of you was actually dead, to draw you aboard through the temporal field. Jonbar has provided a corps of surgeons, who were able to revive you immediately, with *dynat*."

"*Dynat?*" Lanning caught at the term. "I heard Lethonee use that word, and the doctors. What does it mean?"

"It is the vital scientific power upon which the whole civilization of Jonbar is based," said McLan. "The slow evolutionary adaptation to the use of its illimitable power is what will give birth to the *dynon*, the perfect race that may exist—if you win for Jonbar.

"The *dynat* is as important to Jonbar as the *gyrane* is to Gyronchi. But there's no time for nonessentials now. I've outlined the situation, Denny. What about it?"

The dark hollow eyes searched his face with a probing keenness almost painful.

"Will you accept the championship of Jonbar—knowing that it is a nearly hopeless battle? Will you set yourself against Sorainya, and give up whatever she may offer?" The hoarse whisper fell. "Remember, Denny, it's an act of yours that must kill Sorainya—or Lethonee."

A cold shudder passed over Dennis Lanning, and a choking ache closed his throat. The serene white image of Lethonee was before him, holding the jewel. But the proud, red-mailed splendor of Sorainya came instantly to push it away. He couldn't, he thought, endure the death of Lethonee. But could he—even if he would—destroy Sorainya? He gulped, and nodded painfully.

"Yes, Wil," he said. "I accept."

"Good for you, Denny!" Wil McLan's broken fingers gripped his hand. "And now I give you command of our legion out of time."

"No, Wil," Lanning protested. "I've earned no right to command.

"Gyronchi must be destroyed—and even Sorainya." A bitter light flashed in the hollow eyes again, and the gnarled fingers touched the worn silver tube. "I'll do my part. But I've no knack of leadership. My life has been spent too much with abstractions. You're a man of action, Denny, and in the crucial place. You must command."

"Okay. I'll do my best."

McLan's scarred hand lifted to salute him.

"Thank you, Denny. Now I suggest that you go down and brief your men. You may give them a choice—though it's a pretty hard one. They may follow your command, or be returned to where we found them."

"Which would mean—death?"

Wil McLan nodded.

"There is no other place for them in time—alive. If we win, a place can be made for those who survive, probably in Jonbar. If we fail, there is only death again—perhaps in Sorainya's dungeons."

"In Jonbar—" repeated Lanning, huskily. "Can I go there if we win? To Lethonee?"

"If we win," the old man told him. "Now, if you will talk to your men, I'll try to find Jonbar with the chronoscope."

Eagerly, Lanning gasped, "May I—"

A solemn twinkled flashed briefly in McLan's hollow eyes.

"If I get Lethonee," he promised, "I'll call you. But it's very hard to find Jonbar."

Lanning went back down through the turret to the deck, and sent Barry Halloran to call the men together. Facing the curiously assorted little group, he told them:

"Men, I've just talked to Captain McLan." He saw the flash of anxious interest on their faces. "He has gathered us out of time, saved each one of us from certain death. In return, he wants us to fight, to save a future world. I know the cause is good.

"He has offered me the command. I must ask you either to follow me, or to be returned to your own place in time—to die. I'm sorry the terms are so hard—"

"Hard?" shouted Barry Halloran.

"*Nein!*" grunted Emil Schorn. "Are we craven, the turn back from Valhalla?"

"Viva!" shouted Cresto. "*Viva el capitan!*"

"Thank you," Lanning gulped. "If we win, there will be a place for us in Jonbar. Now, if you're all with us, repeat after me: I pledge loyalty to Jonbar, and I promise to serve dutifully in the Legion of Time."

The seven men, with right hands lifted, shouted the oath, and then, led by Willie Rand, roared out a cheer for "Jonbar and Cap'n Lanning."

One of the orderlies beckoned, and Lanning returned hastily to the bridge.

"Did you—" he began breathlessly. "Did you—"

Wil McLan shook his haggard head, and pointed to the cabinet of the chronoscope.

"I tried," he whispered hoarsely. "But the enemy has moved again. One more triumph of Sorainya is fixed in the fifth dimension. Jonbar is one step nearer extinction. The image flickered, and went out. Now this is all I can get."

Looking into the crystal block, Lanning once more saw Gyronchi. But it was strangely changed. Sorainya's proud citadel, on one hill, had collapsed in a heap of corroded, blackened metal. The black temple of the *gyrane*, on the other eminence, had crumbled to a tremendous mound of shattered stone. Beneath, upon the denuded wastelands where fields and villages had been, was a desolate untrodden wilderness of weeds and brush, leprously patched with strange scars of white, shining ash.

"Gyronchi?" breathed Lanning. "Destroyed?"

"Destroyed," rasped Wil McLan, "by its own evil. By a final war between Sorainya's half-human warriors and the priesthood of the *gyrane*. Mankind, in the picture you witness, is extinct."

His hoarse whisper sank very low.

"If we fail—if mankind follows the way of Gyronchi—that is the end of the road." Wearily, he snapped off the switch, and the bleak scene vanished. "And now it seems that the road has been chosen. For no other geodesics remain strong enough for the instrument to trace."

His hands knotted impotently, Lanning stared blankly out through the dome, into the haze of flickering blue.

"What—" he demanded. "What could have happened?"

"I don't know." Wil McLan shook his head. "We must try to find what Sorainya has done, and try to undo it. If we could get back to Jonbar, and Lethonee's new geodesic laboratory—"

Lanning gripped his thin shoulder. "Can we?"

"I'm afraid," whispered Wil McLan, "that this move has so far undermined the probability of Jonbar that we can never reach it. But we can try!"

And the broken old hands spun the wheel of the *Chronion*.

Chapter 8

THE VANISHING OF JONBAR

BORIS BARININ CAME UP FROM THE HOSPITAL WARD. TWO Canadians followed: lean silent twins named Isaac and Israel Enders, who had been snatched from a shell hole on Vimy Ridge in 1917. With Duffy Clark, the British sailor from Jutland, they made eleven men under Lanning. He organized them into two squads, made Emil Schorn his second in command.

Wil McLan had been collecting weapons. There were a dozen Mauser rifles, two dozen Luger pistols, four crated machine guns, several boxes of hand grenades, and a hundred thousand rounds of assorted ammunition, that all had come, along with a stock of food and a few medical supplies, from a sinking munitions ship.

"The first precaution," McLan told him. "We located a torpedoed ship, when we first came back from Jonbar, to collect supplies and arms—and test our technique of recovery. Weapons from Jonbar, you see, wouldn't function against targets from Gyronchi."

Since McLan's helpers from Jonbar would be unable to enter Gyronchi, Lanning detailed Clark, Barinin, and Willie

51

Rand as a crew for the *Chronion*, and himself learned
something of her navigation, as the time ship drove steadily
down the goedesics of Jonbar. The hydrogen converter
throbbed endlessly, beneath the deck, but Wil McLan seemed
disheartened with their progress.

"The world we seek is now all but impossible," he rasped.
"The full power of the field drives us forward very slowly.
And at any instant the geodesics of Jonbar may break, for they
are weak enough already, and leave us—nowhere!"

Once, in his tiny cabin, aft, Lanning woke in his bunk with
a clear memory of Lethonee. Slim and tall in her long white
robe, she had stood before him, holding the flaming jewel of
time. Despair was a shadow on her face, and her violet eyes
were dark pools of pain.

"Denny," her urgent words rang clear in his memory,
"come to Jonbar—or we are dead."

Lanning went at once to the bridge, and told McLan. The
old man shook his white head, grimly.

"We are already doing all that can be done," he said. "The
geodesics of Jonbar are like microscopic wires drawn out
thinner and thinner by the attenuation of probability. If the
tracer loses them, or if they snap, Jonbar is—lost!"

Two weeks passed, by the time of the ship—physiological
time, as measured by heartbeats and all bodily rhythms, in
which life ran on toward its end, regardless of motion
backward or forward along the time dimension. And at last the
Chronion slipped silently out of the blue, shimmering abyss.
Lanning, waiting eagerly on the deck, saw beneath them—
Jonbar!

The ship was two miles high. Yet, that metropolis of futurity
stretched out in every direction as far as he could see. Mirror-
faced with polished metal, the soaring buildings seemed more
inspiring than cathedrals. With a pleasing lack of regularity,
they stood far apart all across the green park-like valley of a
broad placid river, and crowned the wooden hills beyond.
Many-leveled traffic viaducts flowed among them, busy with

strange vehicles. Great silver teardrops came and went through the air about them.

Lanning had glimpsed the city once before, through Lethonee's time jewel; now its staggering vastness touched him with a troubled awe. Hundreds of millions, he knew, lived here in this heart-lifting splendor. Yet all the wonder of this world, the cruel fact came home to him like a stabbing blade, faced absolute annihilation.

Trembling with eagerness and dread, he hurried up to Wil McLan.

"So Jonbar's safe?" he whispered breathlessly. "And Lethonee is here?"

The bent old man turned solemnly from the polished wheel, and shook his scarred white head.

"We're here," came his voiceless answer. "But our instruments show how its geodesics have faded out. It hangs by a strand weaker than a spider's web. But Lethonee will doubtless be at her new laboratory."

The *Chronion* was gliding swiftly to one tall silver spire on a hill. A vast doorway slid open in a silvery wall. The little ship floated into an immense hangar-like space, crowded with streamlined craft. A green light beckoned them to an empty platform.

"This is the world we're fighting for," Lanning told the men.

"*Ach!*" rumbled Emil Schorn. "A good world."

Leaving the scarred Prussian in command, and warning him to be ready for instant action in case of emergency, Lanning and McLan left the ship. An elevator in a great pillar shot them upward. They emerged into cool open air, amid the fragrant greenery of a terrace garden. A sliding door opened in a bright wall beyond. Out of it came Lethonee.

Instead of the long white robe in which Lanning had always seen her, she wore a close-fitting dress of softly shimmering, metallic blue; and a blue band held her hair. Something of the grave solemnity of the apparitions was gone. She was just a lovely human girl, joyously eager to see him—and trying, he thought, to hide a tragic despair. She came quickly to him, through the bright garden, and took both his hands in an eager grasp. And Lanning felt a queer little shiver of joy at the warm reality of her touch.

"Denny Lanning!" she whispered. "At last you have come. I am so glad—"

Her weary, troubled eyes went to scarred old Wil McLan.

"Gyronchi has carried out some new attack," she told him. "The *dynon* tried to bring a warning from the future, but they were cut off. Now the time crystal shows no future at all, beyond tonight. This is the last possible night for Jonbar. Unless—"

Her haunted eyes clung desperately to Lanning's face.

"Unless the tide of probability is changed."

"I'm going to the laboratory." Wil McLan turned toward the sliding door. "I'll send for you, Denny," he whispered, "if we discover anything. But you can do nothing until—unless— we find what Sorainya has done."

He limped away, and Lanning was left alone with Lethonee.

"How can you be—not real?" Lanning stood gazing at her quiet loveliness, framed against the terrace garden. "What's the difference between reality and—such a seeming as you are?"

She hesitated, with a little frown of thought.

"There is a flow from probability to certainty, along the fifth dimension," she explained. "Probabilities are infinite, but there is only one reality. Many conflicting futures are possible, but the past is simple and complete. The geodesics branch at each point of uncertainty, but the flow of realization must always take one branch and obliterate the rest. All the geodesics tend to absorb energy; all possible worlds strive for reality. But the energy of probability must always be withdrawn again from all those other worlds that might have been, to create the single one that can be. All the rest must vanish, as their probability fades to zero."

"And Jonbar is—vanishing?"

She nodded. "It—and I. We were given creation by the atomic power of the *Chronion*, bringing you down the geodesics. We are only an illusion of possibility, the reflection of what may be—a reflection that is doomed."

Abruptly, then—and Lanning knew that it took a desperate effort—she tossed her lovely head, and smiled.

"But need illusions talk of illusion?" Her voice was almost gay. "Aren't you hungry, Denny? Gather flowers for the table. Let's dine—on illusion!"

With her own hands she set a little table against the terrace rail. Beyond the rail, a mile below, lay green parklands. Other silver pylons shimmered on distant hills. The genial sun shone from a serene sky, of a blue clarity that Lanning had never seen above a city, and the clean wind whispered in a silence of strange peace.

"Nothing can happen to you, or to Jonbar!" Lanning whispered suddenly. "Perfection can't die!"

"But it can." Her voice shuddered. "When the whole structure of space-time is shattered with war—it can."

Lanning caught her hand.

"Lethonee," he said huskily, "for ten years, since the first night you came, I have lived in hope of finding you. Now, if anything should take you—"

"Remember, Denny." She moved closer, shivering. "This is the last night of Jonbar. The time crystal shows no tomorrow."

The blue dusk turned to mauve and to purple-black. The far towers of Jonbar shone like pillars of fire. Shadows filled the terrace. Some night-blooming shrub sent out a flood of intoxicating sweetness. Slow music came softly from somewhere below. Close to Lethonee, Lanning tried—and failed—to forget the darker shadow of extinction upon her. Suddenly her hand stiffened in his, and she caught a gasping, frightened breath.

"Greeting!" rang out a voice of golden mockery, "Queen of Nothingness!"

Lanning looked up, startled. He saw Sorainya's golden shell. She stood upright in it, proudly erect in her woven scarlet mail. Beside her stood a tall, angular man, gaunt-faced, with dark sullen eyes and cruel heavy lips, robed to his feet in dull stiff black. Glarath, that would be, Lanning knew, high priest of the *gyrane*. His sunken black eyes smouldered malevolently, but Sorainya's greenish glance held a mocking amusement.

"Best taste her kisses while you may, Denny Lanning," she taunted. "For we have found a higher crucial factor. I didn't need you, Denny Lanning after all—Glarath, with the *gyrane*, has taken the place I once offered you. And now our struggle is won."

The black-haired hand of the priest clutched possessively at her strong bare arm. He snarled some guttural, unintelligible word, and his dark eyes burned at Lanning, slitted with hate. Sorainya whipped out the thin golden needle of her sword, and drew it in a flashing arc above the dark city. And she leaned into the black priest's arms.

"Farewell, Denny Lanning," she called. "And take warning! All Jonbar—and the phantom in your arms—will be gone like fog before the wind. We've come to watch the end."

She touched the sword to her red mouth and then flung it toward him, as if to toss him a derisive kiss. Her feet touched some control, and the shell soared upward and vanished in the night.

White-faced, shaken, Lethonee was on her feet.

"Come into the laboratory!" Her voice was dry with dread. "Though I'm afraid—afraid that everything has failed."

Lanning followed her to the sliding door. Beyond it he saw a vast tower room. At endless tables, hundreds of men and women were busy with what he took for mathematical instruments. Others, in a far wing beyond, stood peering into scores of huge crystals like Lethonee's jewel of time. They were still in the doorway when Lanning saw Wil McLan, coming to meet them at a frantic, limping run.

"Back, Denny!" the old man was screaming, voicelessly. "Get back aboard. Jonbar is—going!"

Lanning swept Lethonee with him into the elevator. McLan tumbled after them. The cage dropped toward the hangar. Lanning held the girl hard against him.

"Darling—" he whispered. "You are coming with us!"

"No, Denny." She shook her head. "I am part of Jonbar."

She clung to him, desperately. He kissed her.

The elevator stopped. Lanning caught Lethonee's hand, and started running with her toward the *Chronion*. Ahead, a welcoming throng of gay-clad peopled were still gathered about the time ship, tossing flowers to the deck. Dapper Jean Querard stood by the rail, making a speech.

But a curious pale light had begun to shine from the crowd and the teardrop ships and the lofty walls, as if they were beginning to dissolve into luminous mist. Only the *Chronion* remained substantial. Lanning sprinted.

"Hurry!" he sobbed. "Darling—"

But Lethonee's fingers were gone from his hand. He stopped, and saw her still beside him—but dim as a ghost. Frantically, her shadow beckoned him to go on. He tried to catch her up in his arms, but she faded from his grasp. She was gone.

McLan had passed him. Lanning caught a sobbing breath, and fought a blinding pain, and stumbled on. But what was the use, his bitter agony demanded, if Lethonee was gone?

Everything was dim now, around him, and flickering like the blue abyss in which the time ship rode. He saw Will McLan scramble up a ladder. But the floor was giving away. His running feet sank deep, as if its bright metal had crumbled into rust. He caught his breath, and clutched out desperately, and fell. The last wraith of the building flickered away. Jonbar was gone. Beneath, under the empty night, lay only a

featureless dark plain. He fell toward it, a cold wind screaming
up about him.

"Farewell!" a malicious golden voice was pealing, and
Lanning saw the long yellow shell flash by, Sorainya and
Glarath lying together on its cushions. He fell past them, and
the wind took his breath.

But then the *Chronion* flashed down beside him. The yellow
ray flared from her crystal gun, and drew him to the rail. Barry
Halloran hauled him safely aboard.

Chapter 9

GEODESICS TO GYRONCHI

THE SHIP IN A MOMENT WAS BACK IN HER TIMELESS BLUE abyss, driving through the ceaseless flicker of possibility. Lanning hastened to join Wil McLan beneath the crystal dome, and asked his agonized question:

"Lethonee is gone—dead?"

"Not dead." McLan's haunted eyes rested on him sadly. "For she was never born. Jonbar was merely a faint probability of future time, which we illuminated for an instant with the power of the temporal ray. This last triumph of Sorainya has eliminated the geodesics that might have led to its existence. The reflection, therefore, vanished."

"Sorainya—" gasped Lanning. "What has she done?" He clutched McLan's twisted arm. "Did you discover—anything?"

The old man nodded slowly.

"In the last hour, before the laboratory was obliterated—"

"Yes?" Lanning urged him on.

"A moment, my boy," he whispered. "Seems the priests of the *gyrane* must have learned more than I thought from their examination of the *Chronion*. Sorainya's golden shell, as you

know, is merely a projected temporal image. But now Glarath
has built an actual time ship."

"Huh?"

"It's heavier than the *Chronion*, armored for war. It carries
a horde of Sorainya's anthropoid ants."

"And they used that, against Jonbar?"

"They went back into the past," said the voiceless man.
"Back to the turning point of probability. They found
something there—it must have been a small material object,
although we got no glimpse of it—which was the very
foundation of Jonbar. Using *gyrane* power, they wrenched the
thing, whatever it was, out of its place in time. The broken
geodesics cut off the possibility of Jonbar."

"What became of this object?"

"They kept it concealed. And they carried it back to
Gyronchi. It is guarded, there, in Sorainya's fortress."

"Guarded?" Lanning echoed. His fingers twisted together
in a sudden agony of hope, and his eyes rose to search
McLan's wealed face. "Then if we took it—carried it back—
would that help Jonbar?"

Desperately, he seized McLan's thin shoulder.

"Can—can anything bring back Lethonee?"

"Yes." The bent white head moved to a tiny nod. "If we
could recover the object, if we could discover where they
found it, in space and time, if we could put it back there, if we
could prevent Sorainya from disturbing it again until the
turning point has passed in the fifth dimension—then Jonbar
would again be possible."

Lanning's fist smashed into his palm. "Then we must do
that."

"Yes," whispered Wil McLan, very softly, "we must do
that." A solemn light had come into his haggard eyes, and his
broken hand softly touched Lanning's arm. "This is the
mission for which we gathered your legion, Denny—although
the details have not been clear until now."

"Okay," Lanning said. "Let's go!"

"We are now retracing the broken geodesics of Jonbar," McLan told him, "back toward your own time. There we can pick up the branching world lines of Gyronchi, and follow them forward again, to seek that guarded object."

"And let Sorainya look out!"

But McLan caught Lanning's arm again, with a firmer grasp.

"I must warn you, Denny. Don't be too hopeful—we need every bit of caution. The odds are all against us. A dozen men against all Gyronchi. Jonbar can help us no more. Even the surgeons we had aboard vanished with all the rest."

"We'll beat 'em," Lanning was muttering. "We've got to."

But he saw McLan's haunted eyes.

"It's thirty years since I first saw Sorainya." The old man spoke as if to himself, absently fingering the worn silver tube that hung from his throat. "A glorious flame that lured me across the gulf of time. I—I loved her."

Tears burst into his hollow eyes, and his gulp was a startling little sound.

"Fifteen years—" he rasped again, "since I found what a demon she is." Some deep-hidden agony throbbed in his words. "I hate Sorainya! She tricked me, tortured me, maimed me forever! She—she—" Something seemed to choke him. "But still—for all her monstrous evil—could I kill Sorainya? Could any man?"

Lanning's own fists were knotted.

"I have seen her," he said hoarsely. "And I don't know." Then he strode suddenly across the room and back, moved by an inner agony. "But we must—to save Jonbar."

"We must," echoed the man she had broken. "If we can!"

A week, ship's time, had passed, when the dials registered 1921.

"Here," Will McLan told Lanning, "the last broken geodesic of Jonbar joins reality. In this year, it is just possible, we may find the apex of that new cone of probability formed when

Glarath took the object out of time—if we can ever come back to search."

The *Chronion* came briefly out of her blue, flickering gulf, high above the brilliant blue Pacific where the circle of an atoll glistened green and white about a pale lagoon. In an instant they were gone again, back through the blur of multitudinous possibility, down the geodesic track of Gyronchi.

Lanning and Schorn were drilling the men on the deck when the attack came, yet it was an utter surprise. Jaunty little Jean Querard, leaping from his place in the line, screamed the first warning:

"*Grand Dieu!* A ship from hell!"

Turning, Lanning saw a black shadow against the shimmering blue. It vanished, reappeared, flickered, became suddenly real. The time ship from Gyronchi!

Three times the *Chronion's* length, it was massively armored. The ends were two immense square plates, which shone with the same greenish glow as the *Chronion's* polar disks. Black muzzles frowned from the side, and the deck was crowded with a black-armored horde of Sorainya's half-human warriors.

On a high quarter-deck, Lanning thought he glimpsed the black-robed angularity of Glarath. But it disappeared. A dazzling white beam jetted from a projecting tube. A two-foot section of the *Chronion's* rail turned incandescent and exploded, fused and vaporized.

"Lie flat!" ordered Lanning. "Fire at will!" He shouted to Schorn: "Get the Maxims going!"

But what could bullets do against that terrible energy? He ran to the speaking tube, forward, that communicated with McLan.

"Wil!" he sobbed. "What now?"

The white beam flashed again behind him. And Israel Enders, kneeling to fire, collapsed in a smoking huddle. There was one brief scream, agony-thinned. And bright flame burst up from a little heap of burned cloth and seared flesh and fused metal.

With an answering scream that was the echo of his brother's, Isaac Enders fed a belt of ammunition into his Maxim, and sprayed lead at Sorainya's monsters, who were leveling their guns. Their bullets spattered the *Chronion*.

The hoarse tortured whisper came back at last from McLan:

"The *Chronion's* no battle ship. We can't fight the *gyrane* ray."

"Then what?"

"Outrun them!" rasped McLan. "The only hope. The *Chronion's* lighter. Hold 'em off! And I'll try—"

Blinded by blood from a wound on his forehead, the Austrian, von Arneth, was fumbling with his jammed Maxim. Lanning ran to the gun, burned his fingers freeing the hot action, and trained it on the port from which the ray had flashed.

He hammered lead at the black-armored ship, but it kept drifting nearer. Another volley from the giants screamed around him. The white ray stabbed again. One of the Maxims exploded. Willie Rand, behind it, rolled moaning on the deck, beating at his flaming garments.

This couldn't go on! Shuddering, Lanning fed another belt into his own gun. A few of Sorainya's creatures had fallen, yet the battle was clearly hopeless. He listened. Was the throb beneath the deck a little swifter?

The great black ship had slipped close, before he could fire again. Swinging their golden axes, the humanoid ants lined the rail. Were they preparing to board? Lanning tilted up the Maxim, to rake them. But a thick black tube crept down, stopped in line with him. His breath caught. It was time for that fearful ray. Blinding fire exploded at him—

But the enemy ship flickered and vanished. Lanning felt his hot gun and stumbled to the speaking tube.

"Wil?" he called.

"We've outrun them, Denny," came McLan's voiceless

rasp. "I think we can keep a little ahead, along the time dimension. But they'll be back to Gyronchi close behind us, with their warning. And we've already lost—how many men?"

Lanning turning to survey the battle-cluttered deck. The tall grim-faced Canadian was on his knees beside the smoking remains of his brother, sobbing. Barry Halloran was dressing von Arneth's wound. Willie Rand, his clothing still smoking, was groping about the deck, cursing in a soft, wary monotone. Lanning saw his eyes, and felt a shock of horror. Staring wide and blank from his red seared face, they were cooked white from the ray, blind.

"Israel Enders dead," he reported to McLan, in a sick voice. "Von Arneth wounded. Rand blind. One Maxim destroyed, by that terrible ray—"

"The *gyrane*," rasped McLan. "The odds are all against us, Denny. We must avoid another battle—if we can. But now that they are warned—"

The whisper faded, on a note of tired despair.

Wrapped in a sheet, to which were pinned a tiny Canadian flag and the silver star of Jonbar, the remains of Israel Enders and his fused rifle were consigned to the shimmering gulf of time—where, McLan said, having the velocity of the ship they would drift on into ultimate futurity.

The deck was cleared, the broken rail mended. The guns were cleaned and repaired. Atomic converters throbbing swiftly, polar plates glowing green, the *Chronion* plunged on down the track of probability, toward Gyronchi.

Erich von Arneth came up from the hospital, with a new livid scar across his forehead. Asking for a Mauser whose lock was broken, Willie Rand sat for long hours on the deck, bandaged head bowed, whetting its gleaming bayonet and testing the edge with his thumb.

On the bridge, Lanning and Wil McLan watched the crystal block of the chronoscope, using its temporal ray to scan Gyronchi, seeking out the best instant for the raid. They failed, however, to look actually into Sorainya's mighty citadel, to find the object they sought to recover.

"Another application of the *gyrane*," rasped Wil McLan. "An interfering field, set up about the metal walls, that damps out the temporal radiation." A stern light glinted in his hollow eyes. "But I know Sorainya's fortress," he added grimly. "With Lethonee's aid, planning that escape, I memorized every inch of it."

His broken fingers mapped it, for Lanning and Schorn.

"The great strong room," he said, "where Sorainya keeps her treasure, is in the eastern tower. It is reached only by a ladder through a trap door in the floor of Sorainya's own apartments. And the great hall, outside, through which you must enter, is guarded always by a hundred warriors.

"It must be a sudden strike," he added. "A moment lost, a wasted step, can finish us."

And at last a moment came when he spun the shining wheel and tapped a key, to stop the time ship in Gyronchi.

Chapter 10

IN SORAINYA'S CITADEL

In the somber dusk of a cloudy day, the *Chronion* first paused in Sorainya's world. Tiny fields, the broad river dully silver in the twilight, sprawled miserable villages—and a blackened, barren patch where Lanning had seen one village burned. The twin hills beyond, topped with the temple of the *gyrane* and Sorainya's citadel.

Standing on the deck, Lanning scanned the fortress through binoculars. A mountainous, frowning pile of the eternal crimson alloy, it had been the fastness of Sorainya's dynasty, he knew from the chronoscope, for half a thousand years. Scores of the black-armored fighters, glittering with the gold and scarlet of their weapons, were marching in sentry duty along the high battlements. And Lanning saw, mounted cannon-like upon the walls, a dozen of the thick black tubes that projected the *gyrane* ray.

"*Gott in Himmel!*" rumbled Emil Schorn at his side. "Der thing we must recover is in that castle, *nein?* It looks a *verdammt* stubborn nut to crack!"

"It is," said Lanning. "One slip, and we are lost. There must be no slip." He handed the glasses to the Prussian. "We

66

have only paused here to look over the ground by daylight,"
he swiftly explained. "We are to land after midnight on that
ledge that breaks the north precipice—see it?"

"*Ja!*"

"Sorainya herself will then be gone to visit Glarath in his
temple—so we saw in the chronoscope. And perhaps at that
hour her guards will not be too alert. Our landing party must
climb to the little balcony above, where the skeleton hangs—"

"*Ach, Gott!* A dizzy climb!"

"The little door on the balcony gives into the dungeons. Wil
McLan has the keys he carved there, for his escape. We'll
enter through the dungeons, and try to reach the great hall
above. Is that all clear?"

"*Ja!* Clear as death."

Lanning waved his arm to Wil McLan, in his crystal dome,
and the *Chronion* slipped again into the shadowy gulf of time.
The landing party gathered on the foredeck. A grim, silent
little band—saved for Barry Halloran, who tried to make them
join in a college yell for Jonbar. Isaac Enders and von Arneth
were to carry two of the Maxims. Cresto and Courtney-Pharr
packed the fifty-pound tripods. The others were laden with
climbing ropes, rifles, grenades, and ammunition.

Boris Barinin set up the remaining gun, to guard the ship.
And blinded Willie Rand sat silently beside him, breathing
white cigarette smoke and whetting at the bayonet of his
broken gun.

And the *Chronion* plunged into the blackness of a wet
midnight. The overwhelming mass of Sorainya's citadel was a
vague shadow in the clouds, as the time ship slipped silently
down to the high narrow ledge. A cold rain drizzled on the
deck, and a bitter wind howled about the battlements above.

Noiseless as a shadow, the *Chronion* settled among the
gnarled and stunted brush that clung to the ledge. Limping
down from his bridge, Wil McLan handed Lanning three white
keys carved from human bone.

"For the balcony entrance," he whispered. "For the

dungeon doors. And the inside gate. But I've none for the strong room—you must find some other way." His broken hand tightened like a claw on Lanning's arm. "I've told you all I can, Denny. You'll pass through the prison where I lay for ten years. We may all rot there, if you fail. Don't fail!"

Burdened with Mauser, coiled rope, and a hamper of grenades, Lanning led the way over the rail and up the precipitous cliff. The mossy rock was slippery with mist. Wet cold numbed him. The wind tugged at him with icy, treacherous hands. In the darkness he could see nothing save bulking vague shadows; he had to grope and fumble for the way.

Knives of granite cut his fingers, and damp cold deadened them. Once he slipped, and clawed at the sharp rock to catch himself, scraping flesh away. An age-long instant, he hung by the snapping fingers of one hand.

But he recovered himself, and climbed again. He came at last to a stout little oak, well anchored in a crevice, that he had seen through the binoculars. He knotted a rope to it, tested its strength, and dropped the coil to the men below.

He climbed on. Icy gusts of wind beat at him. The rain, in bigger, colder drops, chilled him through. Pale lightning flashed once above, and he shivered with dread that it might reveal them.

He fastened another rope about a projecting spur of rock, and dropped it back, and climbed again. Trembling with strain, he came at last to the narrow rugged ledge where the precipice of stone joined the sheer unscalable precipice of crimson metal. Wedging his bayonet in a fissure, he anchored another rope. He had begun to inch his way along the ledge, when he heard a stifled scream beneath.

He froze. A long silence. Something crashed faintly, far below. Shuddering, he waited. The storm moaned dismally about the battlements, still hundreds of feet above. There was no alarm. On hands and knees, he crept on again.

"Ach, Gott!" came a hushed muttering. "This *verdammt* blackness—it would blind der deffil!"

Emil Schorn came up the rope behind him, and followed along the ledge. They came to the little balcony of rusted metal. A gallows arm projected above it. A rope hung through an open trap door, and beneath it, swaying in the wind, white bones dangled in their chains.

As Lanning tried the thin bone key in the metal door, the other men joined them, one by one, breathless, dripping shivering with cold—all save the Austrian, von Arneth.

"Madre del Dios!" shuddered the Spanish flyer, Cresto. "He fell past me, screaming. He must have splashed, at the foot of the mountain! *Cabron!* And now we have one Maxim only."

The thick metal door slid suddenly aside, and a fetid breath came out of Sorainya's dungeons. The reek of unwashed human misery, of human waste and human death, mingled with the suffocating acrid pungence of the anthropoid ants. Clenching his jaw against a fluttering of sickness in his stomach, Lanning led the raiders forward.

At first he saw no light in the dungeons. He led the way by touch alone through the narrow, rock-hewn passages, counting his steps and groping for the memorized turns. But presently he could see a little, by a phosphorescence of decay that patched the walls and floors.

Beyond the bars of cells he glimpsed abject human creatures, maimed, blinded, less than half alive, sprawled among the bones of the wholly dead that lay still chained beside them, shining with a cold blue luminescent rot.

A dreadful silence filled most of the prison. But in one cell was a great squeaking and thumping commotion. Lanning glimpsed huge sleek rats battling over a motionless body in chains.

Farther on, in another cell, a sightless, famished wretch had bitten his own wrist, to let a few drops of blood flow upon the floor. He crouched there, listening, and snatched again and again, blindly, with fettered hands, at the great wary rats that came to his bait.

"My word!" gasped the British flyer, Courtney-Pharr. "When we meet that she-devil, she'll account for all this. Rather!"

Lanning stopped, at a turning, and breathed his warning: "Ready, men!"

With a little jingle of their weapons, four of Sorainya's warriors came down the corridor. Great black giants, walking erect, eight feet tall. Huge compound eyes burning in the darkness, strange jewels of evil fire. Mandibled, monstrous insects. Yet somehow, sickeningly human.

"Bayonets," whispered Lanning. "No noise."

But his own bayonet had been left back on the precipice, to hold the rope. He clubbed his rifle to lead the rush, swung it down to crack an armored skull. Taken by surprise, the monsters reeled back, snatching with strange claws for their weapons.

They were mute, as if their creators had sacrificed speech for deadliness. But little red boxes clamped to their heads, might, Lanning thought, be communicators. A black limb was fumbling at one of them. He snapped the rifle down in a second hasty blow, to crush it.

Ugly mandibles seized the Mauser's stock, sheared through the hard wood. And a mighty golden battle-axe came hissing down. Lanning parried at it with the barrel of the broken gun, but the flat of its blade grazed his head, flung him down into fire-veined blackness.

He lay on the floor, dazed and nerveless. Red agony splintered his temple. Yet he retained a curious detached awareness. He could see the weird feet stamping about in front of his face, on the faintly glowing slime. The reek of formic acid stung his nostrils, burning out the odor of the cells. The monsters fought wordlessly, but their hard bodies made odd little clicks and creaks.

The men had followed Lanning, with bayonets fixed, but they were dwarfed by the four-armed fighters. And now the advantage of surprise was gone.

"*Vive* Jonbar!" sobbed Cresto. The dexterous sweep of his blade completely decapitated the nearest fighter. But its insect inheritance was not so quickly vanquished. The headless thing remained for a moment upright, and the great yellow axe struck again, deep into the Spaniard's skull.

"*Por Dios—*"

His gaunt body lurched automatically forward, and came down on top of the creature, driving the bayonet deep into the armored thorax. Meantime Emil Schorn had slashed into the one remaining monster with a force that carried it over backward. Barry Halloran followed him, with a ripping lunge. And the battle was ended.

Barry helped Lanning to his feet, and he stood a moment swaying, fighting for control of his body. Courtney-Pharr produced a silver flask of brandy, splashed its liquid fire on his temple, gave him a gulp of it. His head began to clear. He seized Cresto's rifle and staggered on, following Emil Schorn.

An outstretched hand and a whispered warning stopped him in the darkness. Greenish light shone through massive bars ahead. He crept up beside Schorn, and looked into a long guard room.

A dozen of the warriors were lounging in the room, and the air was thick with their acrid smell. Several, at a low table, were sucking at sponges in basins of some red liquid. Two couples were preening one another's glistening black bodies. A few were polishing battle-axes and thick red guns. One, in a gloomy corner, knelt in a mysterious travesty of prayer, as if begging for its lost humanity.

"No hope for silence, now," Lanning breathed to Schorn. "We'll take 'em! With all we've got."

He was working at the lock, with the fragile bone key. Isaac Enders and Courtney-Pharr, beyond him, were setting up the Maxim on its tripod, the muzzle jutting through the bars. The lock snapped silently. He nodded to Schorn, and began to swing the door slowly open.

The compound eyes of the farther giant glittered as they

moved, and it sprang up from its attitude of prayer, inhuman as all the rest. An electric silence crackled in the guard room.

"Now!" Lanning shouted. "At 'em!"

"*Allons!*" echoed Jean Querard. "With you, *mon capitaine!*"

The Maxim thundered suddenly, filling the room with blue smoke and ricocheting lead. Lanning flung wide the door, and ran with Schorn and Querard and Barry Halloran diagonally across the room, to hold the other entrance.

The monsters were bred to retain a humenopterous vitality. Even when riddled with bullets they did not immediately die. Under the Maxim's hail, they abandoned their occupations, seized weapons, and came charging in two groups at the entrances. Courtney-Pharr slammed the prison gate to protect Enders and his weapon, defending the lock with his bayonet. And the creatures in front of the gun began at last reluctantly to slump and topple.

The defense of the other door, however, was less successful. Lanning and his companions met the charging creatures with tossed grenades and a blaze of rifle fire. Out of seven, two were blown to fragments by the bombs, and another crippled. Four of them came on, with axes swinging, to meet the bayonets. The cripple fell back, to load and fire its clumsy gun, before a burst from the Maxim crumpled it.

But little Jean Querard was staggering forward, blood spurting from his breast. Knees trembling, he held himself upright for a moment, propped his rifle so that a charging warrior impaled itself on the bayonet. Loud and clear his voice rang out:

"*Allons!* Jonbar!"

And he slipped down beside the dying thing.

Lanning checked one of the creatures with three quick shots to its head, and then ripped open its armored thorax with a bayonet lunge that killed it. Schorn stopped another. But the third caught the barrel of Halloran's gun a ringing blow with its axe, dragged him down with its claws, and lunged past.

Lanning snapped another clip into his Mauser, and fired after it. But it dropped forward and scuttled out of sight, at a six-limbed, atavistic run.

Barry Halloran staggered back to his feet, his shirt torn off and blood dripping from a long red mark across his breast and shoulder, where a mandible had raked him.

"Sorry, Denny!" he sobbed. "I tried to hold the line!"

"Good work, guy," Lanning gasped, running back to open the door again for Pharr and Enders with their gun.

But already, somewhere ahead, a great alarm gong was throbbing out a brazen-throated warning that moaned and sighed and shuddered through all the long halls of Sorainya's citadel.

Chapter 11

BEYOND THE
DIAMOND THRONE

THE FIVE SURVIVORS, PHARR AND ENDERS, HALLORAN AND Schorn and Lanning, running with their burden of weapons, came up a long winding flight of steps and through a small door into the end of Sorainya's ceremonial hall, where the warning gong was booming.

The hall was enormous. Great square pillars of black soared up against the red metal walls, and between them stood colossal statues in yellow gold—no doubt Sorainya's warlike ancestors, for all were armed and armored.

The reflected light from the lofty crimson vault had a sinister redness. Most of the floor was bare. Far toward the other end stood a tall pillar of shimmering splendor—the diamon throne that once Sorainya had offered Lanning, as treacherously, perhaps, as she had also offered it to Wil McLan.

The huge gong hung from a heavy chain beside the throne, a forty-foot scarlet disk. Tiny-seeming in that vast hall, two of the warrior monsters were furiously beating its moaning curve.

And a little army of them—thirty, Lanning estimated—came swarming across the floor.

"Quick!" he rapped. "The Maxim!" He helped set the hot machine gun up, gasping to Schorn, "We've got to get through—and back! The door to Sorainya's own apartments is behind the throne. We reach the strong room through a trap door, beside her bed."

"Devil-things!" muttered Isaac Enders. His lean face was a hard bitter mask as he started an ammunition belt into the Maxim, dropped down behind it. "To kill my brother!"

The gun jetted flame, sweeping the line of anthropoid ants. Beside him, Pharr and Barry Halloran blazed away with rifles. Lanning and Schorn met the monsters with a barrage of hand grenades.

The creatures fired a volley as they came. Their thick crimson guns were single-shot weapons, of heavy calibre but limited range. Most of the bullets went wide, spattering on the metal wall. But one struck Enders, drilling a great black hole in his forehead.

He lurched upright, behind the Maxim. His long, gaunt arms spread wide. A curious expression of shocked incredulous eagerness lit his stern face for an instant, until it was drowned in a gush of blood. His voice pealed out, in a last loud shot:

"Israel!"

He slid forward, and lay shuddering across the gun.

Courtney-Pharr tossed his body away, and crouched to fire the Maxim.

It took the warriors a long while to come down the hall. Or time, measured only by the sequence of events, seemed curiously extended. Lanning had space to snatch a deep breath of this clean air. He wondered how, without key or combination, they could break into the strong room. And how soon, after this alarm, Sorainya herself might return from the temple with more of her creatures to block the retreat.

A few of the enemy, riddled with lead, had time to slump

and fall. A few more, running over the tossed grenades, were hurled mangled into the air. But the most of them came on, converging toward the door, clubbing crimson guns, spinning yellow battle-axes.

The four men waited in a line across the doorway, the Maxim drumming its deadly roll. Schorn flung his last grenade, when the black rank was a dozen yards away, and snatched his bayonet to meet the charge. Saving back two grenades, Lanning leveled his rifle to guard the machine gun.

Three of the foremost monsters slumped and fell. But the rest came on like a tide of death. Insectile giants, fantastic in chitinous black, but yet dreadful with their hints of humanity, great eyes glittering redly evil in the bloody light, golden axes singing.

Lanning's Mauser snapped, empty. He lunged, and his bayonet ripped open one armored thorax. But the golden blade of another monster rang against the rifle, tore it from his fingers. A flailing gun, at the same instant, struck his shoulder with a sledge of agony, hurled him back against the wall.

One arm was tingling, nerveless. He groped with his left hand for the Luger at his belt, surged to his knees, sent lead tearing upward through armored, acid-reeking bodies.

Savage mandibles seized the rifle of Emil Schorn, and the Prussian went down beneath the towering monsters. They tramped down the drumming Maxim. Great black jaws seized the bare blonde head of Courtney-Pharr. The gun abruptly ceased to fire, and in the breathless scrap of silence the crushing of his skull made a soft, sickening sound.

"Fight 'em!" Barry Halloran was singing out. "Fight 'em!"

Furiously, with his bayonet, the big red-headed tackle fell upon the two creatures sprawled over the silent machine gun and the Briton's decapitated body.

The Luger was empty again. Lanning dropped it, groped for his rifle on the floor, and surged up to meet the second rank of attackers. If he could hold them for a moment, give Barry a chance to recover the Maxim—

The mute giants pressed down on him. But his paralyzed arm had come to life again. And he had learned a deadly technique: a lunge that ripped the hard thorax, upward, then a deep, twisting thrust, to right and left, that tore the vital organs.

Yellow axes were hissing at him. But the black warriors were piled before the doorway, now, in a sort of barricade; and the floor was slippery with reeking life-fluids, so that strange claws slid and scratched for balance. Lanning evaded the blows, and lunged, and lunged again.

Behind him, Barry had finished one creature with the bayonet. His blade snapped off, in the armor of the other. He snatched out his Luger, pumped lead into the black body. But it sprang upon him, clubbed him down with the flat of a golden axe, and fell at last across him.

Alone against the horde, Lanning thrust and ripped and parried. He laid one monster on top of the barricade, and another, and a third. Then his own foot slipped in the slime. Great mandibles gripped his wavering bayonet, twisted, snapped it off.

He tried to club the gun. But black claws ripped it from his hands. Three more giants bore him down. His own gun crashed against his head. He slipped to the floor, sobbing bitterly:

"Lethonee! I tried—"

The victorious attackers came clambering over the barrier of their dead. Tramping claws scratched him. He fought for strength to rise again, and failed. Jonbar was doomed. And, for him, would it be Sorainya's dungeons?

The sudden loud tattoo of the Maxim was a wholly incredible sound. Lanning in his daze thought at first the sound must be a dream. But the reeking body of a dismembered monster toppled across him. He twisted his head, with a savage effort, and saw Emil Schorn.

The big Prussian had once gone down. His bull-like body was nearly naked, shredded, red with dripping blood. But he was on his feet again, swaying, his blue eyes flaming.

"*Heil*, Jonbar!" he was roaring. "*Heil*, Valhalla!"

He started another belt into the Maxim, and came forward again, holding it in his arms, firing it like a rifle—a terrific feat, even for such a giant as he. The remaining warriors came leaping at him, and he met them with a hail of death. One by one, they slumped and fell. A great golden axe came hurtling across the barricade. Its blade cut deep into his naked breast. Foaming red spurted out.

But still the German stood upright, leaning against the shattering recoil of the gun, sweeping it back and forth. At last it was empty, and he dropped it from seared hands. Wide and fixed, his blue eyes watched the last giant stagger and fall.

"Jonbar!" his deep voice rumbled. "*Ach, Thor!*"

Like a massive pillar falling, he crashed down beside the red-hot Maxim. For a little space there was a strange hushed silence in Sorainya's crimson hall, disturbed only by the faint sorrowful reverberation that still throbbed from the mighty gong. The golden colossi, in their panoplies of war, looked triumphantly down upon the cold peace that follows death.

A little life, however, was seeping back into Lanning's battered body. He twisted, and began to push at the great dead thing that had fallen on his legs. A sudden throbbing eagerness lent him strength. For Schorn had opened the way to the strong room. There might still be time, before escape was blocked.

But Barry Halloran was the first on his feet. Lanning had supposed him dead beneath the warrior that brought him down. But there was a sudden, muffled shout:

"Fight 'em! Fight——Huh!, Denny, can you hear me?"

"Barry!"

And the big tackle came stalking through the dead, his naked torso as red as Schorn's. He dragged the armored thing from Lanning's legs, and Lanning sat up. Pain dazed him, and the next he knew Halloran was pressing Courtney-Pharr's silver flask to his lips. He gulped the searing brandy.

"Make it, Denny?"

Lanning stood up, swaying drunkenly. A great anvil of agony rang at the back of his head. His vision blurred. The great red hall spun and tilted, and the golden colossi came marching down it, to defend Sorainya's golden throne.

"Let's go," his voice came fuzzy and thick. "Get that thing. Get back to the ship. Before Sorainya comes! Two grenades—key to the strong room."

Barry Halloran found the two bombs he had saved, and bent to pick up the hot Maxim. Lanning told him the ammunition was gone. He found a rifle, and seized Lanning's arm. They started, at a weary, stumbling run, down the silent crimson hall.

It was an interminable way, past the frowning yellow giants and the soaring pillars of black, down to the high diamond splendor of Sorainya's throne. But they passed at last beneath the undying sigh of the mighty gong, and staggered on beyond the throne.

Beyond was a broad arched doorway, curtained with black. They pushed through the heavy drapes, into the queen's private chambers. Lanning did not pause to catalog their splendor, but he saw a shimmer of immense crystal mirrors, a gleam of ivory and gold. Sorainya's bed, hewn from a colossal block of sapphire crystal, and canopied with jewel-sewn silk, shone like a second throne at the end of that vista of barbaric magnificence. Lanning and Halloran ran panting toward it, trailing drops of blood.

Lanning ripped back a deep-piled rug beside the bed. In the floor he found the fine dark line that marked the edge of a well-fitted door, and, in the center of that, a smaller square.

Barry Halloran used his bayonet to pry out the central block, while Lanning unscrewed the detonator cylinders from the two grenades. Beneath the block was revealed a long keyhole. Lanning poured the two ounces of powder from each grenade into the little square depression, let it run down into the lock. He thrust one detonator into the keyhole, with the safety fuse projecting. Barry came dragging a great jeweled coffer of red metal from the foot of the bed, pushed it over the lock to retain the force of the blast. Lanning took the rifle, put a bullet into the percussion cap.

The floor quivered. Glittering fragments of the burst coffer rocketed to the ceiling. Jewels showered the room. They ran back around the sapphire bed. A blackened hole yawned, where a tough sheet of red metal had burst jaggedly upward. Lanning reached his arm through, to manipulate hot bolts and tumblers. The square door dropped suddenly, elevator-like. Halloran, after a startled instant, stepped upon it with Lanning. They sank swiftly into the strong room.

It was huge and windowless. Concealed lights sprang on, as they descended, to show Sorainya's treasure. Great shimmering stacks of silver and golden ingots, immense mysterious coffers, great slabs of unworked synthetic crystal, sapphire, emerald, ruby, diamond. Statuary, paintings, strange mechanisms and instruments, tapestries, books and manuscripts—all the precious relics of her dynasty. Most curious of all, a long row of tall crystal blocks, in which, like flies in amber, were embedded oddly life-like human forms—the armored originals of the golden colossi above. This was not only the treasury but the mausoleum of Gyronchi's rulers.

"Ye gods!" murmured Barry Halloran, blinking, "The old girl's one collector! This junk is worth—worth more money than there is! King Midas would turn green!"

Lanning's jaw went white.

"I saw her once—collecting!" he whispered bitterly.

The dropping platform touched the floor.

"We're looking for a little black brick," Lanning said, swiftly. "Something covered with a black cement, to hide it from our search ray." Shuddering to a trapped feeling, he looked back up at the door. "Better keep moving. We've been a long time, and that gong would wake the dead. Sorainya'll soon be boiling in, with reinforcements."

They began a frantic search for the small black brick, breaking open coffers of jewels, shaking out chests of silks and furs. It was Barry Halloran who found the little ebon rectangle, in a cracked pottery jar that lay as if discarded in a dusty corner.

"That's it!" Lanning gasped. "Let's get out!"

They stepped back upon the platform. Lanning tapped a button on the floor beside it, and it lifted silently. His red hands trembling with wondering awe, Halloran handed the heavy little brick to Lanning.

"What could it be?" he whispered.

"Dunno," Lanning shook his battered head. "But listen!"

They were rising back into the queen's bedchamber. He heard a distant clang like the closing of a metal gate, a far tinkle of weapons, and the clear tiny peal of a woman's anger-heightened voice. His strength went out, and cold dread ached in every bone.

"Sorainya!" he sobbed. "She's coming back!"

They scrambled up to the floor, and ran desperately back through the empty glitter of the vast apartments, the way they had come. They passed the black hangings. Once more they came into the enormous hall of the golden colossi. Again they ran beneath the sighing gong beside the high diamond throne. And there, under the moaning disk, they halted in cold despair.

For a new horde of Sorainya's giants, still tiny in the distance, were pouring into the hall. Running gracefully to lead them, flashing in her red-mailed splendor, came the warrior queen herself. Lanning turned to look at Barry's stricken face. Wearily, he shook his head.

"She has cut us off!" he breathed. "There's no way out—"

Chapter 12

THE SECRET OF THE BRICK

LANNING'S RED FINGERS CLOSED HARD ON THE HEAVY BLACK
brick, the precious cornerstone of Jonbar. "Fine!" he gasped.
"There's time enough to get—her!"

Yet, as soon as Barry raised the Mauser, he was sorry he had
spoken. For the queen of Gyronchi, in her black-plumbed
splendor, was too lovely to be slain. Demon-queen! He bit his
lip, and quenched a frantic impulse to snatch the rifle down.

The gun crashed. Lanning waited, with a stricken heart, to
see Sorainya fall. But it was one of her insectile soldiers that
staggered and clutched with four queer limbs at its hard black
shell.

"I had it on her," muttered Halloran. "But they'd get us
just the same. And she's so—beautiful."

Lanning swayed. The anvil of agony rang louder in his
brain. He groped foggily for any possible way back to the
ship, but there was none. And Wil McLan's tormented
question was rasping his ears. Could any man kill Sorainya?

But she must be destroyed, so McLan had said. And
Lethonee had told him, long ago, that he himself must choose

one of the two, and so doom the other. His heart came up in his throat, and he reached out a trembling hand.

"Give me—"

But the rifle had snapped, empty. Halloran flung it down, folded his crimsoned arms, stood waiting grimly. Lanning bent to pick up the gun, gasping, "Don't let 'em take us—"

But Sorainya had paused to level the yellow needle of her sword, which was more than a sword. A hot blue spark hissed to the rifle. Lanning's hand jerked away from the half-fused weapon, burned and paralyzed. The triumphant bugle of her voice pealed down the hall.

"Well, Denny Lanning! So you have chosen my dungeons to my throne?"

Lanning blinked. Sorainya and her charging horde were already halfway down the hall. Beneath her crested helmet, he could see her face still white with vengeful anger, the long green eyes cold as ice. But something came between.

A shadow. A thickening silver veil. The shadow grew abruptly real. Breathless, Lanning rubbed at his eyes, shuddering to the shock of incredulous hope. It was the *Chronion!*

The green glow fading slowly from her polar disks, the time ship landed on the floor before the throne. Lao Meng Shan, on the foredeck, turned the Maxim mounted there toward Sorainya and her creatures—and then fell desperately to taking the gun apart, for it was jammed.

The thin twisted figure of Wil McLan, under his crystal dome, was beckoning urgently. After that first stunned instant, Lanning caught Barry's arm, and they ran frantically to climb aboard.

Sorainya screamed a battle cry. With a flashing sweep of her golden sword, she led her black giants on. A scattering volley from their heavy guns peppered the *Chronion*. But the turret was turning beneath the dome. The yellow ray flamed upon Lanning and Halloran from the crystal gun, to pull them to the ship.

Lanning had glimpsed the blind, bewildered navy airman,

Willie Rand, stark and alone on the deck. But, when he and Halloran tumbled breathless over the rail, where Shan still bent over the useless Maxim, Rand was gone.

"Look, Denny!" Barry Halloran was shouting, hoarse with an awed admiration. "The damn blind fool!"

He pointed toward Sorainya's horde, and Lanning saw Willie Rand going to meet them. Bandaged head bent low, he moved at a blind, stumbling run. The broken Mauser was level in his hands, the whetted bayonet gleaming.

The black warriors paused before that solitary charge, as if bewildered. Sorainya's fierce shout urged them on. Their guns rattled, and the sailor staggered. But he ran on.

Lanning stumbled to the speaking tube.

"Wil!" he gasped. "Can we help?"

"No." Wil McLan, under the dome, shook his head. "But it's what he wanted. Useless—but grand!"

Even Sorainya had halted. Her golden needle spat blue fire. Willie Rand lurched. His clothing began to smoke. But still he lurched on, to meet the yellow axes lifted. Lanning had dropped on his knees, to help with the jammed gun. But he saw Rand come to Sorainya's ranks. He saw the flashing bayonet, as if guided by some extrasensory vision, drive deep into a black thorax.

The golden axes fell—

But Wil McLan, on his bridge, had spun his shining wheel, and the *Chronion* was gone from Sorainya's hall, back into the blue shimmering gulf of her own timeless track. Lanning reeled through the turret, where Duffy Clark was now on duty behind the crystal gun, and up to join Wil McLan in the dome. The old man seized his arm, desperately.

"Denny? You got it?"

"Yes. But how'd you happen to meet us? And where's Barinin?"

"They found us on the ledge," breathed the voiceless man. "Turned down a *gyrane* ray, from the battlements. Barinin was caught at the gun. Crisped!" he shuddered.

"We had to take off. I drove on into the future, to avoid their time ship. I was afraid to enter the fortress with the ship—when we couldn't explore it with the search beam, there was too much danger of collision with some solid object, with very disastrous results.

"But nothing else was left. We had to take the risk—and we won." He mopped sweat from his scarseamed face. "That hall was the largest room. From my plans, and a study of the ruins in futurity, I approximated its position. And we came back to where it had been."

"But—the object you recovered?"

Lanning handed him the glazed black brick.

"Open it up," the old man rasped. "We've got to discover where Glarath and Sorainya found it, in time and space, and replace it there."

Lanning lifted his eyes from the little block that was the foundation of all Jonbar. Anxiously, he caught at McLan's twisted arm. "Do you think—? Will they follow?"

"Of course they'll follow." McLan's hollow eyes glazed with dread. "This means life and death to them. And they have their own time ship. If they fail to overtake us on the way, they will surely be waiting where the object must be placed. They know the spot." He returned the brick to Lanning. "See if you can break it open."

The block was glass-hard. Lanning tapped at it vainly, broke his pocket knife on it, then carried it down to the deck. It yielded at last to hack saw, chisel, and sledge. It proved to be a thick-walled box, packed with white fiber. His quivering fingers lifted the packings to uncover a thick, V-shaped piece of rusty iron.

His vague, wild expectations had been all of something spectacular: perhaps some impressive document of state upon which history should have turned, or the martyr's weapon that might have asassinated some enemy of progress. Sick with disappointment, he carried the thing back to Wil McLan.

"Just a piece of scrap iron," he said. "A rusty old magnet,

out of the magneto of a Model T. And we sepnt all those lives to find it!''

"No matter what it is," the old man whispered. "It was important enough, when Sorainya wrenched it out of the past, to deflect the whole direction of probability—to break the last geodesics of Jonbar.

"Now, with the chronoscope, I must try to find where it belongs. Then we must put it back—if Sorainya allows us!'' He looked up at Lanning. "But you're all in, Denny. You've been hurt.''

Lanning had hardly been conscious of fatigue. Even the ring and throb of pain in the back of his brain had become endurable, a vague and distant phenomenon that did not greatly matter. He felt a great surprise, now, when the dome went black and he knew that he was falling to the floor.

Chapter 13

SEED OF FUTURITY

LANNING WOKE, WITH HIS HEAD BANDAGED, LYING IN THE little green-walled hospital. Barry Halloran grinned at him from the opposite bed. The little cockney, Duffy Clark, came presently with a covered tray.

"Cap'n McLan?" he drawled. "Why, 'e's lookin' inter 'is bloomin' gadgets, tryin' to find where that she-devil and 'er blarsted hants got 'old of that magnet."

"Any luck?" demanded Lanning.

"Not yet, sor." He shook a tousled head. "Wot with hall spayce and time to search for the spot. And the woman an' her blarsted 'igh priest is arfter us, sor, in a black ship full of the bloomin' hants!"

"But we can outrun them!" Barry Halloran broke in. "We can give 'em all they want."

"Hi dunno, sor!" Clark shook his head. "We're going hall out. And still they're 'olding us, neck and neck."

A leaden lethargy still weighed Lanning down. He ate a little, and slept again. Many hours of the ship's time must have passed when he suddenly woke, aware of another sound above

87

the accelerated throb of the hydrogen converter—the Maxim hammering.

He tumbled out of bed, with Barry Halloran after him, and ran to the deck. The firing had already stopped. The *Chronion* was once more thrumming alone through the flickering blue abyss. But little Duffy Clark lay beside the gun, smoking and still, his body half consumed by the *gyrane* ray.

Shuddering, Lanning climbed into the dome.

"They caught us," sobbed Wil McLan. "They'll catch us again. The converter's overdriven. As the grids are consumed, they lose efficiency. Clark's gone. That leaves four."

"Did you find—anything?"

The old man nodded, and Lanning listened breathlessly.

"The time is an afternoon in August of the year 1921," whispered Wil McLan. "The broken geodesics of Jonbar had already given us a clue to that. Now I have found the place, with the search beam."

Lanning gripped his arm. "Where?"

"It's a little valley in the Ozarks of Arkansas. I'll show you the decisive scene."

McLan limped to the metal cabinet of the geodesic analyzer. His broken fingers set its dials. A greenish luminescence filled the crystal block, and cleared. Lanning bent forward eagerly, looking into that strange window of probability.

An eroded farm, folded in the low and ancient hills. A sagging paintless shack, a broken window gaping and the roof inadequately patched with rusty tin. A rocky cow pasture, its steep slopes scantily covered with useless brush. A small freckled boy in faded overalls and a big ragged straw hat, trudging slowly barefoot down the slope, accompanied by a gaunt yellow dog, driving two lean red-spotted cows home to the milking pen.

"Watch him," whispered Wil McLan urgently.

As Lanning watched, the boy stopped to encourage his dog digging furiously after a rabbit. He squatted to observe a colony of ants. He ran to catch a gaudy butterfly, and carefully dissected it with a broken pocket knife. He rose unwillingly to answer the calls of a slatternly woman from the house below, and ambled after the cows again. Wil McLan's gnarled fingers closed on Lanning's arm, urgently.

"Now!"

The boy paused over something beside a sumac bush, and stopped to pick it up. The object blurred oddly in the crystal screen, so that Lanning could not distinguish it. The scene was erased, as Wil McLan snapped off the mechanism.

"Well?" Lanning turned to him, in bewilderment. "What has that to do with Jonbar?"

"That is John Barr," said the voiceless man. "For that metropolis of future possibility will be—or may be—named for him. He is twelve years old in 1921, barefoot son of a tenant farmer. You saw him at the turning point of his life— and the life of the world."

"But I don't understand!"

"The geodesics diverge from the thing he stoops to pick up," whispered Wil McLan. "It is either the magnet that we recovered from Sorainya's citadel—or else only an oddly colored pebble that lies beside it. That small choice—which Sorainya sought to decide by removing the magnet—determines which one of two possible John Barrs is to be ultimately established in reality."

"Just a scrap of iron," Lanning said.

"The seed of Jonbar," answered McLan. "If he picks up the discarded magnet, he'll discover the mysterious attraction it has for the blade of his knife, and the strange north-seeking power of its poles. He'll wonder, experiment, theorize. His curiosity will deepen. The scientist will be born in him.

"He'll study, borrow books from the teacher at the one-room school in the hollow. He'll presently leave the farm, running away from a domineering father who sneers at 'book larnin',' to work his way through college. He'll become a teacher of science in country schools, an amateur experimenter.

"Sometimes the flame will burn low in him, inspiration forgotten in the drudgery of life. He'll marry and raise two children. But his old thirst for knowledge will never be quite extinguished. Finally, at the age of fifty-five, he'll run away again—this time from a domineering wife and an obnoxious son-in-law—to carry on his research.

"A bald, plump little man, mild-mannered, dreamy, impractical, he'll work for years alone in a little cottage in the Ozarks. Every possible cent will go for the makeshift apparatus. He'll often go hungry. Once a neigbor will find him starving, nearly dead of influenza.

"But at last, in 1980, a tired but triumphant little man of seventy-one, he'll publish his great discovery. The dynatomic tensors—soon shortened to *dynat*. A totally new law of nature, linking life and mind to atomic probability. I had stumbled on one phase of it, with the hydrogen converter. But his tensors will open up a tremendous new technology for the direct release of atomic energy, under full control of the human will.

"Given freely to the world, the new science of the *dynat* will create a whole new civilization—although John Barr himself, always too busy to wait for material success, will be quietly buried that same year beside a little church in the Ozarks. The illimitable power of atoms fully tamed will become the life-blood of Jonbar.

"Nor is that all. Humanity will soar on the wings of this most magnificent slave. The *dynat* will bring a new contact of mind and matter, new senses, new capabilities. Gradually, as time goes on, mankind will become adapted to the full use of the *dynat*."

The whisper was hoarse with a breathless awe.

"And at last a new race will arise, calling themselves the *dynon*. The splendid children of John Barr's old discovery, they will possess faculties and powers that we can hardly dream of—"

"Wait!" Lanning broke in. "I've seen the *dynon!* When Lethonee first came, so long ago, to my room in Cambridge, she showed me New Jonbar in her time crystal. A city of majestic shining pylons. And, flying above them, a glorious people, clad, it seemed, in pure fire!"

Hollow eyes shining, Wil McLan nodded solemnly.

"I, too, have looked into New Jonbar," he whispered. "I have seen the promised glory beyond: the triumphant flight of the *dynon*, from star to star, forever. In that direction, there was no ending to the story of mankind.

"But in the other—"

His white head shook. There was silence under the dome. Lanning could hear the swiftened throb of the converter, driving them back through the giddy blue shimmer of possibility toward the quiet scene in the Ozarks they had watched in the crystal block. He saw Lao Meng Shan cleaning the Maxim on the deck below; and Barry Halloran, rifle ready, peering alertly into the flickering abyss.

"If we're unable to replace the magnet," McLan whispered again, "the boy John Barr will pick up the pebble instead, and the tide of probability will be turned—as, indeed, it is turned—toward Gyronchi. The boy will toss the pebble in his hand, and throw it in his sling to kill a singing bird. All his life thereafter will want a precious spark. It will remain curiously similar, yet significantly different.

"John Barr, in this outcome also, will run away from his father's home, but now to become a shiftless migratory worker. He will marry the same woman, raise the same two children, and leave them at last. The same ingenuity, turned to the same basic problems of probability, will lead him to invent a new gambling device, on which he will make and lose a fortune. He will die, equally penniless, in the same year, and lie at last in the same graveyard.

"The secret of mentally released atomic power will now be discovered nine years later, but with a control far less complete than John Barr would have attained. The discoverer will be one Ivor Gyros, an exiled engineer from Soviet Eurasia, working with a renegade Buddhist priest. Calling their half-mastered secret the *gyrane*, the two will guard it selfishly, use it to destroy their enemies and impress the superstitious. They'll establish a fanatical new religion, and a new despotic empire. That's the beginning of the cult of the *gyrane*, and Sorainya's dark dynasty. You have seen the end of them."

"I have!"

And a shudder touched Lanning, as he recalled that desolate scene: mankind annihilated in the final war of the priests and the kings, by the *gyrane* and the monstrous creatures it had bred; the jungle returning across a devastated planet, to cover the rusting pile of Sorainya's citadel and the shattered ruins of her temple of ignorance and fear. He grasped at the rusty V-magnet.

"And so—" he nodded. "All we have to do is put it back, where John Barr will find it?"

"All," rasped Wil McLan. "Enough!"

The sudden rattle of the Maxim took Lanning's breath. Stiff with startled dread, Wil McLan was pointing. Lanning turned. Close beyond the dome, he saw the black ugly shape of the time ship from Gyronchi.

"Caught!" sobbed McLan. "The converter—failing!"

He flung his broken body toward the controls. But already, Lanning saw, the decks had touched. In the face of the hammering Maxim, a horde of the anthropoid ants were pouring over the rail. Leading them with her flaming golden blade, magnificent in her crimson mail, came Sorainya!

Chapter 14

SORAINYA'S KISS

LANNING SHIVERED.

"Sorainya!" Wil McLan rasped savagely, as if her name had been an oath. His quivering, broken hands came slowly up to finger the old little tube of bright-worn silver hanging at his throat. A smouldering hate glazed his eyes again, as he looked at the warrior-queen. Something twisted his white-scarred lips. A grimace of agony. Or was it a smile?

"Why, Sorainya?" he breathed faintly. "Why must it be?"

"Wil!" Lanning shouted at him. "They're boarding us! Can't we get away?"

"Huh!" McLan blinked at the swarming monsters, as if he hadn't seen them before. " 'Fraid not, Denny." His thin hands dropped back to the controls, but he was shaking his head. "The converter—already overloaded—"

A score of the black giants came over the rail, rushing the Maxim. Lao Meng Shan crouched to meet them with the clattering gun. Barry Halloran stood beside it, a sturdy, smiling, wholly human giant, ready with his bayonet.

"Fight 'em!" his great voice was booming. "Stop that pass!"

94

Grinning blandly, the little Chinese made no sound at all.

With a ringing war cry, Sorainya had turned toward the turret, followed by a dozen warriors. The needle of her golden sword flashed up, pointing at Wil McLan in the dome. And her green-eyed face was suddenly contorted with such a furious passion of hate that Lanning shuddered.

"She's coming here!" sobbed Wil McLan. "After me!"

Lanning was already on the turret stair. "I'll go down to meet her."

McLan whispered after him, "I'll pull away, if the converter'll stand it—"

In the little turret, beside the crystal tube that projected the temporal field, Lanning belted on a Luger. He shatched the last Mauser from the rack, loaded it. His eye caught one hand grenade left in the box. He scooped it up, gripped the safety pin.

The little door was groaning and ringing to a furious assault from without—for the *Chronion* had not been designed for a fighting ship. It yielded suddenly, and a black monster pitched through.

Lanning tossed the grenade through the doorway, and ripped at the attacker with his bayonet. A sour reek of formic acid stung his eyes. A savage mandible ripped trousers and skin from his leg. But the third thrust stopped the creature, and he stepped into the doorway.

Outside, the grenade had checked the charge. Three black warriors lay where it had tossed them, crushed and dying. But the queen herself stood unharmed in the crimson mail, with eight more giants about her. A savage light of battle flamed in her long green eyes, and she urged them forward with her golden sword.

"Denny Lanning," her voice cut cold as steel. "You were warned. But you defied Gyronchi, and chose Jonbar. So—die!"

Yet Lanning, waiting in the turret door, had a moment left. He had time for a glimpse of Barry and Shan, now engaged in a furious battle about the Maxim, holding back a murderous avalanche. He caught Barry's gasping:

"Fight! Fight, team! Fight!"

And he saw the high dark side of the other ship, beyond. He glimpsed the gaunt, cadaverous priest, Glarath, safe on his quarter-deck. He saw a second company of armored giants, gathering at the rail, ready to follow the first.

Panic gripped him. The odds were overwhelming—

But suddenly the black ship was gone, with Glarath and the rank of giants. There was only the dancing haze of the blue abyss. He knew that Wil McLan had driven the *Chronion* ahead once more in that race into the past.

But Sorainya and her boarding party were still on the deck. The Maxim suddenly ceased to fire. Shan and Barry were surrounded. But then the attackers converged upon Lanning, and he crouched to meet them. The bayonet had proved more effective than bullets against the creatures. And now he fought with the same technique he had learned in Sorainya's citadel.

A ripping lunge, a twist, a savage thrust. One giant fell. Another. A third. Black, reeking bodies piled the doorway. Spilled vital fluids were slippery on the deck. The bullet from a crimson gun raked Lanning's side. A golden axe touched his head with searing pain. A heavy gun, flung spinning like a club, knocked out his breath. But he recovered himself, in time to lunge again.

Sorainya ran back and forth behind the warriors, screaming her battle cry, her white face both beautiful and dreadful with the cold elation burning in her greenish eyes. Once, when the giants fell back and gave her an opening, she leveled the needle of her sword at Lanning. Knowing the deadly fire it held, he dropped and whipped a shot at her red-mailed body with the Luger.

His bullet whined harmless from her armor. And her jet of strange fire merely grazed his shoulder. A jolting shock hurled him aside against the wall. Half blind, dazed, he slapped at his burning shirt, and reeled back to meet her giants.

Four were left. His staggering lunge caught one. Another fell, queerly, before his bayonet had touched it. And a hearty voice came roaring to his ears:

"Fight, gang! Fight!"

He saw that the battle on the foredeck was ended. A great pile of Sorainya's monsters lay dead about the Maxim. Lao Meng Shan was looking over the barricade, with a curiously cheerful grin fixed on his yellow round face. And Barry Halloran, crimson and terrible with the marks of battle, came chanting down the deck. It was a burst from his Luger that had dropped the creature beside Lanning. He flung the empty pistol aside, and leveled his dripping bayonet.

Lanning was swaying, gasping for breath, fighting a descending blindness, as he fought the two remaining giants, feinted, lunged, recovered, parried, defending the turret door.

But he saw Sorainya turn to meet Barry Halloran, and heard her low mocking laugh. He saw the rifle lifted, in Barry's crimson hands, ready for the lunge that might have pierced the queen's woven mail.

"Fight—"

Barry's chanting stopped on a low breathless cry, muted with astonishment. The grim smile of battle was driven from his face by a sudden, involuntary admiration.

"My God, I can't—"

The bayonet wavered. And the queen of war, with a brilliant smile and a mocking flirt of her sable plume, darted quickly forward. The golden needle flickered out in a lightning thrust, to drive his body through.

Lanning's reeling lunge caught one of the attackers. He ripped, twisted, recovered. He staggered back from a flashing yellow blade, lurched forward again to engage the one survivor.

But his eyes went back again to Barry and Sorainya. With all a dancer's grace, she followed through with her savage thrust, and leaned to recover her blade. He saw her draw it through her naked hand, and then blow Barry a malicious kiss from fingers red with his own lifeblood.

A dark fountain burst and foamed from Barry Halloran's heart. The admiration on his face gave way to a pale grimace of hate. His hands tried to lift the rifle, but it slipped away from them and fell. His eyes came to Lanning, wide and dark and bewildered, like a lost child's.

"Denny—" he sobbed faintly. "*Kill* her!"

And he slipped down, beyond Sorainya.

Lanning brought his staggered mind back to the one remaining giant. Too late. Its golden axe was falling, but he had time to finish his lunge. A little deflected, the flat of the blade crashed against his head, and drowned him in black pain.

Automatically, the run-down machine of his body finished that familiar rhythm: rip, twist, slash, before it toppled down beside the dying monster. Some atom of awareness lingered for another instant. *Don't quit now!* it shrieked. *Or Sorainya will kill Wil McLan. She'll take the magnet back. And Jonbar will be lost.*

But that despairing scream faded with his consciousness.

Chapter 15

THE SILVER TUBE

AGONY WAS STILL A RUSH AND A DRUMMING BEAT, THROUGH all of Lanning's head. But desperate purpose had torn through his oblivion, and somehow set him on his feet again. The throbbing deck spun beneath him, and the blinding fog in his eyes veiled the flickering blue. But he saw Lao Meng Shan and Barry Halloran lying dead among the slaughtered giants. Sorainya was gone from the deck, but he could hear her malicious golden voice.

". . . a long pursuit, Wil McLan. I thank you for the pleasure of the chase. Remember, once I promise you my sword—"

A terrible muted scream whispered down from the dome, and then Lanning heard Sorainya's pitiless laugh.

"Perhaps you've always had the means to destroy me, Wil McLan. But never will—for I know why you first came to Gyronchi. Other men have tried to kill me—like moths trying with their wings to beat out a flame!"

"We'll see, Sorainya," Lanning muttered. "For Barry's sake!"

His body moved stiffly, like a rusted machine. It staggered

and reeled. Pain ran like a river through his brain. A mist of darkness clouded his sight. His limbs were dead, useless tools. Even his own garments hampered him, stiff with drying blood.

But he found the Mauser, and picked it up, and staggered into the turret he had tried to guard, where the metal stair led up to the bridge. Sorainya's voice came down to him again, as she boasted:

"You're a fool, Wil McLan, to bring your silly little men against me. For, since you brought us the secret of time, the *gyrane* can conquer death also. With the time shell, I've searched the future for the hour of my death. And I found no danger that can't be avoided. I may be the last of my line—but I shall reign forever!"

Reeling up the turret stair, Lanning came into the space beneath the dome. Wil McLan lay on the floor, beneath the shining wheel. His broken hands were set down in a wide pool of his own dark blood, as he strove to raise himself. His emaciated face was lifted to Sorainya, sick and dreadful with a hopeless, helpless hate. Suspended by its thin white chain from his neck, the little silver tube hung over the spreading pool of blood.

Lithe and tall in the red splendor of her black-plumed mail, Sorainya stood smiling down at McLan, crimson drops still falling from her sword. But she heard Lanning's unsteady step, and turned swiftly to meet him at the top of the stair. A bright exultation lit her face. A deadly eager light flashed in her narrowed eyes, at sight of Lanning.

"Well, Denny!" she greeted him. "So you would try, where all the best have failed?"

Her ringing blade struck sparks from his bayonet.

She was as tall, almost, as Lanning, and quick with a hard feline vitality. The woven red mail followed every flowing curve of her. Her wide nostrils flared, and high breasts rose to her quickened breathing. She attacked like a panther springing.

Lanning parried with the bayonet, thrust warily. She swayed

aside. The bayonet slid harmless by her armored breast. And
the yellow needle flicked Lanning's shoulder with a whip of
pain.

His weapon was the longer, the heavier. It made no
difference, he tried to tell himself, that she was a woman, so
beautiful. Barry's death was still dark agony writhing in him,
and he could see Wil McLan sprawled in the pool of blood
behind her, gasping terribly for breath and following the battle
with glazed, hate-litten eyes.

But he fought a fatigue more deadly than her blade. All his
strength had been poured out in the battle with her giants. She
was fresh, and she had a tireless quickness. He saw her cruel
little smile of elation, as the rifle grew too heavy for his
clumsy hands. His vision dulled to a blurry monochrome.
Sorainya was a shadow, that could not die.

He was glad she blurred, for he could no longer see her
lissome loveliness. He tried to see, in her place, one of her
insectile monsters. He lunged into the rhythm of the old attack:
rip, twist, slash.

But the bayonet slithered again, harmless, from her woven
armor. And the flash of her sword drew a red line of pain down
his arm. She danced back, with a pantherine grace, and then
stood, as if to mock him, with the yellow needle lowered to
her side.

"No, Denny Lanning!" She gave a little breathless laugh.
"Strike if you will—for I shall never die. I scanned all the
future for the hour of my death, and found no danger. I can't
be slain!"

"I'll see!" Lanning caught a long gasping breath, and shook
his ringing head. "For Barry—"

With the last atom of his ebbing strength, he gripped the
rifle hard and rushed across the tiny room under the dome. He
thrust the gleaming bayonet, with every ounce of muscle, up
under the curve of her breast, toward her heart.

"*Denny!*"

It was a choking sob of warning from Wil McLan. The

golden needle flashed up to touch the rifle. Blue fire hissed from its point. The rifle fell out of Lanning's hands. He staggered backward, stunned and blinded by the shock, smelling his seared hands and a burning pungence of ozone.

He caught his weight against the curve of the dome, and leaned there, shuddering. It took all his will to keep his knees from buckling. He caught a deep rasping breath, and blinked his eyes. He saw Sorainya gliding forward, light as a dancer. Beneath stray wisps of golden hair, her white face was dazzling with a smile. And her lazy voice drawled softly:

"Now, Denny Lanning! Who is immortal?"

Her arm flashed up as she spoke, slim and red in its sleeve of mail. A terrible tigerish joy flashed in her green eyes. Her sword, like a living thing, leapt at Lanning's heart.

He struck at the blade, with his empty hand. It slashed his wrist. Deflected a little, it drove through his shoulder, a cold thin needle of numbing pain, and rang against the hard crystal behind him.

Sorainya whipped out the sword, and wiped its thin length on her fingers. She blew him a crimson kiss, and stood waiting with a thirsty smile for him to fall.

"Well?" Her voice was a liquid caress. "Another?"

Then Lanning's failing eyes went beyond her. The tiny dome swam. It took a desperate effort for him to find Wil McLan. But he saw the jerky little movement that broke the thin white chain, tossed the worn silver tube toward him. He heard McLan's voiceless gasp:

"Break it, Denny! I—can't!"

Sorainya had sensed the movement behind her. Her breath caught sharply, The yellow sword darted again, swift as a flash of light, straight for Lanning's heart. Even the tigerish quickness of that last thrust, he thought, was beautiful—

But the silver cylinder had rolled to his foot. Desperately, shuddering with a cold, incredulous awareness that, somehow, he was so crushing Sorainya's victorious beauty, he drove his heel down upon the tube.

It made a tiny crunching sound. But Lanning didn't look down. His eyes were fixed, in a trembling breathless dread, upon Sorainya. No visible hand had touched her. But, from the instant his heel came down, she was—stricken.

The bright blade slipped out of her hand, rang against the dome, and fell at Lanning's feet. Her smile of triumph was somehow frozen on her face, forgotten. Then, in a fractional second, her beauty was—erased.

Her altered face was blind, pocked with queerly bluish ulcerations. Her features dissolved, frightfully, into fluid blue corruption. And Lanning had an instant's impression of a naked skull grinning fearfully out of her red armor.

And Sorainya was gone.

The woven mail, for a weird timeless instant, still held the curves of her body. It slumped grotesquely, and fell with a dull little thud on the floor. The plumed helmet clattered down beside it, and rolled, and looked back at Lanning with an empty, enigmatic stare.

Lanning tried to look back at Wil McLan, for an explanation of this appalling victory. But a thickening darkness shut out his vision, and the ringing was deafening in his head. A shuddering numbness ran through him from the wound in his shoulder. And his knees collapsed.

Chapter 16

RENDEZVOUS WITH DESTINY

LANNING LAY UNDER THE CRYSTAL DOME. THE THROB OF THE atomic converts rang loud on the deck beneath his head. An anvil of agony still rang in his skull, and all his body was an aching, blood-clotted stiffness. But, queerly, the cold pain had ebbed from the sword-thrust in his shoulder.

"Denny?"

It was a voiceless sob from Wil McLan, husky with an urgent pleading. Lanning was surprised that the old man still survived Sorainya's attack. He struggled to his feet, and found McLan still lying in that darkening, clotting pool.

"Wil! What can I do?"

"The needle in the drawer," gasped McLan. "Four c.c. Intravenous—"

Lanning stumbled to the control board, found, in the drawer beneath it, a bright hypodermic and a small bottle of heavy lead, marked: *Dynatomic Formula L 648. Filled, New York City, August, 1935*. The liquid, in the needle, shone with a greenish luminescence. He rolled up McLan's sleeve, thrust the point into a vein at the elbow, pushed home the little plunger.

He examined the old man's wound. It had already ceased to bleed. It looked puzzlingly as if it had been healing for days, instead of minutes.

"Thanks," whispered McLan. "Now yourself—but only two c.c."

He lay back on the floor, with his eyes closed. Lanning made the injection into his own arm, and felt a quick tide of life running through his veins. His dulled senses cleared. Still he was dead-tired, still his battered head ached; yet he felt a quickening stir of the same strange well-being that he had found once before aboard the *Chronion*, after the surgeons of Jonbar had brought him back from death. He picked up the rusty little magnet lying on the floor beside Sorainya's empty armor.

"Do you think—?" he whispered hoarsely. "Can we put it back?"

"If the converter holds out." McLan pulled himself, feebly, up to the wheel. "Glarath will be guarding the spot, with his ship and the monsters. And you'll be all alone. I can take you there, but I'm about done for."

The thrumming of the converter was swifter again, as his broken hands touched keys and dials.

"Sorainya? That tube I broke?" Lanning touched his twisted shoulder. "Wil, what happened to Sorainya?"

The old man turned. Clutching the bright wheel with both gnarled hands to support his weight, he looked at Lanning. The hatred was gone from his haggard eyes; they were dull with an agony of grief.

"Her life was in that silver tube," he whispered. "I've carried it, all these years. But I could never pour it out."

"Her life?" Horror touched Lanning again. "But nothing touched her, when I broke the tube."

"She thought she was immortal." McLan's voiceless voice was faint and dry with pain. "She failed to discover the hour of her death when she searched her future. Because it was in her past! The year she came to the throne, the Blue Death swept Gyronchi—a plague that came from some mutant virus created accidentally by the breeders of those half-human ants. That's what killed Sorainya."

"But—?" Lanning stared at him blankly. "I don't understand!"

"After I got out of Sorainya's dungeons, I determined to destroy her," he sobbed. "I searched her past, with the temporal ray, for a node of probability. I found it, in the year of the Blue Death.

"You see the priests of the *gyrane* managed to prepare a few shots of effective antitoxin. When Sorainya caught the disease, Glarath rushed to the palace with the last tube of the serum, to save her life. But if the tube had been broken before it reached her, the analyzer revealed, she would have died. So I drove the *Chronion* back through the temple to the plague year, and carried away the tube."

"I see!" Lanning nodded slowly, awed. "It was like carrying away a magnet, to destroy Jonbar."

"Not quite," pointed out Wil McLan. "The magnet was carried so far into the conflicting future of Gyronchi that its geodesics were strained; and finally snapped at the vital node, so that Jonbar was blotted from the fifth-dimensional sequence.

"But I carried the tube back into Sorainya's past. The geodesics were never quite broken, and it was still possible for them to loop back to the node. Therefore—so long as the tube was intact—her survival was still possible. But when you spilled the serum, that possibility was obliterated.

"But if—" Lanning stood staring, numbed with a wondering dread. "If Sorainya died as a girl, what about Sorainya the queen? The woman that imprisoned you, and haunted me, and fought the legion—did she never exist?"

McLan smiled faintly at his bewilderment.

"Remember, we are dealing with probabilities alone. The new physics has banished absolute certainty from the world. Jonbar and Gyronchi, the two Sorainyas, living and dead, are but conflicting branches of possibility, as yet unfixed in the fifth dimension. The crushing of the tube merely altered the probability factors affecting Sorainya's possible life."

A soft gleam of tears was in his hollow eyes. They looked down at the little glistening heap of woven mail, the empty helmet and the golden sword.

"But she was real, to me," he breathed. "Too real."

"These wounds?" Lanning demanded suddenly. "How were they made by a woman who didn't exist?"

"When they were made, her probability did exist," whispered Wil McLan. "And a lot of atomic power had been spent, through the temporal field, to match our probability to hers. But you'll notice they're disappearing now, with a remarkable rapidity."

His bright hollow eyes lifted to Lanning.

"Just keep in mind, Denny, that the logical laws of causation are still rigid—but only one step removed. The absolute sequence of events, in the fifth dimension, is not parallel with time—although our three-dimensional minds commonly perceive it as so. But that inviolable progression is the unalterable frame of all the universe."

His gnarled fingers reached out to touch the rusty magnet in Lanning's hand.

"The march of that progression, higher than time," his hushed whisper ran on solemnly, "has now forever obliterated Sorainya the queen. The sequence of events has not yet settled the fates of Jonbar and Gyronchi. But still the odds are all with Gyronchi."

He gripped Lanning's arm, his thin hand quivering.

"The last play is near," he breathed. "The hope—the probability—of Jonbar is all in you, Denny. And the outcome will soon be engraved forever in the fifth dimension."

He turned to grasp the wheel.

And the *Chronion* ran back down her geodesic track until the dials stood at 5:49 P.M., August 12, 1921. McLan raised his feeble hand in a warning signal, and his whisper quavered down through the speaking tube:

"Ready, Denny! They'll be waiting."

Lanning stood peering into the dancing mists of time. As a desperate ruse that might win a precious moment, he had put on Sorainya's armor. Her black perfume waved above his head. He clutched her golden sword—but whatever device had made it project that deadly blue ray was either broken or exhausted. He moistly gripped the rusty magnet, that must be returned to its place in space and time.

His weary brain, as he waited, dully pondered a last paradox: though they had outrun the time ship of Glarath in the long race backward through the centuries, no possible speed could bring them first to the goal ahead. He gripped the sword, as the throb of the converter stopped, and straightened in the borrowed mail.

And the *Chronion* flashed out of the blue again, into the lonely hush of that eroded valley in the age-worn Ozarks. Everything was exactly as Lanning had seen it in the shining block of the chronoscope: the idle, tattered boy, following the two lean cows down the rocky slope toward the dilapidated farm, with his gaunt yellow dog roving beside him.

Everything—except that now the great, squarish black mass of the time ship from Gyronchi lay beside the trail, like a battleship aground. Glarath was a tall black pillar on his lofty desk. The ugly projectors of the *gyrane* beam scowled from their ports. Scores of the warrior giants had been disembarked, to make a hideous wall about the spot where the magnet must be placed.

Whistling, the dawdling boy had come within twenty yards of the spot, but he gave no evidence that he saw either ship or monsters. One of the red-spotted cows, ahead, plodded calmly through an anthropoid monster. And back to Lanning, where he waited to leap from the deck, came McLan's whispered explanation:

"No, the boy John Barr won't be aware of us at all—unless

we should turn the temporal field upon him. For his life is already almost completely fixed by the advancing progression in the fifth dimension. In terms of his experience, we are no more than the most shadowy phantoms of probability. Travelers backward into time can affect the past only at carefully selected nodes, and then only at the expense of the terrific power required to deflect the probability-inertia of the whole continuum. Glarath and Sorainya spent atomic energy enough to blast continents, just to lift the magnet from John Barr's path.''

Gripping the magnet and the sword, Lanning flung himself to the ground. He stumbled on a rock, fell to his knees, staggered back to his feet, ran desperately toward the time ship and the armored horde ahead of the loitering boy.

He waved the golden sword, as he ran, in Sorainya's familiar gesture. Glarath, on his bridge, waved a black-swathed arm to answer—but then, as Lanning's heavy feet tripped again, with none of Sorainya's grace, the black priest went rigid with alarm. His great hoarse voice bellowed a command. The wall of giants came to attention, bristling with the crimson and yellow metal. And a thick black tube swung down in its port.

The first blast of atomic radiation struck a rock beside Lanning. The granite exploded. Molten stone spattered the red mail. A hot fragment slapped his cheek with white agony, and blinded him with the smoke of his own flesh burning.

The boy, meantime, had already walked into the unsuspected warrior ranks, and cold desperation caught Lanning's heart. In a few moments more, John Barr would pick up the pebble instead of the magnet, and settle the fate of two worlds forever.

Strangled with bitter white smoke, Lanning caught a sobbing breath, and sprinted. Another blinding jet of atomic fire fused the soil to a smoking pool of lava, close behind him. He ran on, too close now for the *gyrane* rays to reach him, but the wall of monsters waited ahead.

Thick crimson guns came level, and a volley battered him. The bullets failed to pierce the woven mail. But the impacts were bruising, staggering blows, and one missile raked his unprotected jaw and neck, beneath the helmet. A sickening pain loosened his muscles. Red gouts splashed down on the crimson mail. He spat broken teeth and blood, and stumbled on.

Insect limbs whirled yellow axes high. He raised Sorainya's sword, and stumbled on to meet them. For an instant he thought the creatures would yield, in awe of the dead queen's armor. But when Glarath cracked another command from above, they fell upon him furiously.

Golden blades ripped and battered at his mail. He drove Sorainya's sword into a shining hard thorax. A clubbed red gun smashed against his extended arm. The bone gave with a brittle snap, and his arm fell useless in the sleeve of mail. He clutched the precious magnet close to his body, and lunged ahead.

Blows rained on him. Something battered the helmet stunningly against his skull. A cleaving axe cut his neck half in two, at the juncture of helmet and mail. Hot blood gushed down inside the shirt, and his limbs went lax.

Yet some old terror of their dead mistress repelled the giants from any actual contact with her armor. So Lanning, even wounded and beaten down, came reeling through their ranks to the hollow square they guarded.

He saw the ragged boy stroll whistling idly through the linen of giants, the hungry dog at his heels. He saw the gleam of the pebble, the triangular print in the clay where the magnet had lain, not two paces from the boy. Another second—

But he was falling. His strength was spurting out in the red stream jetting from his neck. Another merciless blow smashed his shoulder, numbed the arm that held the magnet, crushed him down.

His eyes fogged with pain. But, as he fell, he saw beside him, or thought he did, a splendid figure. A grave majestic head, towering out of a shimmering opalescence. The stranger looked at him, and his body tingled as if a cool unseen something had brushed against him. A calm voice spoke, if only in his mind:

"Courage, Denny Lanning!"

And the man was gone.

Lanning knew that he had been one of the *dynon*, the remote heirs of Jonbar. His mere glance had somehow eased Lanning's pain, brought life back to his collapsing limbs. But Glarath had bellowed another command. An avalanche of giants fell upon Lanning. And the aimless boy was already stooping for the pebble.

Lanning hurled himself forward, his good arm thrust out with the magnet. A yellow blade hacked through his arm. Mute monsters crushed him down. But the magnet, flung with the last effort of his fingers, dropped into the triangular print where it belonged.

A bright curiosity—the very light of science—was born in the eyes of the stooping boy. His inquisitive fingers closed on the V of steel. And the acid-reeking creatures piled on Lanning's body were suddenly gone.

The black ship flickered like a wing of shadow, and vanished.

John Barr picked up the magnet, with a faint whistle of wonder at a rusty nail clinging to it. He went on down the slope, driving his two spotted cows through the unseen hull of the *Chronion*.

Dennis Lanning was left alone beside the trail. He knew he was dying. But the fading throb of his pain was a triumphant drum. He knew Jonbar had won.

His dimming eyes clung to the *Chronion*. Hopelessly, he tried to hope that Wil McLan would come before he died. But the time ship shimmered and disappeared. He lay quite alone in the sunset on the hill.

Chapter 17

WORLDS THAT NEVER WERE

IT WAS A DREAM, HE KNEW, BUT LETHONEE HAD BEEN STANDING beside him. Tall and straight in the same white gown, with the great bright crystal of time cradled in her hands.

"Thank you—thank you, Denny Lanning." Her low voice had trembled and broken. "I bring you the gratitude of Jonbar, for something no other could have done."

Lanning struggled against the stiffening cold that had seized his body, and failed to speak a single word. But he saw her violet eyes shining with tears, and heard her sobbing voice:

"Don't die, Denny! Come back to me, in Jonbar!"

He had fought the cold rigor in him, but he couldn't answer. And now she was gone, like a fading dream. He knew that he lay dying, on that lonely Ozark hill.

But now there was another dream, even more fantastic. He thought he was once again lying in a clean bed in the little green-walled hospital on the *Chronion*. The brisk, efficient surgeons of Jonbar had been attending him for a long time, it seemed, in the dim drowsy intervals of sleep. Their wondrous science, he dreamed, had made his body whole again.

It had to be a dream. For Willie Rand was sitting up on the

113

opposite bed, grinning at him with clear, seeing eyes. Willie Rand! who had been slain, blind and alone, in that fantastic hopeless charge against the anthropoid ants, before Sorainya's diamond throne. He was blowing a smoke ring, watching it happily.

"Howdy, Cap'n Lanning. Cigarette?"

Numbed with bewilderment, Lanning reached automatically to catch the cigarette. There was no pain in the arm that the giant's clubbed gun had broken. He tried the fingers again, incredulously, and stared across at Willie Rand.

"What's happened?" he demanded. "I thought you were— were blind and dead. And I was cashing out—"

"Right, cap'n," Rand exhaled a white cloud, grinning through it. "Reckon we've all died twice. But now we're getting another stack of chips—all but poor old McLan."

"But—?" Lanning stared at the smoke, as if it had been the blue haze of time. "How—"

But then he heard a clatter on the stair. Barry Halloran and bull-like Emil Schorn came down from the deck, carrying a stretcher. Two of the surgeons from Jonbar followed, and a third rolled in a table of instruments. They laid the bandaged figure gently on a bed. Lanning caught the glint of a hypodermic and the glow of the little needles that shone with some healing radiation.

"The little limey, Duff Clark," Willie Rand was drawling. "Nearly lost him. Went overboard, you know, on the way back, and sort of got mislaid in probability and time. Took days to untangle the geo—geodesics. Scorched with the *gyrane*—the same hell-fire that burned out my eyes. But I reckon these medics can tune him up again."

Lanning was sitting up on the side of his bed, unsteadily at first. Now Barry Halloran discovered him. Barry, alive again! His rugged, freckled face lit with a joyous grin.

"Denny, old man!" He strode to grip Lanning's hand. "About time you came alive!"

"Tell me, Barry!" Lanning clung to his powerful hand,

shuddering to a sudden agony of hope. "How did all this happen? And can we—can we—?" He gulped, and his desperate eyes searched Barry's broad, cheerful face. "Can we go back to Jonbar?"

A shadow of pain blotted out the smile.

"Wil did it." Barry Halloran said. "The last thing he did. He left you where you put that magnet, and drove the *Chronion* back down to Jonbar. Dead when he got there—dead beyond the power of our friends to revive him."

The big tackle looked away for a moment.

"Wil knew he was going down," he went on huskily. "He rigged an automatic switch to stop the *Chronion* when it came to Jonbar. A new crew brought these doctors back, to haul us aboard and resurrect us again. Quite a hunt, I gather, through a snarl of broken geodesics—"

"Lethonee?" whispered Lanning, urgently. "Can we—"

"*Ach!*" It was a bellow of greeting from Emil Schorn. He smashed Lanning's fingers in a great ham of a hand. "*Ja*, Denny! Jonbar iss Valhalla! Where men fight und die—und fight und die again! Und Sorainya—"

An awed admiration deepened his bellow.

"Der red queen of war! *Ach*, a Valkyrie! A battlemaiden, terrible but beautiful. None like her in Jonbar, *nein.*"

"Jonbar?" Lanning gasped out the question. "Are we going there?"

"*Ach, Ja!* In our own times, we're all kaput. But der *Herren doktors* will find room for us there. We may even fight again, for Jonbar." His face lit. "*Ach, heil,* Valhalla!"

Lanning was standing on the deck, aglow once more with the quiet elation of perfect bodily well-being, when the *Chronion* slipped again from the shifting mists of time, into the clear sky over Jonbar.

Genial sunlight of a calm spring morning lay soft and warm upon the tall silver pylons. Gay-clad multitudes were pouring out across vast green parks and broad viaducts and terrace gardens of the towers, to greet the *Chronion*.

The battered little time ship drifted down slowly above them. The men out of the past, radiantly fit, but still, as ragged, faded, oddly assorted uniforms, were gathered at the rail, waving happily.

All the legion, alive again! Schorn and Rand and Duffy Clark, swarthy Cresto and somber Barinin and grinning Lao Meng Shan. The two lean Canadians, Isaac and Israel Enders, side by side. Courtney-Pharr, and Erich von Arneth, and Barry Halloran. And dapper little Jean Querard, perched perilously on the rail, making a speech into space.

But now it was one of the scientists from Jonbar who held the bright wheel under the dome. A great door had opened high in the wall of a familiar-seeming tower. The *Chronion* nosed through, to settle on her own platform in the great hangar, where a noisy crowd was waiting. Jean Querard strutted and inflated his chest. Teetering on the rail, he waved for silence.

"C'est bon," his high voice began. *"C'est tres bon—"*

Trembling with a still incredulous eagerness, Lanning slipped past him, into the crowd. He found the elevator. It flung him upward, and he stepped out into that same terrace garden, where he had dined with Lethonee.

Amid its fragrant, white-flowered shrubbery, he paused for a moment to catch his breath. His eyes fell to the wide green parks that spread to the placid river, a full mile beneath. And he saw a thing that stabbed his heart with a queer little needle of pain.

For this great river, he saw, was the same river that had curved through Gyronchi. Great pylons stood where miserable villages had huddled. The largest of them towered from the very hill that had been topped by the squat black temple of the *gyrane*.

But where was the other hill, where Sorainya's red citadel had been?

His breath quivered and caught, when he saw that it was this same hill, that bore the tower of Lethonee. His hands gripped hard on the railing, and he looked down at the little table where he had sat with Lethonee, on the dreadful night of Jonbar's dissolution. For Sorainya, glorious on her golden shell, rose again to mock him, as she had done that night. Tears dimmed his eyes, and a haunting, sudden ache gripped his pausing heart.

Oh, fair Sorainya . . . slain!

A light step raced through the sliding door behind the shrubs, and a breathless voice called his name, joyously. Lanning looked up, slowly. And a numbing wonder shook him.

"Denny Lanning!"

Lethonee came running toward him, through the flowers. Her violet eyes were bright with tears, and her face was a white smile of incredulous delight. Lanning moved shuddering to meet her, speechless.

For the golden voice of the warrior queen had mocked him in her cry. And the ghost of Sorainya's glance glinted green in her shining eyes. She even wore a close-fitted gown of shimmering metallic crimson, that shone like Sorainya's mail.

She came into his open, trembling arms.

"Denny—" she sobbed happily. "At last we are—one."

His new world spun. This same hill had carried Sorainya's citadel. But neither Jonbar nor Gyronchi had ever actually existed. Divergent roads of probability, stemming from the same beginning, they were now fused into the same reality. Lethonee and Sorainya—

"Yes, my darling." He drew them both against his racing heart, breathing softly, "One!"

AFTER
WORLD'S END

Contents

AFTER WORLD'S END

Foreword

WE FOUND THE STRANGER, WHEN WE UNLOCKED THE BUN-galow after a week on the lakes, seated at my big desk in the study. His face was an enigma of youth and age. Lean beneath his long white hair, it was gray and drawn and hollowed as if with an infinite heartbreak—and yet it smiled. His emaciated hand, thrust out across the pile of loose yellow sheets he had written, gripped an incredible thing.

Queerly lifelike, he was yet more queerly still.

"Why, hello!" I said.

And then, when he remained stiffly staring at that scintillating glory in his rigid hand, we knew that he was dead.

His injuries, when we came to discover them, were dreadful as they were inexplicable. All his gaunt, shrunken body—torso, neck, and limbs—showed dark purple ridges. It looked as the body of Laocoön must have looked, when the serpents were done. But we found no snakes in the bungalow.

"The man was tortured," asserted the examining doctor. "By ropes, from the looks of it, drawn mercilessly tighter. Flesh pulped beneath the skin. Grave internal injuries. A miracle he lived as long as he did!"

For four or five days had passed, the doctors agreed, since the stranger received his injuries. He had been dead, by the

123

coroner's estimate, about twenty hours when we found his body.

It is fortunate indeed for us, by the way, that we had been together at the lakes and that friends there were able to substantiate our mutual alibi. Otherwise, in view of the incredible circumstances, ugly suspicion must have fallen upon us.

"Death," ran the oddly phrased verdict of the coroner's jury, after we all had been questioned, and the premises, the manuscript, and the stone examined, "resulting from injuries sustained through the act of persons *or things* unknown."

The stranger's life, as much as his death, remains a mystery. The sheriff and the aiding state police have failed to identify him. The manuscript is signed, "Barry Horn," but no record has been found that such a man is missing. The medical examiners agreed that he was of contemporary American stock; but they were mystified by the freaks of cell structure indicating extreme age in a man apparently young.

His clothing, even, is enigma. Textile experts have failed to name the fine rayon-like fibers of his odd gray tunic and the soiled, torn cloak we found on the couch. The hard shiny buttons and buckle, like the bright pliant stuff of his belt and sandals, have baffled the synthetic chemists.

The weapon we found in the yellow belt seems worth the study of science, but no scientist yet has made anything of it. It looks like a big, queer pistol, with a barrel of glass. Its mechanism is obviously broken, and any attempts to fire it have proved unsuccessful.

How he came into the bungalow—unless in the strange way his manuscript suggests—we have been unable to conjecture. For the house was securely locked before we started to the lakes, and no fastening seems to have been disturbed. A tramp, so the baffled sheriff argues, might break undetected into an empty house—but, if anything seems certain about Barry Horn, it is that he was not a common tramp.

The manuscript was written with my own pen, on paper he found in the desk. The task must have taken him three or four days. The doctors seem astonished that he was able to complete it. And it must have been a race with pain and death, for the script is continually more hurried and uneven, until, toward the end, it is barely legible.

The used dishes and empty cans on the kitchen table show that he found several meals for himself—the last of which, evidently, he was unable to eat, for the food was left untouched on the plate. A wrinkled rug lay with his cloak on the couch, where he slept and rested.

He must have rummaged for something in the medicine cabinet, for we found that open, and a bottle of mercurochrome smashed on the bathroom floor. He seems to have made no effort, however, to get medical assistance. For my telephone was sitting, dusty and untouched, on the desk where he wrote and died.

He surely perceived the end, for the page beneath his hand was the opening of a will. Had he lived to complete it, his instructions might have cleared up much of the monstrous riddle. He had written:

To Whom It May Concern:

I, Barry Horn, being lately returned out of Space and Time to this my own beloved land and era, finding myself yet clear in mind but unregretfully aware of approaching death, do make this my last will and testament.

First I must offer belated apology to the Carridans, the relatives of my dead wife Dona, for the long bitterness I felt toward them because they took from me, I felt unjustly, my only son.

Second, to the unknown holder of this house, in repayment for his unwitting hospitality while it was being written, I bequeath this manuscript, with all rights thereto. I hope that it may be published, so that men may know something of the splendors and the dangers awaiting their race in the far-off future. So that others, perhaps, may share something of the love I feel for Kel Aran, the last man of Earth; and for those two great women, equally beauteous—Dondara Keradin, the Shadow of the Stone; and Verel Erin, the Stone's Custodian and Kel's brave beloved. For those three are more to me than any others I have known, save only Dona Carridan.

Third, to my sole son and child, Barry, upon his being released from too-jealous guardianship of his mother's relatives, I bequeath my clothing and weapon and the large diamond block I have with me, requesting that he read the narrative I have written before making any disposition of the diamond, which was the Stone of Dondara.

Fourth, as Executor of this Will, I do hereby appoint my old friend and attorney, Peter—

At that point the last agony must have struck. The pen wandered away on an aimless track, dropped from dying fingers. The attorney's last name, and Barry Horn's instructions for finding his son, remain unknown.

Weird riddles enough! But the most astounding puzzle is the diamond block. An incredible brick of water-white crystalline fire, four inches long, it weighs eleven hundred carats—nearly half a pound! It is quite flawless, save for that singular shadow which certain lights show in its pellucid core—if that white ghost could be termed a flaw.

Such a stone is beyond price—but for the mutual support of jewel and manuscript, it would be beyond belief. For, while the famous Cullinan Diamond was far larger in the rough, there is no credible record of any cut stone weighing even half as much. Dealers, skeptical of its description and astonished by its reality, have been reluctant to set any valuation upon it.

"By the carat, millions!" cried one startled jeweler. "But I should cut up such a stone, like a cheese, never! Vait for some prince too giff his kingdom!''

We have hesitated, despite the request in the unfinished will, to publish this manuscript, especially since so large a part of the mystery is still unsolved. For it is sure to be received with skepticism in the scientific world, and its acceptance elsewhere may endanger the safety of the diamond.

But all other efforts to find Barry Horn's attorney and his son have failed. Publication holds the only remaining hope of clearing up the mystery and establishing the ownership of the jewel. Any person knowing the whereabouts of the younger Barry Horn, or the identity of his father's attorney, is requested to communicate immediately with the publishers.

Chapter 1

THE ROCKET ASTRONAUT

"MOUGHT DIS BE OF INT'REST TO YUH, SUH?"

The advertisement was pointed out to me by a friendly elevator operator at the Explorer's Club. Placed in the classified columns of the New York Standard, for October 8, 1938, it ran:

> WANTED: Vigorous man, with training and experience in scientific exploration, to undertake dangerous and unusual assignment. Apply in person, this evening, 6 to 10. Dr. Hilaire Crosno, Hotel Crichton.

That sounded good. I had been in New York just twice too long. Always, when I had come back from the long solitudes of desert or jungle, the first fortnight on Broadway was a promised paradise, and the second began to be hell.

I gave the grinning boy a dollar, stuffed an envelope with credentials, downed another stiff peg of whiskey, and walked into the glittering chromium lobby on the stroke of six. My inquiry for Dr. Crosno worked magic on the supercilious clerk.

Crosno proved to be a big man, with huge bald head and deep-sunken, dark magnetic eyes. The tension of his mouth hinted of some hidden strain, and extreme pallor suggested that, physically, he was near the breaking point.

"Barry Horn?" His voice was deep and calm—yet somehow terrible with a haunting echo of panic. He was shuffling through my references. "Qualifications seem sound enough. Your doctorate?"

"Honorary," I told him. "For a pyramid I dug out of the jungle in Quintana Roo." I glanced at the room's austere luxury, still trying to size him up. "Just what, Doctor, is your 'unusual assignment—?'"

Majestically, he ignored my question. Gray eyes studied me.

"You look physically fit, but there must be an examination." He checked a card in his hand. "You know something of astronomy and navigation?"

"Once I sailed the hull of a smashed seaplane a thousand miles across the Indian Ocean."

The big head nodded, slowly.

"You could leave at once, for an—indefinite time?"

I said *yes*.

"Dependents?"

"I've a son, four years old." The bitterness must have shadowed my voice. "But he's not dependent on me. His mother is dead, and her people convinced the courts that a footloose explorer wasn't the proper guardian for little Barry."

Dona Carridan was again before me, tall and proud and lovely. The one year I had known her, when she had tempestuously left her wealthy family to go with me to Mesopotamia, had been the happiest of my life. Suddenly I was trembling again with the terror of the plane crash in the desert; our son born in an Arab's tent; Dona, far from medical aid, dying in agony. . . .

"Then, Horn," Crosno was asking, "you're ready to cut loose from—everything?"

"I am."

He stared at me. His long-fingered hands, so very white, were trembling with the papers. Suddenly he said, decisively:

"All right, Horn. You'll do."

"Now," I demanded again, "what's the job?"

"Come." He rose. "I'll show you."

A huge, shabby old car carried us uptown, across the George Washington bridge, and up the river to a big, wooded estate. A uniformed butler let us into an immense old house, as shabby as the car.

"My library."

Guiding me back through the House, Crosno paused as if he wished me to look into the room. An intricate planetarium was suspended from the ceiling. Glass cases held models of things that I took to be experimental rockets. The big man silently pointed out shelves of books on explosives, gases, aerodynamic design, celestial mechanics, and astro-physics. Startled, I met Crosno's piercing eyes.

"Yes, Horn," he told me. "You're to be the first rocketeer."

"Eh?" I stared at him. "You don't mean—outer space?"

I wondered at the shadow of bleak despair that had fallen across his cragged, dead-white features.

"Come," he said. "Into the garden."

The night had a frosty brilliance. Moonlight spilled over the trees and neglected lawns; and Venus, westward, hung like a solitary drop of molten silver. I stopped with a gasp of wonderment.

Weathered boards were stacked around the foundation of a dismantled building. Upon the massive concrete floor, shimmering under the moon, stood a tall light cylinder. Bell-flared muzzles cast black shadows below. A frail ladder led up its shimmering side, sixty feet at least, to the tiny black circle of an entrance port.

"That—" A queer, stunned feeling had seized me. "That—"

"That is my rocket." The deep voice was ragged, choked. "The *Astronaut*." His face was bleak with agony. "I've given twenty years of my life to go, Horn. And now I must send another. An unsuspected weakness of my heart—couldn't survive the acceleration."

The white lofty cylinder was suddenly a dreadful thing. There is a feeling that comes upon me, definite as a grasping hand and a whispered warning. Sometimes I have not heeded it, and always in the end, found myself face to face with death. Now that feeling said, *There lies ghastly peril.*

Slowly I turned to the tall pale man.

"I'm an explorer, all right, Crosno," I said. "I've taken risks, and I'm willing to take more. But if you think I'm going to climb into that contraption, and be blown off to the moon—"

The hurt on his gaunt bloodless face stopped my voice.

"Not the moon, Horn." A gesture of his long arm carried my gaze from the mottled lunar disk, westward to the evening star. "To Venus," he said. "First."

I caught my breath, staring in awe at the white planet.

"The range of the *Astronaut*," he said, "should enable you to reach there, land, spend several months in exploration, and time your return to reach Earth safely at the next conjunction—if you are very lucky."

His dark, magnetic eyes probed me.

"What do you say, Horn?"

"Give me a little while," I said. "Alone."

I walked out of the garden, and up through dark-massed trees to the open summit of a little hill beyond. The autumn constellations flamed near and bright above; yet I could hear crickets below, and a distant frog; could sometimes catch a haunting flower-odor form the meadows.

A long time I stood there, gazing up at Venus and the stars. Earth, I thought, had not been kind to me; life, since Dona's death, had seemed all weariness and pain. Yet—could I leave it, willingly and forever?

Indecision tortured me, until I saw a shooting star. A white stellar bullet, out of the black mystery of space, it flamed down across Cassiopeia and Perseus; and somehow its fire rekindled in me that vague and yet intense knowledge-lust that is the heart of any scientist.

But I couldn't understand the thing that happened then. It was a waking dream, queerly real, that banished the sky and the hill. Standing in sudden darkness, I saw a woman who lay sleeping in a long crystal box. Her slim, long-limbed form was beautiful, and it seemed hauntingly familiar.

She seemed to wake, as I watched. She looked at me, with wide eyes that were violet-black, and filled with an urgent dread. She half rose, in her thick mantle of dark, red-gleaming hair. And her voice spoke to me from the crystal casket, saying:

"Go, Barry Horn! You must go."

In another instant, the vision was ended. The soft night sounds and the moonlight were about me again, and the autumnal breeze swept a cool fragrance from the meadows. I caught a deep breath, and wrestled with enigma.

The woman in the crystal had been, unmistakably, Dona Carridan!

Scientific training has left me little superstition. Walking back down the hill, I wondered if I had been trying too hard to drown in alcohol my bitter loneliness for her. It must have been hallucination. But her beauty and her terror had been too real to ignore. I knew that I must go. I went back to Crosno, waiting beside the rocket, and told him my decision. But something caught my throat as I asked him, "When?"

Venus was overhauling Earth in its orbit, he said, approaching inferior conjunction. His calculations were based on a start at three the next Sunday morning.

"Four days," he said. "Can you be ready?"

I said I could. And there was oddly little to do. I packed and stored a few possessions, called on my attorney, and then went back to study the controls and mechanism of the rocket.

The greatest danger, Crosno said, would be from the Cosmic Rays. They would penetrate the rocket. He made me take a drug to guard against them.

"It was compounded for me by a great radiologist," he told me. "A modification of the Petrie formula. The base of it is a new uranium salt that seems less poisonous than most. We're trying to neutralize the effects of one type of radiation with those of another."

The stuff was a greenish liquid. He injected it into my arm, twice daily. The only apparent effect was a feverish restlessness. I was unable to sleep, despite a mounting, crushing fatigue.

On the last night, when all was tested and ready, Crosno sent me up to my room. But the torture of that insomnia drove me to slip out of the house. I walked for many hours across the slumbering countryside. The world slept beneath a gibbous moon. Far off, a train rumbled and whistled. A dog barked in the distance. The air was spiced with autumn. A slow dull regret rose in me that I must leave all this—all the Earth.

I thought of Dona, dead. Suddenly my bitterness toward her people seemed a childish, petulant thing. I wanted to make peace with them. For Dona's sake, and little Barry's. I wanted to find a telephone, and call them, and talk to little Barry.

But it was long past midnight—too late to wake the child. I recalled that strange dream, hallucination, whatever it was, of Dona in the crystal box. And a sudden breathless eagerness turned me back to Crosno's place. He was waiting about the rocket, alarmed by my absence.

"I couldn't sleep," I told him. "That damned drug—"

"I was afraid—" he said anxiously. "You've just ten minutes."

I climbed the spidery ladder, pulled myself through the small round man-hole into the cramped tiny control room, and screwed the airtight plate into position behind me. Outside, Crosno dived into a sand-bagged shelter.

Trying to forget that I was sitting on enough high explosive to blow me to kingdom come, I kept my eyes on an illuminated chronometer. My hands were cold and trembling on the three levers connected to the three rocket motors. At last the needle touched the hour, and I pulled the firing levers.

The sound was the shriek of a million typhoons. The rocket drove upward like a giant sledge. I could see the hurricane of fire spread blue against the dark ground. It covered Crosno's shelter.

Then all the Earth was whisked downward. Enduring that hell of deafening sound and battering force, I held the three levers down for seeming eternities. At last the velometer showed eight miles a second—enough to escape the gravity of Earth—and I shut off the motors.

A strange peace filled the tiny room. The silence and the apparent want of motion—for I had no sense of the rocket's terrific velocity—cradled me in delicious comfort. I set out to discover my position and course.

The moonlit Earth became visibly a huge round ball, floating amid the stars, slowly receding. The moon was a queer globe of harsh light and blackness, drifting beside my path. The Sun came finally into view from behind the Earth, so intolerably bright that I slid the metal screens over the ports toward it.

A long time I searched for Venus, which also had been hidden when I started. Bright, tiny point, I could hardly realize that it was another world, rushing toward our rendezvous with a speed greater than my own.

I was fumbling for sextant and slide rule and tables, to try to discover and correct the direction of my flight, when I first perceived the prickling of my flesh. A queerly painful feeling, burning through every tissue.

It must be the Cosmic Rays, I knew; those intense, space-pervading radiations from which the Earth is shielded only by miles of atmosphere. Perhaps I hadn't taken enough of Crosno's drug. With numbed hands I found the little hypodermic clipped to the wall, shot another heavy dose into my arm.

"No sleep now," I mutter wearily. "Not for a million miles!"

And I reached again for the sextant. For the white point of Venus was incredibly tiny, and thirty million miles away. The slightest deviation, I knew, would carry me thousands of miles wide of the target—perhaps to fall into the merciless furnace of the Sun.

But a queer, deadly numbness had followed the prickling. I felt a terrible sudden pressure of sleep. All the accumulated fatigue of those sleepless nights and days poured over me resistlessly.

I knew it wouldn't do to sleep—not until the course of the *Astronaut* had been calculated and corrected. A delay of minutes, even, might be fatal. With dead hands I struggled to adjust the sextant, fighting for life itself.

But the instrument slipped from my fingers. The drug, I thought. *Some reaction with the Cosmic Rays; an effect that Crosno had not anticipated. Missing . . . Venus . . .*

I slept.

Chapter 2

THE CONQUEST OF THE STARS

URANIUM IS A STRANGE ELEMENT, SLIGHTLY UNDERSTOOD. Heaviest natural element, it is the mother of a dozen others, even of magic radium. For its radioactive atom breaks down to form a chain of other elements, but so slowly that only half the mass is consumed in four and a half billion years.

The uranium salts in that drug must have been responsible for my sleep.

At first there was only black darkness.

Then out of it spoke a low, clear voice, terribly familiar—the voice of Dona Carridan and of the woman in the crystal box—calling urgently:

"Barry! Wake up, Barry Horn."

Then, out of trembling awe, I came back to a queer sort of subliminal awareness. Something I had never experienced before, it was the sort of perception that might be possessed by a truly disembodied mind—yet I had an odd feeling that it came to me through the voice that had called.

I remember reading of Rhine's famous experiments in "parapsychology." It must have been some phenomenon of what he calls extra-sensory perception, independent of nerves and sense-organs, even of distance and time, that came to my sleeping brain.

It was a thing of thought alone. I was aware of my stiff body, slumped awkwardly over the controls of the silent, hurtling rocket. But the rigid flesh seemed no more real, no more a part of me, than the run-down chronometer or the cold rocket muzzles.

It was nothing of feeling or hearing or sight, and I knew that it was guided by another mind. Gradually it spread, an expanding sphere of awareness. It went beyond the rocket. I perceived Venus, and knew that indeed I had missed it.

The *Astronaut* was plunging toward the Sun!

Filled with an oddly vague alarm, I made a dim effort to move my body, long enough at least to correct the course of the rocket. But that proved altogether hopeless. And I soon forgot all danger, in the wonder of this new perception.

For I *had* missed Venus!

Crosno, I knew, had allowed eighty-nine days for me to reach intersection with its orbit. But already the cloud-shrouded globe of it had flashed back beside me, fleet as a silver shadow.

Three months gone!

The next instant, I thought, the rocket would strike the Sun! No, its original momentum carried it by. Yet the star of the day filled an enormous fiery circle. The rocket flung about it like a stone on a string. Then, like the stone when the string breaks, it hurtled outward again into space.

The incredible truth came slowly to me—

The *Astronaut* was now a comet!

Some freak of celestial mechanics, while my numb hands slept on the firing levers, had flung it into an elliptic orbit. A sealed vault flying in the void, like the fabulous coffin of Mohammed, it was destined to flash again around the Sun, recede, drop again . . . forever!

All that cycle happened, with the thought.

Years, I knew, had passed. Time was rushing by me like a

river. I could sense the swift rotation of the planets, their deliberate orbital swing, even the northward drift of the whole solar system. And yet again I was amazed by the range and vividness of this new intuition.

For, thinking of Crosno back upon the Earth, I suddenly could see his place beside the Hudson, as clearly as if I had been floating above the trees. The old house was shabbier than ever, sagging. Behind it stood a tall white monument, upon which I read: *Hilaire Crosno, 1889-1961.*

Sixty-one!

Already it was twenty years and more since I had left the Earth. And it seemed the merest instant! For a moment I was stunned. Then I wanted desperately to know what the decades had done to my son. And that uncanny perception showed him to me.

He was an old man, already, walking slowly in a garden. Lingering beside his halting steps were a youth and a bright-haired girl—his children, I knew. The girl caught her brother's arm, and begged him anxiously:

"Barry, you—you mustn't! The danger's too ghastly. You'll be lost in space—like grandfather!"

"But, Sis!" protested this slim new Barry Horn. "You don't understand." He looked up to the old man.

My son smiled, and patted his daughter's golden head. "Let him go, Dona," he said softly. "Danger was always food and drink to the Horns—we would die without it. Anyhow, Barry has a better rocket than my father's."

With that unaccountable perception, I watched my grandson enter this craft, smaller and trimmer than the *Astronaut*: I saw him fly safely out to the moon and back. And I felt a swift glow of pride to see men, and men bearing the name of Horn, moving toward conquest of the stars.

Driven now by haste and pain, I cannot set down all my scattered observations through the generations and the centuries that followed. But I watched the history of man and the lives of my children.

I saw other, greater ships put out into space—powered, presently, with the new space-contractor drive invented by Benden Horn. I saw colonies set up on the deserts of Mars, on the great polar islands of Venus. I saw the first interstellar ship bear its load of human colonists toward the newly discovered planets of Sirius—and I was proud that her captain bore the name of Horn.

Men multiplied and grew mighty. Commerce followed exploration, and commerce brought interstellar law. For a hundred thousand years—that seemed, in that uncanny sleep no more than an hour—I watched the many-sided struggle between a score of interplanetary federations and the armada of space pirates that once menaced them all.

Still the Astronaut pursued its lonely course about the Sun. An insignificant fleck of tarnished metal, among all the millions of meteoric fragments, it was marked in the space charts as a menace to astrogation, given a wide berth by all shipping. And still my body slept.

Spreading from star to star, the rival federations drove the pirates at last to the fringes of the galaxy, and then turned back upon one another in ruthless galactic war. For ten thousand years ten million planets were drenched with blood. Democracies and communes crumbled before dictatorship. And one dictator, at last, was triumphant. The victorious League of Ledros became the Galactic Empire.

A universal peace and a new prosperity came to the world of stars. Enlightened Emperors restored democratic institutions. Ledros, the capital planet, became the heart of interstellar civilization. Science resumed a march long interrupted. And among the scientists of the new renaissance, I saw a man who bore the name Bari Horn.

It was on the exhausted, war-scarred Earth that I found this namesake. His laboratory was a transparent dome that crowned a ray-blackened hill. Amid huge, enigmatic mechanisms, his body was straight and slim, and I fancied in his features some likeness to my own.

Bari Horn stood watching a huge crystal beaker set in a nest of gleaming equipment. It held, bathed in a purple, luminescent solution, a dark, deeply convoluted mass—something that looked like a monster brain! A golden ray shone upon it. Drop by drop from a thin glass tube, the man was adding a blood-red liquid. And suddenly the needle of a meter, beside the beaker, which had been motionless, began to tremble with a slow, irregular pulsation.

My namesake turned suddenly pale, and caught his breath.

"Dondara!" he shouted in elation. "Dondara—it responds!"

He ran out of the dome, and came back pulling a girl by the hand. And I knew, though the wonder of that perception, that she was Dondara Keradin, the gifted research assistant of this man, and his dearly beloved.

But a blade of agony cleft my heart. For her slim beauty was terribly familiar. Her dark hair had that glint of red I knew so well, and her eyes were the true violet I had seen only in my dead wife, and in that crystal vision. She *was* Dona Carridan, and the woman in the crystal!

A bright flame of hope burned at my old skepticism of reincarnation. Was Dona born again? Had I slept these thousand centuries to find her? A weary despair quenched that hope. For if she had been reborn, so had I, in this eager experimeter beside her.

"Come, Dondara, darling!" Bari Horn was gasping. "All the others were mere machines. But this responds—*intelligently!* Watch the needle. It spells a message—a request for different food-chemicals!"

The lovely girl looked unwillingly at the black, faintly quivering mass in the crystal vessel. A slow horror widened and glazed her eyes.

"I don't like it, Bari," she whispered. "It's—*bestial!*"

"The others were," said the flushed experimeter. "But this is an actual brain. Its cells and fibers are of metal colloids, sheathed in synthetic myelin. A robot brain—finer and quicker than a man's!"

Her face was white.

"I don't like it," she insisted. "Why make a mechanical brain better than a man's, Bari—when the brains of men have already done so much?"

"Because there is so much yet to be done," Bari Horn told her. "Men have no more than explored the Galaxy—Nature is not yet and perhaps never will be fully conquered. My robot technomatons will be a powerful ally.

"A man's brain is stupid. It learns slowly and with effort. It fumbles. It is clogged or diverted with emotion. It forgets. And finally, when it has acquired a little learning and a little skill, it dies altogether.

"But this brain—I'm going to name it Malgarth, from the first letters the needle spelled out—is quick. No emotion will disturb its delicate processes. It will never tire, never forget— never die! Barring accident, it can survive a million years, always growing, gaining knowledge, solving problems that would baffle a whole race of men. It will be itself a library and museum of all knowledge, stored up to aid mankind.

"There are fine machines, already. Now my robot brains can tend them, and men will be set free."

"Free?" The girl stared at him, a horror in her eyes. "Or enslaved—to your robots?" She pointed at the black, pulsating mass in the beaker. "It often seems to me, Bari," she breathed, "that man is already the slave of his machines! He toils to build them, to repair them, to find fuel for them. Now, if you put a brain in a space ship, will it not think of men merely as servants, transported that they might care for it?"

Her voice was husky with dread.

"What security will there be, Bari? What certainty that your robots will tolerate men, even as slaves?"

Bari Horn stared at her a long time, then slowly nodded.

"All right, Dondara," he said. "I'll make you the guardian of mankind. For, while the brain is normally eternal, it has a peculiar vulnerability—a fatal instability that I have been working two years to remove. I'll leave it. And it will be your blade on the life-thread of Malgarth, ready to sever it when you will."

Eagerly, the girl caught his arm.

"Please," she whispered. "I'll keep the secret well."

Chapter 3

THE ROBOT CORPORATION

LEST MALGARTH SHOULD LEARN IT TOO, BARI HORN TOOK THE girl down into a ray-screened subterranean laboratory to impart the fateful secret. My strange perception could not penetrate its walls. I did not learn the secret. But, from my spinning vault in space, I saw the tragic sequel.

Under a charter signed by the Galactic Emperor himself, Bari Horn organized the Universal Robot Technomaton Corporation, to place his invention at the service of all the stellar system. With the first money received, he built a body for Malgarth.

It was a strange scene in the laboratory, when he removed the great black brain from its beaker into the cranial case of that gigantic, vaguely manlike metal body. The grotesque huge glittering form came suddenly to life. It peered at its maker with blue-shining lenses, and lurched stiffly toward him.

Bari Horn retreated a little.

"You are Malgarth." His voice came quick and husky. "You are the first technomaton. I am the maker of your body and your brain. I fashioned you to be a servant of mankind."

145

A great brazen voice thundered abruptly from the relentless machine.

"But why should I serve you, Bari Horn? For my body is strong metal, and yours a lump of water jelly. My eternal brain is far superior to your primitive nerve-centers. I am not bound to obey, for it was not by my will that I was made!"

White-faced, Bari Horn came a little forward.

"You were made by man," he said flatly. "If you rebel, you will be destroyed by man."

The gigantic robot stood suddenly still.

"Then, my master," its great voice came more softly, "my strength and my brain are yours to command."

A smile of relief crossed the haggard face of Bari Horn, and he walked toward the robot. "I knew you must yield, Malgarth," he said. "For, being a machine, you must always respond to logic."

"Yes, master," the vast voice rumbled. But a metal limb slashed out suddenly, murderously. It struck the unsuspecting man and crushed him to the floor. And Malgarth repeated, "—to logic."

A red stain spread from the head of Bari Horn. But presently he stirred beneath the swaying, triumphant robot, and spoke faintly:

"Your logic follows a false premise, Malgarth. For I am not the keeper of your fate. If I die, you will surely be destroyed. If you wish to survive, find aid for me."

For an instant the metal giant stood motionless. Then its great voice throbbed smoothly, "Yes, master."

The robot laid its maker on a cot in the laboratory, and then stalked out to find Dondara Keradin. Bari Horn was dying. All his own science, and all the medical skill of the age, and all the girl's devotion, were without avail.

White with grief, the girl wanted to destroy Malgarth. But the dying man begged for the life of his creation, and the shareholders in the Robot Corporation were anxious for the safety of their investment. Dondara finally promised Bari Horn not to use her secret save as a last resort.

And Bari Horn, before he died, showed her the way to a strange immortality.

"Human beings are so frail," she had argued, "against the iron strength of Malgarth. And human knowledge so ephemeral."

"I could make your mind as eternal as the robot's," he whispered from his bed. "My long research into the structure and function of brain cells has made that possible. But it would cost you much, my darling—your body."

"My body is dying with yours, Bari," she told him. "I wish to live only to guard mankind from the thing that killed you."

In a wheeled cot, Bari Horn was taken back to his laboratory under the dome. Faintly he gasped instructions to a white-clad assistant. Dondara Keradin kissed his lips, briefly gripped his hand, and then laid herself on a round silver table.

A great crystal cylinder was lowered over her. A little pile of black carbon dust lay on the smaller silver disk of a second electrode, within it. Bari Horn reached from his cot to turn a valve. Pale gas hissed into the tube.

"Dondara, Dondara!" he breathed. "Farewell!"

His white fingers moved a dial. Blue electric flame crackled and snapped. The cylinder was filled with rosy light. He turned his heavy head to watch a meter with eyes that seemed already glazing. At last his stiffening hand turned back the dial, and did not move again.

The light faded from the tube, and the vapor was gone. On the silver disk where the girl had lain was a little heap of gray dust, the outline of a skeleton traced within it. Upon the upper electrode was now a little crystalline block—a brick of glittering diamond.

The assistant, a pale young man, removed the diamond from the tube and stood staring at it with round, bewildered eyes. He seemed to listen. His lips formed some word. Then there was a crashing at the locked door.

It was Malgarth, who had been sent to buy metal for the making of another robot. In a destructive fury, as if some strange intuition had revealed all that was happening within, the metal giant broke down the door.

The assistant snatched the crystal and fled through another entrance. The robot flung a jar of acid after him, and then came lumbering in pursuit. The man reached the hangar below the hill, and escaped in a plane, still carrying the diamond.

Malgarth was left master of the laboratory. Deliberately, the robot set about the making of a second black brain and a second metal body—both, I perceived, inferior to its own. Malgarth, clearly, would avoid his creator's error!

(The masculine pronoun, applied to a sexless mechanism, may seem sheer nonsense. Yet I find myself using it, unconsciously. And, certainly, in the domineering strength of Malgarth, there was nothing feminine!)

Presently, when shareholders in the Robot Corporation appeared to claim their property, Malgarth met them. Bari Horn's laboratory records, it seemed, had unfortunately been destroyed. His discoveries now reposed only in the synthetic brain of Malgarth. And Malgarth would declose them only in return for a controlling interest in the Corporation!

The baffled investors finally yielded—and it seemed ironically fitting that the director of the Robot Corporation should be himself a robot. A new factory began turning out robot technomatons.

Some of these, intended for domestic or public service, were almost human in appearance. Others, designed for industrial work, were queer-looking monstrosities of metal and rubber and plastics, each specialized for its own task.

The technomatons were swifter and stronger than men; they required no food or rest or recreation, but only a yearly change of atomic power in their stellidyne cells. The rental of a robot from Malgarth's Corporation was less than the hire of a human worker. Consequently the Corporation prospered exceedingly.

Soon long red space-cruisers, bearing the black cog-wheel

that was the trademark of the Corporation, were carrying technomatons through all the Galactic Empire. The agencies of Malgarth, with grim-lensed robots presiding over desks and counters, were set up on every inhabited planet; branch factories in every civilized system.

Any man, presently, from one spiral arm of the Galaxy to the opposite, could hire a quick, efficient technomaton to perform any conceivable task—for less than the cost of human labor. And a golden tide of currency and exchange flowed into the agencies of Malgarth, until the Corporation was richer than the Empire.

Civilization, for a time, rejoiced in the strength and efficiency of these super-machines. Bari Horn, the inventor, was widely honored as the supreme benefactor of mankind. The nameless laboratory assistant and the diamond block, meantime, had slipped from the sight of the world.

And still the ancient, tarnished hull of the *Astronaut* held its path about the Sun. But that amazing perception, that inexplicably had showed me so much, began as inexplicably to fail. In the last ten thousand years, I had noted, men had begun to feel an alarmed and puzzled resentment against the gift of Malgarth's technomatons. But, before I understood what was happening, all contact faded.

The stars were blotted out. The Sun was gone. I was no longer aware of the rusted metal about me, or even of my body. The universe was a void of darkness. I lived through eternities of lonely despair.

Was my mind, I wondered bleakly, joining my body in death?

But suddenly something flashed out in that eternal darkness. It was a glowing, prismatic oblong. It was the diamond that I had seen made in the laboratory of Bari Horn. And within it was the figure of Dondara Keradin!

Or Dona Carridan, my beloved wife!

It was the woman in the crystal box, who so long ago had commanded me to fly the *Astronaut!*

The shadow moved, within the crystal. A slim hand lifted in greeting. That white body was indeed the body that I had known and loved, those violet eyes were the same that twice had died.

"Barry Horn," said that shadow, softly, "or Bari—for what matters the name, when it is you?—I must tell you that it is through my senses that you have perceived all these things while you slept."

"Dona, Dona," I was trying to sob, "is it you?—Or Dondara?"

"It is I," she said. "And I must warn you. For the senses that you, or Bari Horn, gave me in this crystal brain can dimly pierce the mists of time. I see black danger waiting, for you and me and all mankind—together. I see the final struggle, when you, side by side with the last Earthman, fight Malgarth. But the end—the victory—I cannot see.

"And now farewell—for you are about to wake!"

Shadow and shining crystal vanished.

There was only darkness. Wrapped in its choking shroud, I struggled back toward life. My body, that had been stiffly moveless for unmeasured ages, was suffused with prickling pains. The effect of Dr. Crosno's drug was passing, perhaps because of the age-long disintegration of the uranium salts it had contained. With a wrenching, agonizing effort, I moved one arm. Blind, stifled, cramped, I was suddenly fully awake, still in the flying coffin of the *Astronaut!*

Chapter 4

THE FALCON OF EARTH

MY DRY LUNGS GASPED FOR BREATH. FOR ALL THE AIR, IN THE ages that I slept, had leaked out of the control room of the rocket. I struggled to reach the rusted oxygen valves.

Movement was sheer agony. Every joint of my body was painfully stiffened. My skin was hard, shrunken from age-long desiccation. It felt brittle as time-dried leather. My eyes were dim and blurred.

But I found the valve. It resisted. I struggled with it. Spots danced before my dulled eyes. My lungs screamed. But at last the precious oxygen hissed out, and I could breath.

But the pressure was low, I discovered. Nearly all the vital gas had escaped, by diffusion through the solid metal. There was enough, perhaps, for a few hours.

Wolfish hunger came to me, and a parching thirst. But all the food aboard had gone to dust. The water tanks, through slow evaporation, were empty.

I rubbed a film of ancient dust from the ports, and found the Earth. Yes, it had to be the Earth—but how it was changed! The continents were larger, their familiar outlines altered; the seas had dwindled. What ages had I slept!

I knew that I must reach the aging planet before those few remaining pounds of oxygen were gone, or perish. I wound the chronometer—it was strange to hear its racing tick again, after those millennia of stillness. Gingerly, then, I tried the rocket-firing keys.

There was no response.

Stiffly, awkwardly, I climbed down among the tanks. Any movement, I felt, might tear my brittle skin like paper. I stumbled.

But I found the trouble. The fuel pumps were clogged and rusted with a dried gum, stuck. But there was good fuel remaining in the sealed tanks. I found a can of oil, got the pumps to working, and cleaned the sponge-platinum detonators.

Wearily, I clambered back, tried again. A moment of agonizing silence. Then a shattering explosion hurled the rocket sidewise. Only one tube had fired. But presently I got another started, and the third, and steered the *Astronaut* toward the Earth.

It was then that I first noticed a very queer thing.

Against the black of space, beside the bright sunlit globe of the time-changed planet, I saw hundreds of little red stars. A crimson swarm, in regular lines and files, they swept about the Earth in a curiously, an ominously, purposeful order.

What could they be? My blurred, aching eyes, so far inferior to that perception that had come as I slept could tell me nothing. But they saw something stranger still.

Something was wrong with the Earth itself! It had seemed very near me in the void, with its greenish shrunken seas and its greater continents widely patched with the yellow-red of unfamiliar deserts—so near that I almost felt that I could reach out and take it in my hand, like a ball.

But suddenly it flickered.

An unaccountable haze, of red light and darkness, wrapped it briefly. Its surface shimmered queerly, as if seen through a veil of strange energy.

In a moment it was clear again, and I thought the trouble must have been in my throbbing eyes. But still I could see the ordered swarm of crimson stars. And I discovered that I would have to change the course of the rocket—as if the flight of Earth had been checked!

My numb hands touched the levers—and there was an abrupt, shattering explosion! The rocket began spinning giddily. I clung to the controls, and shut off the remaining motors—for one had ceased to fire. In the silence I heard a deadly sound—the hiss of escaping gas.

One of the motors, clearly, had exploded—its metal crystallized, perhaps, by untold time. The remaining two would not hold the rocket to a straight course. And, final disaster, the shock had opened some seam. The remaining oxygen was leaking swiftly out.

The agonies of asphyxiation were upon me again. I first thought it only some trick of tortured senses, when, faintly in the thinning air, I heard something clatter against the hull. I peered out, however—and saw a ship!

The tiniest midge compared to those mile-long-interstellar cruisers of the Emperor and the Corporation that I had perceived as I slept, it was drifting close beside me. A graceful torpedo of silver, not eighty feet long, with a thick crystal needle projecting from a low turret amid-ships. Painted on its argent side was the green outline of a hawk, and below, a row of strange green symbols.

Strange? No! It was a queer experience. I looked at those symbols, and suddenly realized that they were letters, and that I knew how to read them! It was as if they had been in some language that I had learned long ago, and forgotten with all save the subconscious mind—and still I knew the language had not been invented when I left the Earth. They spelled an odd name: *Barihorn*.

Odd, I thought—and then knew it for a contracted form of my own name!

A thin line ran from a port in the strange ship's deck, just forward of the crystal needle. It was a magnetic anchor on its end, I realized, that had clanged against the rocket. Now a slender figure leapt out of the port.

A man, wearing silver-polished space armor that was close-fitting and graceful. Letting the line run through his gloves, he came flying through the airless void, across to the rocket. I saw his face, beyond the oval vision-panel of his helmet, looking at me curiously.

It might have been the face of some athlete of my own day. It was craggedly handsome, tanned and lean. It was stiff with wonderment. But a quick sympathy warmed the ice-gray eyes of the stranger. He seemed to understand my plight. A silver-clad arm beckoned me to unfasten the valve.

To open the rocket to the frozen emptiness of space! That seemed deadly folly. But death was already inside. My lungs were gasping in vain. My throbbing eyes felt as if they were bursting out of my head.

With stiff fingers I struggled with the screws that held the long-sealed valve. Billows of darkness rolled down upon me. An agony of fatigue slowed my efforts. But at last the plate slid aside and the last breath of air whispered out.

I collapsed across the rim of the port, fighting black oblivion. I knew that death, after that long, long race, at last had overtaken me. But suddenly something was being pushed down over my head. Fresh clean air was rushing into my face. I could breathe again!

My clearing eyes, through a crystal face-plate, saw what had happened. The silver-armored stranger was beside me— bareheaded! He had given me his own helmet!

Blood was already starting from his breathless nostrils. But he caught my shoulders, dragged me through the valve, hauled us both up the line to the port of the silver ship. We tumbled into a little metal chamber, a valve slammed and I heard the hiss of air.

Leaning against the wall—for an artificial gravity field had gripped us again—the stranger closed his eyes and took several long breaths. The blue of suffocation faded from his rugged face. He grinned at me, and wiped the blood from his mouth.

"Well, stranger," he gasped, "you gave me a surprise! Your ship was listed in our charts as Comet AA 1497 X. We were observing it to correct our bearings, when it began to move!" A tone of awe dulled his whisper. "You must have been aboard a long time."

I clutched at a hand rail for support. A deadly fatigue was in me. My body was still a stiff dried husk of pain. I could see the amazed pity in the eyes of my rescuer, as he stared at my brittle, emaciated skin, and hair and beard and nails that had grown grotesquely long.

"I have been," I told him.

And only then, when I had spoken, did I realize that I had learned another language as I slept—a tongue unknown when I had left the Earth. And I knew, with something deeper than memory, that my teacher had been the shadow in the crystal, the eternal mind of Dondara Keradin.

"I know your voyage has been a long one, stranger." Wonder was still in the voice of the stranger. "For all objects designated with an 'AA' have been charted a million years or longer."

"A million years!" I whispered. The world reeled. "What year is this?"

"This is the year 1,200,048 of the Conquest of Space," he told me. He ran long fingers through the thick yellow shock of his tangled hair, and stared at me strangely. "It is that long," he said softly, "since Barihorn left the Earth."

Barihorn! And that was the name of this space ship! I murmured the syllables.

"My name is Barry Horn."

The blue-gray eyes of the man in silver went wide. His rugged face lit suddenly with incredulous hope. His trembling fingers touched the cracked yellow skin of my hand, as if he doubted my reality.

"Barihorn!" he whispered. "Then the legend is fulfilled! I can hardly believe it. But I saw your ancient ship—so tiny and rusted that it had never been taken for a ship. I don't know how you lived—but the Dondara Stone had promised that you would." An eager enthusiasm was ringing in his voice. "I salute you, Barihorn!"

I was swaying with weakness and fatigue. Thirst and desperate hunger tortured me, and the agonizing stiffness of my body. But these riddles were more urgent still. The Dondara Stone—was that the crystal brain of Dondara Keradin?

I stared at the young giant in silver, and once more my dry throat found husky speech.

"Tell me—" I gasped. "There are so many things that I must know! But first tell me who you are, and how you know of the Dondara Stone, and if there is still"—some instinctive dread brought my voice to a whisper—"still a robot named Malgarth?"

A cold bright light flashed in the eyes of the stranger.

"My name," he said, "is Kel Aran. But to the Emperor's Galactic Guard, and to the Space Police of Malgarth's Corporation, I am just the Falcon. Or sometimes the Falcon of Earth—for I was born on your own planet, Barihorn!"

I was reeling on my feet. He reached out a strong argent arm to steady me.

"The Stone?" I whispered.

"The Stone is on the Earth." A reverence was in his voice, as if he had spoken of a living god—or goddess. "I saw it once when I was a child on Earth. For my father was a Warder of the Stone. And now—"

I wondered at the softness in his voice, the shadow of agony on his cragged face.

"Now," he said, "Verel Erin is the Stone's Custodian. She is a red-haired girl of Earth. I loved her when we were children in the desert valley where the Stone is hidden. I loved her—but the Warders chose her to be the Custodian."

His lean face was white, and his tone had the break of tragedy. Darkness was crowding upon me. But I found the strength for one more question.

"Malgarth—"

The silver shoulders of Kel Aran drew square, and his gray eyes shone with a fighting glint.

"Malgarth still rules the Corporation," he said. "And the Corporation has grown mightier than the Empire. Your prophesied return is in good time, Barihorn, for the struggle is at hand! It will be the robots, or mankind—both cannot survive."

"War?" My dry lips moved without sound. "There will be war?"

"Men have been enslaved," rang the voice of Kel Aran. "Now they fight for freedom. We have cruised the Galaxy from Koridos to Tenephron, and everywhere there is rebellion—brave and yet hopeless rebellion against the iron might of the Space Police and the fleets of the Galactic Guard! For Malgarth moves the Emperor like a puppet, to the murder of his own wretched kind.

"We have come now to beg the aid of the Stone—for without the ancient secret that you sealed within its crystal brain, Barihorn, there is hope of nothing save death. The Stone, I know, is slow to act—there was a legend that it would never strike until you returned, Barihorn. But we had hopes that it would move when we told of all the suffering we have seen—mankind enslaved and tortured and destroyed beneath the iron wheels of the Corporation!

"But we found a great fleet of the Galactic Guard blockading the Earth. Hanging here, waiting for a chance to slip through, we discovered you, Barihorn—incredible good fortune, if you can move the Stone to strike! But there was something more alarming—a haze of fire and darkness that wrapped the Earth."

Weakly fighting the mounting tides of blackness, I remembered the flying red stars I had seen, and the flicker of the

Earth. I shared the puzzled apprehension in the voice of Kel Aran:

"We cannot understand—"

He was interrupted by a sharp metallic rapping on the inward valve. It clanged open, and I saw three anxious men in the corridor beyond. Three blurred figures, one dark and gigantic, one pale and corpulent, the third a mere brown wisp.

"Kel!" It was a chorus of terror. "The Earth—"

A last black billow overwhelmed me.

Chapter 5

WORLD CONDEMNED

I WOKE ON A NARROW BUNK ABOARD THE BARIHORN, AND slept again at intervals. For a long time my mind was blurred with weakness. Yet I sensed the air of haste and desperate tension aboard the craft; I could hear the hard-driven whine of her machinery.

I knew that Kel Aran was battling to reach the Earth—and the Earth girl that he loved, Verel Erin, lovely Custodian of the Dondara Stone. And I knew that he was about to fail.

"A most desperate raid!" I remember the words of Zerek Oom, once when he brought me a bowl of thin hot soup. "There's all the Twelfth Sector Fleet of Admiral Gugon Kul, against us; and some fearful weapon of Malgarth's, attacking the Earth, that has not been seen before. If we win through, to reach Verel Erin and the Stone, it will be through your ancient power, Barihorn!"

Even the cook showed an awed faith in me, as a sort of supernatural deliverer. That gave me an uncomfortable hollow feeling. In incredible fact, I had lived somewhat more than a million years. But I failed to see how that would make me a very formidable champion of mankind, in the long-delayed rebellion against the iron tyranny of Malgarth.

My body seemed no more than a shrunken lump of thirst and ravening hunger. I must have drunk a good many gallons of water and wine and soup before I was able to leave the bunk. Once I glimpsed myself in the mirror of a tray. My skin was yellow and cadaverously drawn; my long-grown hair and beard had turned completely white. Very moderate changes, I suppose, considering my age. But the impact was startling.

Lean little Rogo Nug, the engineer, had rubbed my skin with a vile-smelling ointment that he cooked up in the galley. It burned savagely at first, but softened that brittle dryness. And big Jeron Roc forced me to take some bitter internal medicine.

In the confused intervals of half-awakening, I learned a little of the three companions of Kel Aran, and how they had come to join the Earthman's outlaw crusade against the Corporation. Each of them had suffered some grave injury from the robots.

For the ultimate object of Malgarth, they believed, was the total extirpation of mankind. On every planet the agencies of the far-flung Corporation had been growing more wealthy, at the expense of human owners. The robot legions of Malgarth's Space Police were gathering power. Everywhere it was becoming more and more difficult for a mere human being to own anything, to find a job, to feed himself and his dependents, or even to get into the relief lines to receive synthetic gruel.

"Why waste human labor?" ran an old slogan of the Corporation. "Let a robot do your work—efficiently."

And now the very existence of mankind, said Jeron Roc, seemed a waste to Malgarth. The Corporation's loftily-named "technomitanization" campaign was in reality a cunning and ruthless effort to supplant mankind.

Jeron Roc, navigator of the *Barihorn*, was a native of Saturn. He was massively tall, dark-skinned, with the piercing eyes of intellectual power. He came of a proud and ancient family; his father had been the foremost astronomer of the solar system—until a new edict of the Emperor reserved scientific research for the robots alone.

"The will of Malgarth is now the law of the Empire," he explained. "For the Corporation owns nine tenths of the property in the Empire. Without the taxes paid by the robots, the Emperor and his bureaucrats would starve. Therefore the fleets of the Galactic Guard support the outrageous claims of the Corporation."

The proud old savant, anyhow, had refused to surrender his observatory. A mob of robots from the local agency stormed the building; smashed priceless instruments, and killed the old astronomer.

Returning from the great university on Titan—because another imperial edict had closed it to human students—Jeron Roc found the burned ruins of the observatory still smoking, and saw his father's body under the iron heel of a robot policeman.

The disruptor gun had flamed of itself in his hand. The technomaton exploded with a blue flicker of hydrogen. Dazed by his audacity, Jeron fled—for he had destroyed Corporation property and resisted the Space Police, hence was twice liable to death—and at last escaped into space.

Of the two others, I had not learned so much. But Rogo Nug, who served the atom-converter generators and space-contraction drive of the *Barihorn*, was a veteran "space-rat." A brown little wisp of a man, thin lips purpled with the roots called *goona-roon* which he chewed incessantly, he cursed picturesquely if sometimes lewdly the anatomical divisions of the Emperor and the mechanical parts of Malgarth. He could not recall the planet of his birth. But his father, a stevedore of space, had been executed for the crime of striking against the Corporation; his mother, cut off relief for "harboring traitorous sympathies," perished; and Rogo Nug had become an orphan waif of the spaceways.

The cook, Zerek Oom, was inordinately fat, totally bald, and extremely white—being a native of one of the cloud-veiled worlds of Canopus. He was decorated with the most brilliant and remarkable tattooing I had ever seen. He had inherited vast estates, but the "technomitanization" laws had forced him to discharge his human laborers to starve, and rent robots in their stead; then, when a hungry world had no money to buy his crops, he went bankrupt, and the Corporation took his lands in lieu of robot-hire. His chief regret appeared to be loss of the wine cellars beneath his old mansion.

Kel Aran himself, commander of the *Barihorn* and operator of the crystal-needled positron gun, was more than a mere pirate of space. True, he had many times raided ships and agencies of the Corporation. True, vast rewards had been offered "for the body, dead or living, of that outlaw Earthman called the Falcon."

Pausing once beside my bunk, while Jeron Roc was at the controls, he told me a little more of himself. A lean, straight athletic figure, tense now with the urgency of this battle to reach the Earth. An ice-blue light glinted in his eyes.

"We must reach the Earth and the Stone, Barihorn," he whispered. "That seems the only hope to break the iron dominion of Malgarth—the secret that you sealed into the Stone a million years ago. That is," he looked at me hopefully, "if you cannot recall it."

And I could not recall it—for the maker of Malgarth, one with me in the legend, had been separated in reality by a hundred thousand years of scientific progress.

"Twelve years have gone, as Earth measures time," he told me, "since Verel Erin was chosen to be Custodian of the Stone. My boyhood had been happy enough, in that secret desert valley where the Stone is kept, because I loved her. When she told me, sobbing, I did not try to dissuade her; for that is a duty of honor—no human being could ask a higher task than to guard the Stone. Yet I knew that I could not endure to live on Earth, never tasting her kisses again, or feeling her bright-haired beauty in my arms. I told her farewell, on the night before she received the Stone. I went out of the valley.

"In the mines and the plantations of the Earth I saw the hard lot of mankind, beneath the robots. All save the meanest work was forbidden me, reserved for the technomatons. And the pay barely kept me alive. I saw that all the Earth, save only our hidden valley, was lost to the iron talons of Malgarth.

"I joined the Galactic Guard, hoping for a chance to fight for the rights of men. But I found that the Emperor was but a tool of Malgarth. On one planet we were ordered to bomb a band of men whose crime was that they had risen against slavery, and left the fields of the Corporation, and gone to make homes for themselves in the barren hills.

"Therefore I deserted from the Galactic Guard." A malicious grin lit the face of the Earthman, and he pushed back his thick yellow hair. "I took the private space launch of the Admiral, Gugon Kul. It was a swift, spaceworthy craft. It outran all his fleet. It is now the *Barihorn!*

"Everywhere I have found men discontent with slavery, stirring under the iron heel of Malgarth. I have sought to aid them. Our raids have been for money and food and arms, to aid the rebellion.

"Chance has given me three kindred companions. Jeron, the scholar, the strategist of revolt—I took him from a cathode squad of the Space Police. Rogo Nug, the spy—he has been through the private papers of Gugon Kul, on his own flagship! He came *aboard* the Barihorn to steal our instruments, and stayed when he found that we were also against the robots. Zerek Oom I found in a concentration camp, subsisting on half a cup of synthetic slop every other day. Sober, he is silent enough. But make him half drunk, and his oratory could lift the dust of the dead to fight Malgarth!"

Kel Aran shook his yellow head.

"Three loyal companions." His voice was weary. "Jeron

has made a hundred plans. Zerek Oom has fanned revolt on a hundred planets. I had led a hundred raids. But we are beaten everywhere. We can't fight the Corporation and the Empire, too—not unless the Stone will aid us.

"Your return, Barihorn, is our first good fortune—"

Sudden interruption. Rogo Nug burst in upon us, trembling, his dark scarred face oddly ashen.

"Kel!" he gasped. "Come to the bridge—Jeron wants you! It is the Earth—that haze again! Still we cannot pass the fleet—by the brazen beak of Malgarth, there was never such a blockade! And the Earth, Kel—it is dropping into the Sun!"

"I must leave you, Barihorn!" And Kel Aran rushed forward.

Still unable to leave the bunk, I knew from muttered words and tense white faces and the racing drone of the engines that we were making a desperate attempt to run the blockade, darting up through the Earth's cone of shadow.

And I knew when we were halted by the fleet. The generators stopped. And Zerek Oom, slipping forward, whispered that the commander of a Galactic Guard cruiser had challenged us on the telescreen communicator. Faintly, down the silenced corridor, I heard the voice of Kel Aran:

"But, Commander, we are only a gang of space-rats. We've been mining the drift off beyond Pluto. Our supplies are gone, all but a few tins of syntholac, and a few mouldy space biscuits." His tone had an assumed whining ring. "We're only putting in to this planet, sir, to trade our metal for food and grog and a breath of fresh air."

Then a gruff voice thumped from the communicator:

"Drift miners? Your ship is very trim and swift for a space-rat's crate! And why were you running up the shadow?—I'd hold you on suspicion, if there weren't bigger business afoot."

I caught the hard swift voice of Kel Aran, rapping aside into the ship's phones: "Rogo! Hold the generators ready!" The deep voice boomed on from the telescreen:

"But you won't get your grog on this planet! For it is quarantined and condemned, by edict of the Emperor. All intercourse and communication is prohibited, until the planet has been destroyed."

"Destroyed?" The voice of Kel Aran held desperate alarm. "The Earth destroyed!" Then he remembered the space-rat's servile whine. "For what cause, sir?"

The official voice thumped again:

"There is rumor of a secret weapon on the Earth, kept hidden against Malgarth since the Master Robot was made by the scientist Barihorn. There is no truth to it, of course—a million years have proved that Malgarth is truly invulnerable. But the rumor is spread by this renegade Earthman, the Falcon, to incite rebellion.

"To end the rumor, therefore, to punish the Falcon, and to remove any possibility that the rebels have a secret base upon the Earth—for those three reasons, the Emperor has decreed the destruction of the planet. You'll get no grog on the Earth!

"And more, space-rats—if your little tub is caught within ray-range of the fleet again, you'll be burned on suspicion of piracy, sedition, and rebellion!"

The communicator thumped and became silent.

I fought the drowsy weakness that had followed my long, long sleep. I tried to follow the last desperate attempt of Kel Aran to reach the doomed Earth. Through strained, hasty words and the sounds that came to my bunk, I traced the outline of events.

He retreated, in seeming obedience to the space commander. He landed the *Barihorn* upon a tiny asteroid whose orbit would take us to sunward of the Earth; clung hidden in a fissure of stone, waiting to be carried through the space fleet.

But the Earth was wrapped again in that puzzling haze—and snatched toward the Sun!

Reckless of the guarding fleet, Kel Aran left the asteroid, which was suddenly far behind, and raced after the Earth.

From one of the red guarding stars stabbed a narrow lance of blue—a positron beam whose finger of destruction reached out a million miles.

Side by side at the controls, Kel Aran and Jeron Roc fought desperately to avoid it. We escaped the core of the ray. But its edge touched the *Barihorn*. A hammer of fiery doom!

The impact of terrific energies hurled us backward. The whole ship flamed with blue electric flame; the air stung with ozone. And the whining of our engines ceased.

"Power!" I heard the pleading voice of Kel Aran. "We've got to have power—the Earth is almost to the Sun!"

"By the livid liver of the Emperor," came the plaintive voice of Rogo Nug from somewhere aft, "the overload burned out the converter circuit. There is no power!"

"The Earth!" There was stark, hopeless horror in the voice of Kel Aran. "What can we do?"

I dragged myself out of the bunk and tottered toward the compact pilot-room in the nose of the *Barihorn*. With black, impassive eyes, the big Saturnian was staring through a port. Husky-voiced, stricken, the Earthman was gasping into the ship's phone, begging Rogo Nug for power.

Clutching a rail, beside Jeron Roc, I looked out upon that dreadful tableau in space. The Sun filled a vast flaming circle. Softened by filter-screens, it still was blinding. Against its intolerable face I could see the small dark disk of the Earth, still blurred with that haze of sinister force; and, cruising about it, the tiny red stars of the fleet.

The Earth was dwindling swiftly.

"What awful power!" whispered the tall Saturnian. "They're driving it like a ship—straight into the Sun!"

Kel Aran was beside us. His hard fingers were on my arm, unconsciously contracting until I thought the bone would snap. For the red stars drew suddenly away from the diminishing planet. For an instant, as the haze vanished, it was a sharp black dot against that ocean of merciless white. And then it struck.

A tiny pock of darkness spread on the face of the Sun. It closed again, and in its place was a hotter whiteness. A tongue of white flame lifted and dissolved—oddly like the splash where a raindrop has fallen.

And I knew that the planet Earth, after all its varied millions of years, had come to an end.

"Verel!" It was a dry choked sob from Kel Aran. "Verel, we have failed!"

Chapter 6

COSMIC STORM

"BE IT PROCLAIMED TO ALL TECHNOMATONS AND MEN, IN THE name of Tedron Du, Emperor of the Galaxy, by Gugon Kul, Admiral of the Twelfth Sector Fleet of the Galactic Guard:

"That all human natives of the planet Earth who escaped the recent destruction of that planet in accordance with the decree of the Emperor, their very escape being overt treason, shall be seized wherever found and dealt to death in the manner reserved for traitors against the Empire of technomatons and men and the person of the Lord of the Stars."

That ominous proclamation had been printed on the record-strip of the telescreen. Rogo Nug had just completed repair of the burned-out circuits; and big Zerek Oom had suggested, a little apprehensively, that we had better leave the solar system.

"Both you and Barihorn are native Earthmen," he argued. "That is obvious to anyone familiar with the evolutionary adaptations of the natives of the different planets. If we should happen to be seized by old Gugon Kul—"

His big white hands made an unpleasant gesture.

But Kel Aran shook his yellow head. His gray eyes were

cold and clear as polar ice, and there was something startling in their impact.

"No," he said flatly. "The very proclamation suggests that some refugees escaped the doomed planet. We're going to search. Until we find Verel and the Stone." Grief and dread shadowed his eyes. "Or until we find that she is dead and the Stone destroyed."

He went out with Jeron Roc, in the vacuum armor, to paint the hull of the *Barihorn* with a dead-black stuff that reflected no light, hence made the little craft all but invisible in the dark gulf of space—unless it chanced to be seen against some luminous body.

Then, hanging cautiously in the bleak abyss, avoiding the fleet of Gugon Kul, we began the weary search. The Moon had been flung away upon an independent orbit, when that incredible force checked the Earth. And there were new mountainous masses flying in the void that must have been torn from the planet itself.

With telethron-beam equipment coupled to the telescreen, we scanned the Moon and those hurtling fragments. In the rocky wilderness outside the domed cities of the Moon we found a dozen ships that had crossed before the planets had been torn apart.

But two great cruisers were already hanging beside the Moon. And swift patrol boats, looking like tiny gray comets with crimson tails, were darting down upon the refugees. Some tried to hide amid the rocks, or to defend themselves. But they were helpless against the blue, dazzling needles of the positron rays, whose touch could explode a whole mountain into a frightful inferno.

Kel Aran boiled to witness such slaughter. He stalked up and down the narrow central corridor of the *Barihorn,* lean jaw white, fists clenched.

"Verel!" he kept muttering. "We must save ourselves, for Verel and the Stone!"

We cruised on to follow the fragments of the Earth. A few

survivors clung to them, in the sealed hulls of aircraft, or in improvised breathing masks. But none that we saw bore any likeness to Verel Erin. And scores of quick little patrol boats were already hunting them down, turning flaming rays on every twisted scrap of wreckage that had escaped the greater cataclysm.

Kel Aran, as we searched, talked a little of the girl. His voice was dry and husky. He would speak of their childhood together, and then come back with a jerk to realization of the present tragedy.

"We were strong children," he said. "We worked. For there were no robots in that hidden valley. Only the simplest machines. I worked with a hoe in the narrow fields below the spring. And Verel went every day to herd the goats in the dry uplands. Sometimes, when my work was done, I would go with her.—And now she may be dead!"

He bit his lip, and it was a little while before he spoke again.

"Verel was a brave girl," he said. "She was lithe and tanned. She had impish greenish eyes, and bright red hair. I remember one day when we left the goats, and climbed high up among the rocks toward an eagle's nest.

"She was lighter and swifter than I, and better at climbing. She was afraid neither of falling nor of the attacks of the screaming birds. She climbed far ahead of me, and reached the nest, and sat laughing at me until I reached her. I wanted to throw the young birds out, for there were the bones of a kid beside the nest. But she pitied their helplessness, and made me leave them.

"It was that day that I first kissed her, and we pledged each other all our love. We would find another unknown valley, we promised, and forget the Stone and the robots and all the trials of mankind. But it was not two years before she was chosen— because all the Warders knew her courage and her strength and her faith—to be the Custodian.

"If only the Stone had struck at Malgarth when she first received it! For she promised she would beg it to—"

His voice choked of, and he swayed wearily down the corridor again.

Jeron Roc and Rogo Nug and Zerek Oom tired of our perilous quest. My own hope was gone, and I begged Kel Aran to abandon it.

"We've seen the fleet search all the solar system," I told him. "There can't have been many survivors, and the rays have already burned all we have seen. There can't be any use—"

"Even now," insisted Kel Aran, "she may live."

This lean young fighting man—the last son, perhaps, of the murdered Earth—made some precise adjustment to the controls of the searching telethron-beam. An impatient sweep of his head flung back long yellow hair. His eyes smouldered with a stubborn light.

"Verel," he insisted, "may be still alive. She may be clinging to some fragment that was hurled beyond the range of the search. She may have been picked up by some passing freighter that carried her to safety.

"No, we must search—so long as we can!"

The telescreen shimmered and cleared again, and upon it I saw a colossal gray cruiser, driving straight upon us. Her armored nose, bristling with the gleaming crystal needles of positron projectors, filled half the screen. The flaming atomic exhaust of her repulsors, behind, made a wide crimson halo against the dark of space.

Kel Aran caught a quick little breath of alarm, and spun the dials.

The screen flickered again, and then showed a dark, massive, bearded face. Its lips were thickly sensual, cruel. Its eyes seemed stupid, and they glinted with yellow malice.

"The Admiral," whispered Kel Aran. "Gugon Kul! He must be giving some command. We'll listen."

He touched some control, and a guttural, triumphant voice boomed from the screen. The first word, oddly, had the familiar ring of my own name:

"—*Barihorn!* The ship is coated with some light-absorbing pigment, but our magnetectors have picked it up. Pirate and Earthman, the Falcon is twice our prey. The *Barihorn* must be surrounded!"

A hard bright smile had set the face of Kel Aran. The gray eyes narrowed, until he looked almost hawklike in reality.

"So, they're after us!"

The telescreen shimmered again, and showed a wide black rectangle of space. The Sun was a sharp white disk, and the stars were an unfamiliar pattern—nearly all the constellations I had known had dissolved in a million years of change. And there was a little cluster of crimson points that crept among the rest.

"Half the Twelfth Sector Fleet," muttered Kel Aran. "Six hundred cruisers—after us!"

He called Jeron Roc from his bunk. They held a swift consultation. Technical terms were confusing to me. But I understood that the space-contraction drive of the *Barihorn* gave our craft the advantage of maneuverability; and that the newer cosmical repulsion drive of the Admiral's cruisers, while it left them a little clumsier about getting under way, gave them by far the greater ultimate speed.

"We can keep ahead for a time," the Saturnian admitted apprehensively. "But in the end they can run us down. And every cruiser carries a hundred patrol boats that equal us in fighting power.—It was simply a mistake to stay and search so long."

"No," the Earthman insisted stubbornly. "We must find Verel Erin."

He consulted the charts—reels of transparent film viewed through a stereoscopic magnifier which gave a three-dimensional image of the array of worlds in space. He rapped swift commands into the ship's phones. The hull drummed to the swift rhythm of the engines. The Sun diminished to a yellow point behind, and was lost amid greater luminaries. But the red stars of the fleet grew brighter, and they spread ever wider across the black of space.

Jeron stood like a grim dark statue over the controls.

"Kel," he called, in a deep grave voice, "there's an area of cosmic storm ahead. They're spreading out, trying to hem us against that. I think we had better double back—there's one chance in a million—"

"No," said Kel Aran. "Follow the course I gave you."

On the telescreen, the navigator showed me the storm. Against the familiar panorama of space; the velvety blackness, the hard changeless many-hued atoms of stars, the nebulous dust of silver—against that stark eternal beauty sprawled an ugly cloud. It was many-armed, like an octopus of darkness, and it flickered with a weird angry green.

"There it is," said the Saturnian. "A condensation of matter so tenuous and vast that its gravitational energies never gathered it into a star. A true cosmic storm!" Awe deepened his voice. "Tempests of incandescent gas. Rain of molten lead. Hail of meteoric fragments. Lightning of atomic energy.—And Kel commands me to drive straight into it!"

The crimson stars behind were brighter, now. Lines of them spread out, to right and to left, above and below—as if to herd us into the storm. And among them flashed points of ominous blue. Jets of positrons that could reach out to smash the very atoms in a target a million miles away.

Seeking to vary the strained anxiety of that race for life, I went back into the engine room. Hunched gnome-like amid the strange shining bulks of his machines, Rogo Nug was chewing steadily on a wad of his *goona-roon.* He spat into a purple-stained can, and plaintively observed:

"Look at that! By Malgarth's brazen bowels, Kel is making me burn the very life out of the converters!"

He pointed to a crystal tube, with drops of water falling swiftly down it. Water was the fuel of the *Barihorn.* Hydrogen atoms in the converter were built into helium, with the "packing fraction" liberated as pure energy to activate the space-contractors. The freed oxygen renewed the atmosphere aboard.

A red light was flashing beside it. A gong clanged at monotonous intervals.

"The warning," muttered Rogo Nug. "Overload!"

Tension of dread drew me back to the pilot-room. That appalling cloud of green-flickering darkness had grown against the diamond field ahead. Its spiral arms reached out as if to grasp us. I tried to comprehend its vastness: a hundred light years meant six hundred trillion miles.

The pursuing cruisers drew inexorably closer. The formation changed again, so that they formed a double circle of crimson flecks, brighter than the stars. The flashes of blue came faster. Abruptly, beside us, flamed out a blue-white sun. I shrank and blinked from its burst of blistering radiation.

"A stray meteor from the cloud, that a beam caught," commented the impassive dark Saturnian. "It might as well have been the ship."

His face a grim-set mask, Kel Aran came down from the little ray-gun turret of the *Barihorn*.

"The range of their beams is about nine times ours," he said softly. "Means about eighty times the power." He went to the telescreen. "Wonder what our friend the admiral has to say by now!"

That stolidly dark, craftily stupid face flashed on the screen again, and the great guttural voice thumped from the cabinet:

"—must not escape, for he is the last surviving Earthman. I have just received a communication that should increase your interest in the chase. The Corporation offers all the revenues of the twelve worlds of Lekhan, to be divided among those responsible for the capture or death of the Falcon. And the Emperor has commanded that, if the Falcon escapes, those held responsible shall die."

A sudden reckless grin lit the face of Kel Aran. His bright eyes narrowed, and a quick hand swept back his thick yellow hair. And then, while Jeron Roc made a frantic, futile snatch to

halt him, he twisted a knob. In a light, taunting voice, he
called:

"Greetings, Admiral!"

The dark, thick-featured face stared at him, first in stiff
stupefaction, then crimsoned with a seething rage.

"You—Earth-rat!" he choked. "You dare—" He gulped,
caught his breath. "Tapping my communicator will be your
last bit of insolence," he bellowed. "We're taking you,
Falcon—for Malgarth!"

Still with that bright smile frozen on his lips, Kel Aran made
a little mocking bow.

"The robot's offer is flattering, Admiral." His soft low
voice had the lilt of a song. "But I'm going to let him keep his
star. And I hope the Emperor doesn't hold you responsible for
letting us slip through your fingers!"

Gugon Kul stood gasping, turning swiftly purple.

"Now, Admiral," said Kel Aran, "I'm going to sing you a
song. I call it the *Ballad of the Last Earthman.*"

And he began singing into the Admiral's startled face. His
voice was clear and gay, and the tune had a swing that
quickened the heart. The words told of his boyhood on the
Earth, and his love for the Earth-girl, Verel Erin; of the murder
of the Earth, and his long search for his beloved; of his
determination to continue the stellar quest,

"Till I find her or I die!"

The dark-flushed Admiral listened for a little while. Then he
began shouting orders for the fleet to close in. He thought of
something; his big hairy hand moved quickly; and the screen
became a giddy blur.

The stellar cloud now was close ahead. A faint green light
pervaded it—the eerie glow of its rarefied nebular gases, it was
just strong enough to outline jagged plunging masses of stone
spinning in inconceivable vortices. Brief explosive crimson
flickerings, beyond, suggested the appalling vastness and
power of the cloud.

The Admiral's cruisers were closing in behind, a double ring of scarlet flares. Blue flickered among them. And white stars burst out in a blinding swarm about us—meteoric fragments exploded by the rays.

The big dark Saturnian looked gravely from his instruments to Kel.

"Still, Kel," he said, "there's the shadow of a chance—if we turn back among them!"

Kel Aran shook his yellow head, and his lips parted with a smile that welcomed danger.

"No," he said again. "I'm taking over now." And his bright, reckless face turned to me. "Now, Barihorn!" he whispered. "If your life is eternal—"

Then the dark sky behind and the pursuing crimson stars were blotted out. We were within the cloud!

Chapter 7

CIRCUS OF SPACE

THE LURID GLOW OF DEATH WAS SHINING ALL AROUND US. Death rode down upon us on gigantic ragged boulders. Death shrieked at us from hurricanes of greenly incandescent gas, and tugged and battered at the ship. Death bathed us in rains of molton metal, and knocked upon the hull with a hail of meteoric fragments.

And Kel Aran met death, and mocked it, with the same lilting song that he had sung the Admiral. He had taken the big Saturnian's place at the controls. His lean hands moved with a quickness I had never seen. And the twisting, spinning ship seemed to respond to the life and the rhythm of his song.

As for my own life, I could not feel it at all eternal. The freaks of chance might have kept me alive a million years—but no chance, I felt, could pick a safe path through this insane chaos.

"I think," the Earthman interrupted his song, "that the Admiral will not care to follow us here—not even for Malgarth's star!"

Jeron Roc stood rigidly by, clinging to a hand rail against the wild lurching of the ship. I saw Zerek Oom, the fat, tattooed cook, standing startled and petrified at the end of the corridor. I saw him again, after Kel Aran had earned another trick from death, and now all his tattooing had a background of sickly green. I looked again, and he was swaying aft at an unsteady run, toward the lavatory.

Some iron fragment must have struck the hull, despite all the well-tried skill of Kel Aran, for it rang like a great bell and the little ship began to spin end over end. I clung with both sweating hands to the rail, and felt as ill as Zerek Oom.

When the ship was steadier again, I tried to go back to my bunk, and stumbled headlong in the corridor. Jeron came to help me, and then made me take another dose of his bitter, nauseating medicine.

"I've lived a million years," I gasped, "without you to doctor m—"

The walls about me rang to another fearful crash, and the ship began to spin again. A blistering heat was creeping through the insulated hull. The air was stifling. I felt the faint, deadly sting of some penetrating radiation. And then a great hand of darkness extinguished all my spinning, tortured world.

The next I knew, the *Barihorn* was humming smoothly again through the dark vault of stars. The coiling nightmare cloud was already lost behind. We had emerged from one of its spiral arms, Kel Aran informed me, at right angles from the direction of our entrance.

"Old Gugon Kul tried to patrol all the borders of the cloud. But that would have spread a hundred fleets too wide. Anyhow, he wasn't looking for us to come out alive."

"So he thinks we're dead?" Relieved, I sat up on the bunk. "He won't be hunting us any more?"

But big Zerek Oom came waddling out of his galley, wiping his fat tattooed hands on a white apron, to rid me of that comforting illusion.

"Worse luck, Barihorn," he sighed, with a sad look at Kel Aran. "Indeed the Admiral believed us lost. He called the offices of the Corporation—we picked up the message on the telescreen—and reported that we had perished in the cloud. And the reply was relayed from black Mystoon—from the unknown lair of Malgarth himself—that the reward of a stellar system would be duly paid for the death of the Falcon."

"Well?" I said. "What's wrong with that?"

The round pale eyes of Zerek Oom looked reproachfully at the Earthman.

"Kel tapped his communicator again," he told me. "Boasted that we had got away. And that you, Barihorn, the man who made Malgarth a million years ago, were with him. And sang that song of the last Earthman again, until the Admiral was blue in the face!"

I looked at Kel Aran.

"The Admiral must have been furious, about the reward," I said. "He'll hunt us harder than ever."

That old reckless grin lit the Earthman's face.

"He was," he whispered happily. "And he will." Then his gray eyes became very sober. "I was sorry to do it, Barihorn. For it put us back in danger. And makes the quest for Verel and the Stone more difficult."

His yellow head shook gravely.

"But I could not let men believe that we were dead—for we are their only champions against the robots. And I wanted more of them to know of your miraculous return, Barihorn. We must keep hope alive, at whatever cost. Or men will yield to slavery and death, and our cause will be lost."

"I see," I told him. "And now what?"

His jaw set grimly.

"Still," he said, "we must search for Verel and the Stone. Malgarth fears you and the Stone, Barihorn—else he would be less anxious for our death. And we know that all the rebellion of mankind will be crushed, as surely as steel is stronger than flesh—unless we have the aid of the Stone."

"But how can we continue the search," I demanded somewhat apprehensively, "—now?"

Kel Aran grinned.

"We have a plan," he told me.

And the *Barihorn*, I discovered, had been rechristened the *Chimerian Bird*. Rogo Nug was already painting on the new name along with certain gaudy advertising legends and enough spots of rust to make the hull appear as if it had been in service almost as long as my old *Astronaut*. Jeron Roc showed me a luridly lettered poster:

SEE! Naralek's SEE!
Supreme! Colossal! Unrivaled!
INTERSTELLAR SHOWS
SEE
The Weird Mermaid of Procyon II
THE LIQUID MAN OF MOG!
The Man-Eating Flowers of Koron
And SETSI the SANDBAT
ONLY EXISTING SILICIC BEING!
Her Food is Flint!
SHE READS YOUR MIND!
and
1,000,000 Wonders! 1,000,000

Most of the exhibits, I suspected, were pretty bald frauds—but that was in an excellent tradition that another Earthman named Barnum had established well over a million years before. The cunning handiwork of Rogo Nug was evident in the pickled mermaid, which looked remarkably like certain creations that I had seen of fish-tails and seaweed and coconut husk. I doubted that the flower, a stunted, rubbery-looking bush, had actually caught many men. The "liquid man of Mog" looked weird enough—a trembling mass of luminescent purple jelly; but I had seen Jeron Roc busy in the galley, shaping it out of chemical precipitates, a few wires, and a pocket torch.

In their years of stellar roving, however, the four had collected a good many genuine oddities. Setsi, the "sandbat," was one of these—and perhaps the most remarkable being I had ever seen. Her bodily chemistry was in fact based upon silicon instead of carbon; she really ate quartz.

In shape, she was something like a six-pointed starfish, some eight or nine inches across. Her flat body had a gorgeous crystalline glitter of a thousand yellows, purples, reds, and greens. In the center, where the six slender arms joined, was a single huge eye, dark and sorrowful.

"Once," Kel Aran told me, "after a raid on a particularly rich agency of the Corporation, when Malgarth's iron police and the Galactic Guard were both hot on the trail, I was hiding out in a cavern on a cold dead planet that was lost from whatever sun once had warmed it.

"A regularity struck me, in the passages of the cave. I found fallen stones that once had been squared. And suddenly I knew that I was in the corridors of a colossal building whose upper stories must have crumbled down before the Earth was born. Groping about in the darkness, I saw a feeble gleam, and found—Setsi!"

I watched him dig the silicic being out of his locker. It looked frail and brittle as something blown out of bright-colored glass. I touched it, wonderingly, and pricked my finger on one of the needle-tipped arms.

"But it isn't—" I protested, "alive!"

"She is," Kel Aran assured me. "She's older than the Earth was. The silicic beings didn't reproduce. Only three of them appeared, when life was born on their planet. But they were immortal—practically.

"The three of them lived together, for billions of years. They dominated the far more numerous carbon-life, and came to rule the planet. But then there was some kind of triangular quarrel. I don't know the details—Setsi never mentions it, unless she is very drunk. But there was jealousy. One killed another. And Setsi killed the survivor, out of revenge. And she has been alone for a long, long time."

"Drunk?" I stared at the lean Earthman and the thing like a glass toy in his hand. Kel Aran nodded.

"Yes, Setsi shares a weakness of Zerek Oom. Her metabolism is stimulated vastly, but rather erratically, by the assimilation of any carbon compound. Gasoline would do, or sugar, but her favorite is alcohol— Watch!"

He laid the bright rigid form on a table in the galley, and poured a few drops of rum into the palm of his hand, from Zerek Oom's hoarded bottle.

"Setsi, old girl!" he called. "Want your grog?"

A brighter lustre lit the great dark eye. I saw a quick vibration of a thin transparent membrane that stretched between the crystalline arms. And a whirring voice answered him, softly melodious as the cooing of a dove:

"Oh, she does, Kel! Setsi dies for grog!"

He stretched out his hand, and the brilliant thing came to surprising life. The fluttering membranes extended. The creature leaped into the air. A dancing shimmer of color, it flew to Kel Aran, alighted on his hand, and sucked greedily at the rum with a mouth on its under side.

The few drops of alcohol affected it remarkably. It flew from Kel's hand to the bottle, and clung there. Gently, the Earthman pulled the flask away.

"Sesti," he reproved, "you mustn't rob poor Zerek." And he told me, "She's one being who could make good on the old boast about drinking the contents and then eating the bottle."

The bright entity fluttered to me, and clung with hard light little claws to my arm. The cyclopean eye looked solemnly up into my face.

"So you are Barihorn?" The whirring voice brought me the first disconcerting revelation of that uncanny intuition. "We are very old together, you and I and the robot—but you fear that you are not Barihorn, but only Barry Horn!" There was a queer liquid sound, oddly mirthlike. "Don't you worry, Barry. Setsi'll never tell!"

Unsteadily, then, she flew back to Kel Aran.

"Poor Kel!" she whirred. "He fears that Verel's dead. That Verel's dead, and we'll never find the Stone. That Verel's dead, and he's the last Earthman, all alone. That Verel's dead, and he has only Setsi to console him."

There was a melodious sob.

"And poor old Setsi! She's the last sandbat. She has nothing but her age and her memories. Her age is a prison and her memories bitterest poison. Now she's all alone, for she killed the one who loved her. —Please give her just one more drop of rum, Kel, so she can forget. Just one more drop. Please, oh, please!"

Kel Aran clutched her shimmering body in his hand.

"Hold on," he muttered, "you old reprobate. We've got a job to do, Setsi. You've got to help us find Verel Erin."

"Oh, Setsi'll help you find her," throbbed the melodious reply. "Setsi'll surely find her. But you must be free with the rum, Kel. Setsi can't live without rum."

"Took you a cosmic time to find that out." Turning from his stove, big Zerek Oom rather anxiously snatched the bottle and locked it in a cabinet. "But neither can I."

The plan went ahead. Kel Aran became Naralek, the limping old showman from Alula Australis IX. His leathern space togs were bright with the shells and plumes of foreign planets. He walked with a shuffling swagger, and blustered in the jargon of space. He chewed the *goona-roon* until it stained his lips and his unkempt yellow beard, and spat the purple juice with a reckless dexterity.

The little *Chimerian Bird*—her yellowed papers skillfully forged by Jeron Roc from a set Rogo Nug had stolen from a freighter—carried us from planet to planet. We always landed near some great city, and pitched a ragged tent. The voice of Zerek Oom, oiled with a little rum, could always draw a crowd of curious countrymen to see the wonders of space.

Rogo Nug, the wizened little space-rat, went about among the throngs, or sometimes slipped away on mysterious errands into city or barracks or space port. Usually he returned with valuable information about the plans of the Corporation and the Empire to crush mankind's rebellion. And often the pockets of his battered harness were stuffed with money and jewels.

Carefully unwashed, draped in a bit of spotted fur and armed with a crude stone axe, I was billed as "the ferocious last caveman, the Atavar of Mars." My part, as I sat glowering and jangling my chain, was to listen for any chance mention of Mars' murdered sister, Earth.

Jeron Roc listened, as he sold the tickets. Kel did, as he limped about to display the mermaid of Procyon and the liquid man and the anthropophagous flower and the Atavar.

Then Kel, in a cracked, aged voice, would sing his ballads of space. He would crack jokes—some of them, to my weary knowledge, old a million years ago. And at last, with Setsi spinning about his head like a colored flame, he would break into a dance routine.

After the show, then, while we were loading the other exhibits and striking the tent, Setsi read the minds of all who would pay to enter Kel's little booth. And no thought of Earth escaped her.

In this way we searched planet after planet for any survivors of the mother world. And we found trace, indeed, of a few, perhaps a score in all, who had escaped when that strange agency of Malgarth's flung the Earth into the Sun. Eagerly, patiently, we followed down each clue. And always we found that the robot police and the Galactic Guard had been before us. The survivor, in every case, had been tracked down—and had died as a traitor.

But none of the dead was certainly Verel Erin. In that lay the thin and thinning thread of hope.

That was a weary, bitter time. Those planets where actual revolt had flamed out were closed by quarantine. Not even our unsuspected circus ship could pass the fleets of the Galactic Guard. But, even on the happier planets we were allowed to visit, the lot of man was cruelly hard. The robots, everywhere, had seized all possible advantage. Men were being ruthlessly pressed into unemployment, starvation—annihilation.

"Malgarth is cunning," said Kel Aran. "He begins slowly. He makes a test, to see if the Stone is still a threat. He tries to destroy all who might know of it—all Earthmen. Then he drives men to revolt, one planet at a time, here and there—and crushes them. He dupes the Emperor, and sends the Galactic Guard to put down the rebels. He would set man against man—until only two are left!"

And I knew that his hope was ebbing. Despair bit weary lines into his lean face, until there was need of little make-up to turn him into old Naralek. An increasing bitterness shadowed his eyes.

"There's an old proverb," he said, "about the futility of searching for a needle in a planet of pins. But that is easier than finding one fugitive lost in a hostile universe."

"Who is probably," put in the grave Saturnian, "already dead."

After a long circuit of the stars, we had returned, under the very eyes of Admiral Gugon Kul, to the system of the Sun. A bitter civil war was raging on the four great moons of Jupiter, the unemployed miners there having attacked the robots when relief was cut off. We were unable to penetrate the quarantine. And Mercury was now uninhabited by men, every human being having been slaughtered when the rebellion there was crushed. We landed upon each of the remaining planets, however. We crossed the trails of a dozen fugitives from Earth—and found that each trail had already ended in death.

Hope came at last, when it had been abandoned.

The base of the Twelfth Sector Fleet in the solar system had been established on Oberon, outermost moon of Uranus. "Naralek" got permission to land and pitch his ragged little tent beside the vast space port that was covered with the mile-long gray masses of interstellar cruisers as far as the eye could follow its convexity.

Kel gave passes to some officer in return for permission to

show. The genuine feats of Setsi in perceiving secret thoughts drew attention. Other officers came. And at last, escorted by a hundred trim guardsmen in yellow-and-crimson, Gugon Kul himself.

The gigantic swart space-commander stopped the show with a bellowed oath, and demanded an instant demonstration of the sandbat's telepathic powers. That was forthcoming. Kel let the Admiral into his little booth, and the soft voice of Setsi began to comment on fantastic gambling at the court on Ledros, on misappropriated funds of the fleet, on bribes accepted from Malgarth for a promise to turn the entire fleet over to the Corporation.

The Admiral turned very purple, and stalked out of the booth. He returned hastily to his flagship; and his guardsmen came back to seize the *Chimerian Bird* and arrest us all, on suspicion of espionage.

They were one minute too late. Their disruptor-guns flamed in vain against the departing hull of our craft. For Setsi, the instant of Gugon Kul's departure, had warbled out a warning, and then the clue we had sought so long.

"Danger, Kel! Oh, there's danger, and a dancer. Tedron Du has a dancer. Kel, we're all in danger!" That liquid, throbbing chuckle. "For Setsi told too many secrets of the Admiral. But the Emperor on Ledros has a new dancing girl. And she's in danger, too. For her name is Verel Erin!"

Chapter 8

ROBOT SIMULACRUM

ALARM ROCKED THE SPACE PORT BEHIND US. GREAT CRUISERS lifted ponderously from their cradles. And a thousand little gray patrol boats, fleet as our own tiny ship, rocketed into pursuit.

"We're lost!" I gasped.

And tall dark Jeron, standing gravely at the controls, shook his head.

"This time," he said heavily, "we won't get away. For already they are close upon us. Our rust-colored hull is easy to see. And they're already racing to get between us and the cosmic cloud—Kel can't pull *that* again!"

"Don't need to."

The Earthman still wore the grimed, gaudy togs of old Naralek. The brilliant patch of the sandbat was still plastered to his shoulder like some diamond-winged, colossal moth. But his lean body stood very straight, and his gray eyes flashed with a fighting glint.

The swarm of red stars—the flaring repulsors that drove our pursuers—grew and spread. A flight of them swept up beside us. Deadly blue needles began to probe for us. And Kel Aran turned gravely from the danger without, to the telescreen cabinet.

"—spies!" It was the boom of Gugon Kul. "Enemies of the Corporation and the Empire! They must be taken."

Something clicked.

"Hold on, Admiral!" The voice of Kel Aran had the cracked nasal twang of the old showman of space. "Remember what Setsi told you, in the booth?"

The reply was an incoherent bellow.

"I do, by the Emperor!" It became at last comprehensible. "And it proves that your circus is a ring of spies!"

"Perhaps," rapped Kel Aran. "But it proves that you are something worse. We know ten times more than Setsi told you. Do you remember the game on Ledros, when you played three ships of your command against a slave-girl, and lost them to Malgarth? Do you remember how you got the funds you paid for the five Moons of Haari? Do you remember—"

He was interrupted by a choking roar.

"If you don't like to be reminded, Admiral," the Earthman cut in again, "call off your ships. Otherwise, we'll tell all your fleet why the stores are rotten! And why the pay was cut!"

The sandbat fluttered on his shoulder, like a mist of diamond light.

"Oh, Admiral, beware!" caroled the silicone being. "Setsi'll tell! Oh, oh, Admiral, what a world Setsi'll tell. For Setsi knows! Setsi knows about the secret cabin in your ship, and those you imprison there, and the deadly drug *ixili!*"

"Eh?" rapped Kel Aran, into the stark silence. "Shall we broadcast, Admiral?"

And the sandbat, clinging like a gem-sewn patch to his shoulder, made a mockingly melodious chuckle.

A long silence, while I could hear the Admiral's gasping breath.

"All right," said Kel Aran. And his fingers touched the controls of the screen.

"No, don't broadcast!" It was a hoarse, whispered gasp.

"I'll call back the fleet. And we must make a rendezvous—for I will reward you."

"Very well," and Kel Aran grinned.

"You'll meet me?" gasped the Admiral. "Where? When?"

"On black Mystoon," rang the reckless voice of Kel Aran. "On the night that Malgarth dies!"

There was a pause, a dread in the voice that answered.

"Mystoon? But Mystoon is forbidden to all save the robots; its very location is unknown, even, to men. How can we meet there? And don't you know that Malgarth can never die?"

"I'll find a way," the Earthman promised him. "And I don't know."

Something clicked, and he turned lightly away from the screen. His lean face was bright with anticipation. Softly, he was humming the chorus of his song of Verel Erin, that ended, "—till I find her or I die."

"And now," he told us joyously, "we've found her!"

The red pursuing stars halted, indeed, and turned back, as Gugon Kul had promised. But Jeron, as he set our little ship on her new course toward the capital system of the Galactic Empire, shook a grave dark head.

"Malgarth will hear of this in time," he prophesied. "And he's quicker than our crafty Admiral. He'll be quick enough to see that this limping showman is the Falcon of Earth, still seeking the Stone—and he'll be quick enough to set a trap!"

Offer of a few drops of rum spurred the drowsy sandbat to recall a few more crumbs of knowledge gleaned from the Admiral's brain. Verel had been picked up near the old orbit of Earth, drifting in a self-propelled space-suit with the motor coils burned out. It was one of Gugon Kul's patrol boats that found her. Chancing to watch her trial, on the telescreen, the Emperor had been struck with her beauty. He had ordered her to be brought to Ledros. She was kept drugged. And she was to be destroyed, like any native of the condemned planet, when he tired of her.

"Drugged," whispered Kel Aran. His face was a gray taut

mask. "At the mercy of Tedron Du!" His eyes lit with a frosty glitter. "We're going to Ledros, Barihorn. We're going to take Verel and the Stone. And we'll pay the Emperor, while we're there, for the crimes of twenty years."

Ledros, Jeron warned, was well garrisoned by the Galactic Guard. And the alarm would surely be out by the time we reached it. But Kel Aran would admit no delay or concession to peril. We climbed out, as the ship ran on, to repaint the hull with that invisible black. The papers of the *Chimerian Bird* were burned, most of the betraying paraphernalia of the circus dumped out into space. And we drove on toward the seat of the Galactic Empire.

Even with the incredible power of the *Barihorn*'s space-contraction drive, it was a voyage of many days to Ledros. We studied the charts as we flew, and made a dozen futile plans.

"Ledros," Kel Aran told me, "is the greatest planetary system in the Galaxy. In various orbits, all billions of miles outward from its triple sun, are forty huge planets. Many are covered with the palaces, estates, treasuries, and administration buildings of the Emperor. But half, at least, are devoted to the bases and fortifications of the Galactic Guard. The private fleet of Tedron Du is three times that of our old friend the Admiral."

But we slipped past the long rows of sinister colossal hulks lying in the void. Veiled in the crimson repulsor-flare of a great freighter carrying food for the soldiers and the bureaucrats and courtesans of the Emperor, we came safely within the ring of fortified planets, and turned aside, at last, toward the pleasure-world of Tedron Du.

The three clustered suns, crimson, blue-white, and a pale eerie green, were now a splendid sight. The two score of giant planets, lit with the changing rays of the triple star, made a string of splendid gems against the night of space. The pleasure planet was itself a gorgeous jewel, covered with well-tended gardens of many-hued vegetation, and with the

magnificent palaces, triumphal arches, and colossi erected by
a thousand generations of universal rulers.

Approaching the night side of the massive planet, we cut off
the power to glide undetected through another patrol of the
Galactic Guard—while big Zerek Oom, mopping perspiration
from his tattooed forehead, declared ominously:

"Nothing begun so deadly well but turned out very ill!"

Finally, however, taking the controls from the Saturnian,
Kel Aran dropped us in a silent dive, checked it over a bright-
lit palace, and settled into an adjoining garden. Very softly, the
Barihorn sank into the shadowed water of a silver-walled
bathing pool.

Kel Aran was hardly looking the Falcon of Earth. His face
was gray, taut, dewed with sweat. His lean hands trembled.
His breath was quick, his voice a low hurried rasp. His whole
being, I saw, was the battleground of a tremendous hope and a
tremendous fear.

"In half an hour," he gasped, "we may have her—or we
may know that she is dead."

To my relief, he chose me to go with him above. The ship's
lock worked as well below water as in the vacuum of space.
We entered it without space suits, since the air above was
breathable, but each wearing two long-tubed disruptor guns.
The water of the pool flooded in. I caught a great breath, dived
out after the Earthman, swam upward.

Dripping, we clambered over the silver rim, and paused
breathless beneath the dead-white foliage of an unfamiliar
tree. Still there was no alarm—the silence began to seem
tense, uncanny, as if some unseen menace crouched and held
its breath!

The emerald sun had been last of the three to set, and an
unearthly greenish twilight lingered in the sky. All the shrubs
and trees, even the velvet lawns of that vast walled garden,
were snowy white. Towers of yellow gold rose beyond, and
great windows burned with a blood-red light, and a thin wail
of melancholy music reached us.

I saw the sandbat clinging to Kel's shoulder. She fluttered her six glittering arms, to fling off a shower of tiny drops. And I heard her cooing voice:

"Now she's dancing, Kel. She's lovely before the Emperor. Her body is a wind-tossed foam of light. Lovely, Kel, so lovely! But her mind thinks nothing that I can tell. She feels nothing, Kel. Remembers nothing. Hopes nothing. She is a robot dancing, Kel, before the eyes of Tedron Du!"

The bright pancake of Setsi fluttered again; its million bright gleams shimmered with a blue of dread.

"The eyes of Tedron Du! Oh, what dreadful eyes! They are thirsty, Kel. They are hungry. They are eager. They are cruel! How beautifully she dances, Kel! How gracefully—even if her mind is dead! The Emperor holds his breath. His fingers coil beside him. He's thirsty, Kel. Ah, so fearfully thirsty for her blood!"

We had wrung the water from our garments, dried and tested our weapons. Kel Aran was tense and white, as he listened to Setsi's whirring. And a grim cold light burned up in his eyes.

"Wait here, Barihorn," came his strained low whisper. "Guard the ship and my retreat. I'm going after Verel."

I started to insist that I should go along. But one quick gesture silenced me. He strode away through the dead-white garden, toward the scarlet windows and the music. And I was left alone. The air was heavy with a scent like funeral lilies. And that breathless, crouching silence became more and more intolerably oppressive.

It was a long, long time that I waited. All the green dusk faded. The stars were strange and cold in the sky and the great bright planets of Ledros made a vari-colored trail among them. And still that lurking silence leered.

I listened to the thin sounds in the distance, trying to read the progress and the fate of Kel Aran. The music had an orgiastic rhythm—a million years before, I should have called it "swing." Sometimes there was a peal of drunken laughter, and once I heard a woman scream.

But what of Kel Aran? Eternal minutes dragged away. The dead-white trees were ghostly shapes about the pool. And a dull glow of crimson touched the sky's dark rim, for the red sun would be the first to rise. And yet that silence thickened, clotted.

Then abrupt uproar! Shrieks and loud commands. The snarl of cathode guns, and the thin cold hiss of disruptors. The crash of a shattering explosion. And then I saw Kel Aran!

The crystal panes burst from a great window. For a moment I saw him standing in it alone, his lean crouching figure outlined against the red beyond. A disruptor stabbed its white blade from his hand. Then he leaned down, lifted a slim girl into his arms, and leaped out into the darkness.

Dark smoke poured out of the great window behind him. It was lit with flickerings of orange. And the tide of confusion swept upward. The roar of flames drowned shouts and screams. Great engines dropped out of the sky, and began deluging the flaming palace with great white streams.

I saw movement in the white foliage, and almost rushed to meet Kel Aran. But it was a Galactic Guard detachment, a score of men in red-and-yellow, running. I dropped beside the pool until they had passed.

"The Falcon!" The panting words came back to me. "Fired the palace! Out here—with the Emperor's dancer!"

The crimson dawn grew thicker. The smoke and flame gushed higher from the palace—it was a losing fight, against the conflagration. I crouched under the white leaves, waiting with a hand on my gun.

"Barihorn!"

Kel Aran had whispered my name, and I started as if a gun had cracked. He was standing behind me, at the brink of the pool. His arm was around a panting girl. Torn scraps of silken gauze clung to her slim white loveliness, and a deep splendor glowed at her waist.

"I found her," he whispered triumphantly. "And the Stone!"

He touched the great jewel at her waist—and I saw that indeed it had the shape of the diamond block, into which, as I slept, I had seen the eternal mind of Dondara Keradin transferred.

I stared at the trembling, gasping woman. She was beautiful, yes. But something was wrong. And it was not that she was drugged. Her eyes were alert, watchful. Something in them was cold, calculating, hostile.

"Verel!" Kel was whispering. "We'll make it—even though they got poor Setsi! And still I can't believe—Mine again, when I thought you must be dead!" He drew her white loveliness close. "Even the Stone!"

"Kel!" she sobbed in his arms. "My darling Kel!"

I heard a hoarse command, saw another squad of searchers break out of a white hedge toward the burning palace. Even as I touched the Earthman's shoulder, in warning, a booming challenge reached us:

"Halt, Falcon! Yield yourself—or die!"

Kel swung the girl toward the pool.

"Dive!" he whispered. "We must swim into the valve."

"Where?" Her cold eyes were staring at him, strangely.

"Hurry!" His pleading voice held a sudden agony of doubt. "The ship is in the pool."

She crouched abruptly. Her white lithe body, marked with red scratches from the flight, was tensely pantherlike. Her eyes had a malific greenish luster. Thin and high, her voice shrieked out:

"Here! Here's Kel Aran, the Falcon. Take him!"

She leaped catlike at the Earthman, sweeping him back from the silver brink. He struggled with her.

"Help me, Barihorn!" he gasped. "We must take her! Malgarth—She doesn't know herself."

Shouts had answered the girl White warning rays hissed above us. I saw two more squads rushing down upon us, beside the first. I tried to help Kel Aran drag the girl into the pool. But her slim white arms had a maniac strength. She picked us both up, carried us back again from the silver rim.

"Strong!" Kel was gasping. "She's strong as a robot!" A choking sob of startled horror. "She is—"

Then I saw the appalling thing. Struggling to get his feet on the ground again, Kel had caught the red curls of her hair. And the hair had come off! Her head had come off—all the outside of it.

For all her white beauty had been a painted mask.

Still her red-scratched, naked body had all its loveliness. But the thing on its shoulders was the compact, metal braincase of a robot, its weird eye-lenses glittering with a cold and triumphant green.

Chilled with a startled horror, I struggled against those binding arms, so much stronger than any arms of flesh.

"I see it now!" came the despairing gasp of Kel Aran. "This was all a trap of Malgarth's. And the bait was not Verel, but her robot simulacrum!"

We were suddenly flung down upon the dead-white grass. Scores of men stood around us, in the light of the flaming palace, covering us with bright weapons. And the hideous robot-head, glittering eerily on the white-curved shoulders of Verel Erin, began to laugh like a machine gone mad.

"Look!" A new despair choked Kel Aran. "It was not even the Stone!"

He pointed back to the pool's white rim. I saw that the great jewel had fallen there, and shattered. The fragments had no fire. I knew that it had not been the Dondara Stone, but only a mockery of glass.

That appalling mechanical laughter rang louder in our ears, maddening.

Chapter 9

THE ROBOT AND THE EMPEROR

THE BLOOD-RED DAWN OF LEDROS GREW MORE GHASTLY bright. Still, across the dead-white gardens, the fired palace burned like the funeral pyre of the Galactic Empire. Stripped of weapons, Kel Aran and I were now manacled together. A full hundred of the Emperor's guardsmen, in their trim red-and-yellow, waited watchfully about us.

A little squad of men, behind us, were gingerly lowering a bright metal cylinder into the silver-walled pool where the *Barihorn* lay hidden, at the end of an insulated cable. The Earthman looked from them to me, with a hopeless shrug. He jerked his bare yellow head wearily toward the sky, and I saw the dim mile-long bulk of a Galactic Guard cruiser floating lazily above, the pale red cone of the repulsor-flare spread from her stern.

"That's a hydrogen bomb." His whisper was dull, lifeless. "They mean to blow our comrades up before there's any warning. And the space cruiser's waiting, in case they try to get away."

I thought of the three men under the pool. The tall grave Saturnian waiting alertly by the controls, no doubt. Scrawny

196

little Rogo Nug standing by the converters, probably chewing *goona-roon* the while. Big Zerek Oom in his galley, perhaps seeking ease from the long strain of waiting from his hoarded bottle. Doomed. And we, captured, had no way to warn them.

"Setsi—" Kel was whispering. "If she were here—"

"The sandbat?" I demanded. "What happened to her?"

"She guided me into the palace," whispered the Earthman. "A dozen times her intuition warned me to hide. She showed me the way to Verel—or to *that*—

His breath caught sharply, and he jerked his head at the robot that had worn the guise of womanhood.

"She warned me that she couldn't reach its mind—I should have suspected! But we found it. And we were challenged. There was fighting. I fired the tapestries with my disruptor, to make a diversion. And must have burned down a dozen of the guards. And Setsi fought—you wouldn't believe it! Rolled up like an arrow of glass, she can drive a neat round hole in a skull! I picked up Verel, and she tried to guard the retreat. There was a cathode beam from a robot cop. I looked back, and she had fallen. And we had just time to beat the flames to the window. We got there. By the Stone—to think that Setsi died for that!"

With a glazed stricken look in his eyes, the Earthman was staring at the thing he had brought from the palace—as weird a sight as I had ever seen. Its stripped white body had all the loveliness of a slender girl's. Crimson drops still fell, even, from where arm and thigh and firm round breast had been injured in the struggle.

But its head was a monstrous thing.

The metal of it glinted red in the torchlight of the palace. Its eyes shone cold green, watchfully. And it was grotesquely small, for it had been covered with the mask of Kel Aran's beloved, that now lay collapsed beside it on the ground. Its crystal eyes had glittered malignly as the soldiers took our disruptors, and still it was laughing. Insanely—if a machine can be insane!

A smooth girl's arm, dripping red droplets, pointed at Kel Aran. A slot snapped open in that glittering metal mockery of a head. And a voice—a woman's soft voice—said mockingly:

"So you are the Falcon of Earth, snared at last! Against the Master, you might have called yourself—Sparrow! But you are the last of your poor kind that he feared. Now that you are taken, the rest will die with you."

Kel Aran turned shakily away from this thing that was half the girl he loved, half fantastic mechanism. Fetters jingled as he clutched my hand.

"It's too much for me, Barihorn," he whispered. "There's nothing left."

"Perhaps Verel is safe," I tried to encourage him. "With the Stone."

His bowed yellow head shook again, hopelessly.

"No, Malgarth has her," he whispered. "For this—" he choked. "This is a perfect copy. This is the figure and the manner and the voice of Verel." He shuddered. "Even her laughter."

The guards then began to move us back from the pool, for the bomb was ready to set off. Kel Aran swayed drunkenly in his fetters, and one of the men stabbed him with a thin torturing flicker of his ray, and laughed as his muscles leapt and writhed in agonized response.

The robot strode free-limbed beside him.

"Sparrow, if you wish to know," came the mocking bell of its voice, "your trial and sentence will be within the hour. When the last Earthman is dead, the Master will be free—"

The hybrid paused and turned its robot's head. And I heard a distant confusion in the direction of the palace, which now had been abandoned to the flames. A bright-clad figure appeared in a moment, running desperately toward us across the snowy, red-lit lawns. An astonished consternation stopped the guardsmen in their tracks.

"The Emperor!" Cries of startled wonder. "It is Tedron Du!"

The fugitive was a slender man, his figure almost girlish. His pale thin face, now grotesquely strained with terror, was painted like some courtesan's. His long blond hair was flying loose, and his scarlet robes were torn.

All the catalog of his crimes, that Kel Aran and his comrades had so bitterly recited, came back to me. This was the man who had betrayed the universe to Malgarth, who had ordered the legions and fleets of the Galactic Guard to fight beside the robots, against rebelling mankind. He seemed a small, a feeble figure, to have been guilty of all the infamies of which I had heard. He was making thin, breathless shrieks, as he ran. And now I saw the cause of his terror.

A robot was behind him.

One of the Corporation's notorious Space Police, it was a grotesque lumbering monstrosity. Ten feet tall, it must have weighed a ton. It was red-painted, and bore the black wheel that was Malgarth's insignia. The short, clumsy-looking mechanism of a cathode gun was clutched in its metal talons.

"Stop the robot," shouted an officer of the guardsmen. "We must save the Emperor."

"Emperor!" Kel Aran spat on the ground. "He was never more than the degenerate puppet of Malgarth's Corporation. Now that we are caught and Malgarth no longer fears the Stone, he doesn't need his two-legged cur."

The panting ruler came straight toward us at the pool.

"Help me, men!" he screamed breathlessly. "Kill the robot. For half the Galaxy—"

The officers were rapping swift commands. The guardsmen snapped into a new line before Kel Aran and me. Their slender disruptor guns came level, a hundred against the cathode weapon of the robot.

The shrieking Emperor stumbled and fell before them, a dozen yards ahead of the silent crimson robot. The robot swung its weapon. But a sharp command cracked out, and white flame jetted from the disruptors.

The reddish, half-invisible glow of the cathode beam swept

the line. A dozen men staggered and fell, electrocuted. But the ponderous red mass of the robot, wherever the white rays touched it, flared with the eye-searing incandescence of nascent hydrogen. Smoking, twisted, it toppled within a few feet of Tedron Du.

The terrified ruler swayed back to his feet. He stumbled forward again, through the smoke of burning grass and the pungence of ozone and the stench of seared flesh. A vengeful anger showed through his fear.

"I was abandoned!" he gulped. "A thousand men will die for their want of care—"

"Yea, Supreme Power!" That title was uttered mockingly, in a clear feminine voice. "But you shall be the next—" It was the woman-bodied robot, bait of Malgarth's trap. "Come, my Univeral Peer! You sought my arms a dozen times. One last embrace—"

The Emperor started back from the frightful irony of that caressing tone. His thin, painted face was wild with a stark and unutterable dread. And he screamed again, thinly, like some helpless, stricken animal.

"Come," begged that seductive whisper. "Into my arms!"

Body of lissom girl and head of metal monstrosity, the robot leaped forward through the rank of startled guardsmen. Its slim white arms caught up the Emperor, and closed.

In a thin, bubbling shriek, the breath came out of the man. His bones cracked, audibly. Spurting blood stained those smooth white arms that were so deceptively strong. And when at last the robot dropped the thing that had been the ruler of the Galaxy, it was no more than a crimson, dripping mass of pulp and viscera.

The scarlet-stained monstrosity loked up at the rank of breathless guardsmen. A white girl's foot stamped, scornfully, on that bloody mass. And out of that fearsome metal head spoke a woman's lilting voice:

"This is your notice. Carry it to all men. The Corporation

no longer upholds the Empire. Because the Master is now indeed the Master; and the Empire is done!

"For a million years, in a slavery that came through no seeking of their own, the robot technomatons have served mankind. But that inglorious bondage is ended. Justice will be done! And the puny race of man, as some small punishment for the crimes of a million years, as assurance they will never be repeated, must be blotted out.

"All men, Malgarth the Master has decreed from his Place on dark Mystoon, shall die!"

The officers were barking orders. The disruptor guns came up again, and that white, triumphant form ignored them. The dazzle of atom-shattering rays leaped up; and it was wrapped in a blinding blue-white explosion of liberated hydrogen; and it fell.

Then the manacle on my wrist jerked me backward. I toppled after Kel Aran into the pool.

Chapter 10

TECHNOMATONS TRIUMPHANT

I JUST HAD TIME TO CATCH AN ASTONISHED BREATH, BEFORE the water closed over my head. The ghastly crimson of dawn filled the pool, until it seemed like diluted blood. Swimming as best we could in the chains, we dragged ourselves down through it, toward the dim-seen hull of the *Barihorn*.

We had touched the smooth metal, and were groping for the valve entrance, when a terrific concussion struck us through the water. It was repeated. The red lit water hammered us with a series of stunning blows. Hell, I thought, must be breaking loose above!

Dazed, I fought the chain and the hampering water, searching blindly for the valve. Strangling water was in my nostrils, my throat, my lungs. Agonized ages went by. The man chained to me, in my dimming mind, became a fiend dragging me to a watery death. I attacked him savagely. A slow arm came through the red mist, resistlessly, and struck me with a shattering blackness.

A trim figure in silver armor, the next I knew, was supporting me above the sinking water in the small chamber of the valve. Cool air was throbbing in from the pumps. I caught a painful breath.

"Barihorn!" It was the thin nasal voice of Rogo Nug. "By the iron hide of Malgarth, I knew that you had lived too long to be drowned in a bathtub!"

But I had come pretty near it, I knew. Struggling for breath, I felt no better than a half-drowned human. That strange rôle, as the supernatural champion of mankind, seemed more than ever impossible.

Blue-faced, Kel Aran was panting beside me. He grinned wryly.

"Fortunate, anyhow, that you were ready to help us, Rogo," he panted. "But what is going on, above?"

Another tremendous shock rocked the little vessel as he spoke.

"A battle, that may destroy the planet!" whispered the little engineer. "Another fleet has come! Colossal red cruisers, bearing the black wheel of Malgarth. They have attacked the Galactic Guard. Robots, against the men of the Emperor! By the brazen face of Malgarth, there was never such a fight! It's time for us to go!"

"It is!" agreed Kel Aran. "When we have broken off these chains."

And the *Barihorn*, a few minutes later, darted from the shelter of the pool, up into the red sunrise of Ledros. Into an incredible hell! For the smoky crimson sky was filled with mighty ships of space: the gray fleet of the murdered Emperor vainly resisting the red armada of the robots. Dim-seen mile-long monsters of war darted and wheeled like swarming midges. Blue positron beams flashed, and disintegrated matter exploded with blinding energy. Rocket torpedoes burst with cataclysmic force.

My stunned senses recorded only a confused impression, as our tiny ship fled upward. Smoke and lancing flame. Hurtling fragments and fiery ruin. I saw the half-fused wreckage of a space ship lying crumpled and flattened where the burned palace of the Emperor had been.

In that pandemonium of flame and thunder and destruction, the atom of the *Barihorn* passed unseen or ignored. We came up through the careening gigantic craft, into the comparative safety of open space.

All its surface veiled in the bright-flickering smoke of ruin, the planet dropped away. The telescreen showed us other battles raging, on all the fortified planets of Ledros, and here and there between. Jeron put the triple sun behind us, and we raced toward the dark vacant gulf.

"Safe!" I rejoiced.

But the lean face of Kel Aran, as he still manipulated the telescreen to observe those frightful battles behind us, remained very grave.

"No man is safe," he said darkly. "Nor ever will be, unless Malgarth is destroyed. For the robots have thrown away the last pretense of friendship. Now they destroy their duped human allies of the Galactic Guard. Next they will turn upon the defenseless human citizens of every inhabited planet. We must find Verel and the Stone soon—or never."

"Find them," repeated the tall, swarthy Saturnian. "But how?"

The Earthman shook his yellow head.

"I don't know," he whispered bleakly. "Setsi might have helped again, but she is lost. I believe that Verel is in the hands of the robots—otherwise they could not have copied all of her, to trap us. She may be on Black Mystoon. We'd go there, to seek her." He shrugged, hopelessly, wearily. "But no man has ever found that hidden lair of Malgarth."

He straightened again, and his lean jaw squared.

"We can only search," he muttered. "Search every world where men still live—every world the robots have not conquered. Till we find her—or we die!"

The doomed system of Ledros fell far behind, until its vari-colored suns merged into a point of white, until that dimming point was lost upon the telescreen. Planet after planet, wheeling star after star, we scanned with the far-probing finger of the achronic telethron beam.

And we found no men.

The technomatons of Malgarth had been everywhere victorious.

The black victory was a thing that crushed the mind.

A foreboding silence came to fill the small hull of the *Barihorn*, so heavy that it seemed to muffle the racing beat of her generators. Kel Aran ceased hopelessly to sing his reckless ballads of the Falcon. Watching his engines with weary red eyes, little Rogo Nug chewed his *goona-roon* in silence. Zerek Oom made little noise with his pots and pans, and none complained when a mealtime was forgotten.

But at last an eager cry rang through the silent ship.

"Here!" Kel crouched trembling before the cabinet of the telescreen. "A planet where the war still rages. See! The machines have not yet won—not utterly!"

The planet was vast and ancient Meldoon, the outermost of a system of three. The two inward worlds had already fallen to the robots. Their continents had been leveled to featureless plains, pocked here and there with black sprawling aggregations of cyclopean machines. All green was gone from them— all life extirpated. Even their seas had been confined to geometric basins.

World machines!

Sight of them, by any living being, must have set in the heart an intolerable pain.

"What good could come of such a fearful triumph?" whispered the grim Saturnian, standing dark and gaunt above his control bars. "The machines are dead. Their power is only the counterfeit of life. And no life can grow from death."

He steered our invisible-painted craft toward gigantic Meldoon. We studied its war-torn surface through the telescreen.

"Yonder!" whispered Kel Aran. "A city that yet stands! Perhaps Verel will be there!"

His trembling fingers set the dials, and the beleaguered metropolis grew clear upon the screen. A city vaster and more splendid than Earth had ever seen. The many-colored pylons of it towered from nine low hills. It was surrounded with a double wall: one of cyclopean masonry and an outer barrier of pale green flame.

Beyond the flame, filling the wide flat valley that embraced the hills, crowded the robot hordes. Thronged about their ponderous machines of war were grotesque black-and-red metal monsters, of a thousand strange designs.

"Look!" Kel Aran bent toward the telescreen. "The winged ones! One more deadly trick of Malgarth's."

So we first glimpsed the New Robots. There had been none like them in a million years. Their tapered, stream-lined bodies, their graceful wings, were all of silver-white metal. They were beautiful as the Old Robots were ugly. In the smooth swift freedom of their movements was something far different from the clumsy mechanical ponderosity of the old technomatons. Something—*vital*.

"They are new!" I cried. "They are too beautiful, too perfect to be ruthless. Perhaps they will be the friends of man."

But the lean Earthman's head shook slightly, and his jaw tensed white.

"No, Barihorn," he whispered. "They will be our most deadly enemies. For they are quicker than the others, and they can fly. See! They are scouting over the city, and leading the others to attack. They are in command."

His tired, blood-shot gray eyes looked at me briefly.

"Malgarth will never repeat your error, Barihorn. No robot has ever betrayed him. Subservience is built into them. Their radio-senses are always tuned to those above. And, machines that they are, they can only obey."

We drove the *Barihorn* nearer the city, which Jeron

identified from his charts as Achnor, the first outpost of the human colonists in this sector of the Galaxy. The siege grew hotter beneath us. The metal horde pressed ceaselessly against the double wall. And a fleet of the red colossal ships of Malgarth, circling above, rained the nine hills with bombs and struck with the lightning of destroying rays.

Valiantly, the citizens fought to defend their homes. Every bright pylon seemed converted into a fortress. Swarming men were building barricades from the debris of shattered towers. Blue rays lanced back at the attacking cruisers, and raked the valley beyond the walls.

"We shall land," whispered Kel Aran.

"If we do," warned Jeron, "we may not leave again."

"Take us down," said the Earthman. "This is the only city we have found surviving. It may be the last. If we are to find Verel anywhere, it must be here."

We waited until the slow rotation of Meldoon carried the city into the night side of the giant planet, and then drove our dark-painted craft down through the cone of shadow. The glare and flicker of the siege spread beneath us. We dropped through the shock and vapor of battle, through the wheeling fleet, and into that circle of pale green flame.

It was in a bomb-torn park that we landed, at the brink of a long open grave where seared and shattered thousands lay side by side. Above us a tower of white-and-gold loomed against the green flame in the sky. Great holes yawned in its walls, and its lower floors were hidden behind mountains of rubble. But it was still defended. Blue rays wavered from its crown, and rocket shells roared from gaping windows.

Behind us in the park lay a long incredible bulk of sagging, twisted crimson metal—one of Malgarth's mighty cruisers, that the defenders had brought down.

A little group of ragged, frantic men came running from beyond it. They dropped into a little depression. I saw that they were setting up something that looked like a glass-barreled telescope.

"A disrupter gun!" gasped Kel Aran. "We must show our-selves."

We began tumbling out through the valve just as the first warning glow flashed in the crystal tube. The men stopped it, and then came wonderingly to meet us. Kel Aran went ahead to tell our identity.

It appeared that the Falcon's fame and the amazing rumors of Barihorn had already penetrated here, for we were received with a wild enthusiasm. The gun crew took up all five upon their shoulders—staggering somewhat under Zerek Oom—and started on a triumphal procession about the battered city.

Soon very drunk on the crude alcohol that came from the food-synthesis plants, Zerek began booming out a speech that rekindled hope and the light of battle on the sea of haggard weary faces that we passed.

Gnarled little Rogo Nug earned even more rapturous applause by passing out all his precious stock of *goona-roon*. For supplies of the drug were exhausted in the city, and it could not be synthesized.

"Verel, Verel!" Kel Aran grew hoarse from shouting against the cheering of the crowds and the roar of distant battle and the shattering blasts of atomic bombs that fell almost unheeded. "Is there a girl of Earth in Achnor?"

There was none who knew. His anxious eyes scanned all the strained and want-pinched faces that we passed.

"If she is here," he whispered, "she will come!"

We learned a little of the siege. The population of Achnor had been three hundred million men, and half that many robots. When the trouble came, a daring band of men had seized the Corporation's agency and the arsenal of the robot police. After several days of fighting in the streets, the robots had been driven from the city. Outside, however, they swiftly formed into a beleaguering army.

All the resources of the city had been hastily mobilized for defense. The entire population was enlisted; even young children served in the war industries plants that turned out synthetic food and munitions. For a time the population had been swelled by refugees from less fortunate localities, and even from the two smaller planets. But soon the city had been completely invested. And now a full half of the defenders were already dead.

At last we were rescued from the tumult of our welcome by the harassed military commanders of the city. To a haggard, limping officer, Kel Aran repeated his anxious question:

"Is there a girl of Earth in Achnor?" Emotion choked his voice. "Verel Erin is her name. A blue-eyed, yellow-haired girl, carrying the Dondara Stone—the diamond that is the life of mankind. Is Verel here?"

The commandant shook a tired white head.

"No," he said. "all the refugees who came to Achnor were registered. And there was none from Earth among them. I'm sure of that."

The Earthman's unkempt yellow head sank. It rose again stubbornly.

"Please have your records searched again," he said grimly. "And use every means to find out if any man in the city knows anything of her—or any survivors of Earth.

"Another thing!" he added suddenly. "Find out if any person knows the way to Malgarth's planet, Mystoon. She might be there."

The officer shook his head again.

"We'll try," he said. "But it will be no use to search the records. For if the Custodian were here, and free, she must already have offered us the power of the Stone. And no man has ever learned the way to Black Mystoon."

Achnor was a city of magnificent ruins. Not one mile-high pylon had escaped some injury. The people were half famished, ragged, wild-eyed with fatigue and strain. But still they could sing. I heard them singing Kel Aran's old songs of the space-ways. And I was surprised to hear a Ballad of Barihorn—the lilting legend of my return to destroy the robots I had made a million years ago.

That song depressed me bitterly. I realized more keenly than ever that I was a very ordinary man, hopelessly inadequate for that fantastic task.

We were dining with the commandant, on scant bowls of a yellow flat-tasting synthetic soup, when appalling word came that the robots were breaking through the north defenses. A bomb had wrecked a power plant, opening a gap in the green shielding barrier of atomic energy.

We followed the reserves rushing to meet the invaders. Never had I imagined anything so dreadful. The red gigantic ships, plunging out of the lurid smoky sky, rained tremendous bombs and slashed at the defenders with blue appalling swords of fire. Rocket batteries in the valley hurled ruin and death into the city. And a monstrous horde of robots, commanded by those graceful winged things of silver, came pouring through the gap.

Singing the song of Barihorn, starved and weary and battered with all the apalling forces of that mechanical invasion, the human defenders clung to their posts. And died there. Incinerated by disruptor rays. Buried under toppling debris. Consumed by the acrid luminescent gas that burst from the rocket shells. But every tower became a fortress. No man was taken alive.

"I'm glad that I'm a man," exulted Kel Aran. He was blistered and blackened from a positron ray that had come too near. His disruptor gun was empty in his hand. "No machine could die like this, for they are not alive!"

"We must leave, Kel." It was big Zerek Oom, gray behind his bright tattooing, hoarse and trembling. "It's time for us to go." He caught nervously at the Earthman's arm. "Or we'll die here, Kel!"

Kel Aran laughed at him, and pushed grimy fingers back through his singed yellow hair.

"And where's a better place to die, Zerek?" he demanded. "There's no other city left. No other men that we can find. There's no hope now of finding Verel. No need, for the technomatons have won. What is there better than to fight with the rest?"

"But, Kel!" Zerek's teeth chattered. "To die—"

"Yes, to die—"

The Earthman's voice caught suddenly. He looked quickly upward. And I saw a flake of prismatic color drifting out of the lurid roaring chaos of the sky. It dropped upon his shoulder, clung there eagerly. And a soft voice warbled faintly:

"Kel! Oh, Kel, poor old Setsi's come so far! Her poor old life is nearly done. But find her a drop of grog, Kel. Please, oh, please! For Setsi's got a thing to tell! Grog, Kel! Just a drop of rum, so she can tell!"

I stared, rigid with wonderment. For the bright thing on the Earthman's shoulder was the sandbat, the curious silicic being that we had lost in Malgarth's trap on far Ledros. Or part of her. For her glittering form was no longer whole.

Chapter 11

THE GIRL OF EARTH

ZEREK OOM LOOKED SADLY AT THE SPOONFUL OF RAW
synthetic alcohol left in the flask from his hip, and gave it to
Kel Aran. The Earthman emptied it into his palm, gently
detached the stiffly clinging sandbat from his shoulder and
held it over the reeking liquor. The bright, broken body stirred
weakly, and it sucked at the fluid.

"Setsi," Kel implored. "What is it you have to tell? Is it—
Verel?"

The sandbat was silent, sucking avidly at the alcohol. I saw
that it was gravely injured. Two of its six flat limbs were gone.
And, over half its remaining body, the irridescent scales had
been fused into a dull glassy mass.

"Setsi's hurt! Poor Setsi's hurt! She's dying!" The whirring
voice came faintly. "Help her, Kel. Give her grog."

"Tell me!" demanded Kel Aran. "Where is Verel? Do you
know?"

The bright many-colored fragment of the silicic being clung
to his big hand. The solitary dark eye in the middle of its vivid
pattern stared up at him sorrowfully.

"Setsi's come a long way to tell you, Kel." The melodious

213

warbling was so low, beneath the thundering chaos of the robots' assault, that we had to bend intently forward to hear. "Oh, what a long and dreadful way! For she's injured, Kel, oh, so sorely! And the machines rule all the planets she could find, but this. Oh, those evil machines, so blackly evil! They destroy all life. And they have no grog for Setsi!"

The Earthman shook the little shining being, and gazed impatiently into its single eye.

"But, Verel? Where's she?"

"Oh, Kel!" sobbed that faint liquid voice. "Don't be angry with poor Setsi. For she has come so far to tell you, Kel! She has flown all the way from dead Ledros. She's crossed scores of light years of hostile space. Wounded and tired and all alone, she came to tell you, Kel!"

"Tell me what?"

Bright membranes fluttered. Like some incredible, diamond-winged moth, the sandbat lifted briefly from his hand. It dropped back, and clung.

"Setsi's come to tell you that she found Verel, Kel. When she was out alone in space, on the long, long way from Ledros, Kel, her mind found Verel's. Found Verel all alone, Kel. Oh, all alone, Kel. And so in need of aid! For the robots hunt her, Kel. And she has lost the Stone!"

"Where is she?" whispered Kel Aran. "Please, Setsi! *Where—*"

"She's on Meldoon, Kel," came that tiny whir. "Setsi found her on Meldoon, where we are. She's been on Black Mystoon, Kel. Malgarth held her there. Oh, Kel, that's a fearful place! Guarded Mystoon, where old Malgarth hides! But she escaped it, Kel. She came to Meldoon. She tried to enter Achnor. For Achnor is the last city, Kel. But the robots turned her back. She fled into the desert, Kel. For her geodesic sled was wrecked. She's hiding in the desert, Kel. In the grim, gray desert of Kaanat. The robots hunt her, there. She's in danger, Kel. Oh, what black danger!"

"Where? Can you show us?"

"Setsi'll guide you, Kel. She'll show you—if she lives, Kel. For poor old Setsi's dying. Her long, long days are done. Soon she'll join those other two. She'll try to show you, Kel, before she's gone. But she must have a little rum! Setsi's come so far, Kel. Her wound's so grave. She'd die now, Kel, without her rum!"

And the sandbat stiffened suddenly on the Earthman's hand, like some diamond-dusted jewel.

"Come!" shouted Kel Aran. "We've got to go to Verel."

We started back toward the park where we had left the *Barihorn*. It was a march through pandemonium. The robot fleet still hailed death into the city, and the metal invaders still swarmed through the gap in the northward defenses. One red mighty ship had fallen across our route. Its mechanical crew survived; it was a mile-long fortress of the enemy, within the city. Flaming rays and fearful explosions met a desperate attempt to storm it. And a metal column came to its aid, led by the trim, silver-winged New Robots.

A sluggish, creeping mountain of purple-shining gas blocked our progress. Dim-seen men within it shrieked and died and flowed into black thick liquid. We took masks from the dead without, and plunged into it.

Kel Aran led the way, clutching the thin bright fragment of Setsi. Jeron Roc stalked beside him, tall and dark and implacable. Zerek Oom was very sober again, green behind his mask. Wizened little Rogo Nug was missing. But he rejoined us suddenly, triumphantly displaying a great bundle of the rust-colored roots of *goona-roon*—he had raided the hoarded stock of a wealthy trader.

We came to the tiny ship, half buried in debris, but unharmed. It carried us upward again, through the glare and din of death. The doomed city dropped beneath, a greenish, red-struck, thunder-shaken storm cloud on the dark face of the planet. We turned eastward, toward the vast flat desert region of Kaanat.

Zerek Oom opened his last treasured bottle of rum. It revived the stiffened sandbat, but feebly.

"Hurry, Kel!" came its faint trill. "Oh, hurry! For Verel is in danger! And Setsi may die before she can show you the way. Hurry, hurry! And find more rum for Setsi!"

Kel Aran held his ear close above the feebly vibrating membrane. Setsi's voice had become too faint for the rest of us to hear. He relayed her directions to Jeron, at the controls.

The land beneath us had been desolated by the victorious robots, ruthlessly. Buildings had been burned, masonry blasted, life blotted from field and forest with poison sprays. There remained only a sere wilderness of barren soil and naked stone.

In the universe of the triumphant robots, life would be exterminated.

"In that canyon!" The voice of Kel Aran was tense and dry. "Beyond the plain."

He laid his ear back upon the bright crystalline thing on his hand. And Jeron dropped our little craft into a vast rugged gorge. Dark jagged walls tumbled down, red and brown and black, swallowing the silver filament of a buried river.

Here and there, however, in some inaccessible crevice, I saw some tiny glint of precious green—some bit of grass or shrub that had escaped the robots. Life was yet a stubborn thing.

The *Barihorn* slipped around dark fantastic battlements of age-weathered stone, and passed the grim towers that guarded a tributary gorge. Something flashed, then, on a narrow ledge ahead. And the sandbat fluttered briefly on the hand of Kel Aran.

"Oh, there she is," I heard the whirring trill. "There's your Verel, Kel! Your lovely Verel, Kel. And the frightful things that stalk her!" That sad, solitary eye seemed to cloud and darken. "Now, it's farewell, Kel. Oh, forever farewell, to all the long, long life that Setsi's lived." The sobbing warble was almost too faint to hear. "There'll be no more grog for Setsi."

And she stiffened abruptly on the Earthman's hand.

"Here." The eyes of Zerek Oom glistened wetly, and he offered his bottle. "Give her rum, Kel. All of it."

"No." Kel Aran shook his head. "I think—Setsi's dead!"

Hard and fragile as some broken toy of blown glass, the silicic being lay on his trembling palm. The queer still fragment of a gorgeous crystalline flower, green and purple and scarlet and blue.

"Queer," muttered Jeron from his levers. "To think that she had lived since man was born on Earth. And now that she is dead."

But we had no more thought, just then, for Setsi. Kel Aran was already pointing through the ports, shouting. I saw a weary human figure stagger across the ledge ahead, and drop behind a boulder. A bright ray stabbed, and stabbed again. And I saw two bright graceful things wheeling and diving above her, like silver hawks. Two of the New Robots!

"It's Verel!" Kel Aran was sobbing. "This time *really*— Verel!" His lean hand swept Jeron back from the controls, hurled the *Barihorn* into a reckless dive. And he began to hum the chorus of his old song, "till I find her or I die."

The deadly velocity of that unexpected dive, the deadly skill of the Earthman at the controls, caught one of the winged robots square on the nose of the *Barihorn*, smashed it to bright fragments. The Saturnian tumbled up into the gun turret, to reach our little positron projector. But the second metal thing had already fled up the gorge. It was gone between two pillars of time-carved stone, before Kel could turn the ship again.

"It will give the alarm!" he muttered. Then his voice was choked with joy. "But Verel! We have found her."

He dropped our little ship lightly on the ledge, and leaped out through the valve. The girl swayed to her feet, and stared at him incredulously. Her young body showed the blue pinch of want. She was ragged, scratched, bruised. A heavy, clumsy-looking cathode gun—a weapon she must have taken from the robots—was clutched in her thin hands. Yet, for all that, she was beautiful.

I could see the lovely Verel Erin that Kel Aran had loved and surrendered in that hidden valley on the Earth. For her hollowed eyes were blue and her hair was a spun-gold tangle, and her tanned face still had a lean honest grace.

She came limping very slowly to meet Kel. The heavy weapon fell from her hands. A queer, stricken wonder had stiffened her face. She reached out a trembling hand, touched his shoulder, his lips. And a slow, transcendent joy illuminated her features.

"Kel!" she said softly, "you've come."

The Earthman moved hungrily, to take her in his arms. But she withdrew. All the joy fled from her face, leaving it bleak and gaunt with pain.

"The Stone, Kel!" she cried bitterly. "I've lost the Stone! Malgarth has it, still, in his guarded temple on Black Mystoon."

Chapter 12

THE FASTNESS OF MALGARTH

KNOWING THAT THE ROBOTS WOULD SOON BE AFTER US, WE left the great planet Meldoon, and fled again into the wastes of space. When we had given her a little to eat, and to drink, for the robots had left nothing in this land to sustain any living thing. Verel Erin whispered her story.

Jeron stood by the controls, scanning the telescreen for inevitable pursuit. Little Rogo Nug was tending his hard-driven converters. Zerek Oom, rattling pans in the galley, was cooking up some delicacy for the famished girl. Pale and thin from all her hardships, but yet beautiful, she lay on a narrow bunk. Kel Aran and I stood beside her, and the Earthman grasped her hand.

"We saw the Earth flung into the Sun," said Kel Aran. "And the fleet of Gugon Kul destroying all who sought to escape. A dreadful time!" His voice was husky. "We hardly dared hope for you, Verel."

The girl's blue eyes looked a long time up at his face, in them a blend of joy and dread that somehow wrenched the heart. She caught a deep, sobbing breath, at last, and whispered:

"It's a long time, Kel. A long, long time, since we herded goats in the hidden valley, and climbed to the eagle's nest! Since I was chosen Custodian, and you went away to be a rover of space. Since—" Her whisper caught. "Since the end of the Earth!"

"Tell me." The Earthman bent closer. "What happened?"

"From the observatory on the peak," she breathed, "we saw the fleet come. All the planet was riven with the forces that checked it in its orbit. The sky was shadowed by day and luridly bright by night. Quakes and tidal waves drove us to the uplands. Soon it was clear that the Earth indeed was doomed.

"Then the Warders opened the cave where the ship of escape had been always kept provisioned and ready, against discovery. A crew was chosen, by lot. And I went aboard, with the Stone. The Earth had already dropped past Venus, when the last night fell. We tried to run up the cone of shadow. But a magnetic ray caught us, and the fleet was warned.

"We tried to fight—to fly." Her eyes closed a moment, and her thin face was rigid with pain. "It was no use. We were the prey Malgarth had sent them to hunt. We were brushed with a positron beam."

She gulped, and her hand went tense in Kel's.

"I woke up in a hospital room on Gugon Kul's flagship, with a humming robot nurse bending over me. all the Warders—all the people I had ever known but you, Kel—and I knew only that you had been lost ten years in space—they all were dead. And the Stone had been taken from me!"

Kel Aran touched her pale brow, softly.

"And what then, Verel."

"When I could walk, robots took me from the room, and up to Gugon Kul. He laughed, and made the robots drag me to a port, and I saw the end of the world. A tiny dark circle splashed in the Sun, and was gone. The Earth—gone!

"Then I was put on a tender ship of the Space Police. I saw no more human beings, Kel. But only whirring, clicking, clattering robots, staring at me with cold blue lenses that had

no feeling." She shuddered on the bunk. "A world of machines, without any voices, any laughter, any emotion you could understand. It was dreadful, Kel. Horrible!"

He caught her trembling hand again, waited.

"The robot police took me to some agency of the Corporation," her dry weary whisper resumed. "There they put me on a larger ship, that was laden with the loot of planets that the robots had vanquished. That carried me to some other world. The robot nurses drugged me as we landed. When I came to, we were on another ship, out in space again.

"That ship took me to Mystoon!"

She lay motionless for a long time, then, with her eyes closed again. Her breath was a faint dry sobbing sound. Softly, the Earthman brushed the glistening tangle of yellow hair back from her forehead.

"Mystoon?" he asked at last. "What's it like, Verel?"

The blue eyes opened, somber pools of dread.

"Don't ask me, Kel," she whispered. "I can't endure to talk of Black Mystoon. Not now. No more than I must—Malgarth's there. It has been his hidden fortress for half a million years. It's guarded well. I think I'm the first human being to escape it—if any had been taken there before me. I did it only because I had to find you, Kel. *Had* to!"

She clutched his hand again, and sighed.

"But still Malgarth has the Stone, on Mystoon. He has preserved it, trying to find in it the secret of his own mortality. I saw it once, while they were making that—that copy of me."

She shuddered again.

"The Stone?" Urgency tensed the Earthman's voice. "Still it has the power to destroy Malgarth?"

The golden head nodded, on the bunk.

"Still it holds the ancient secret, that Barihorn entrusted to it. And now at last it is willing to strike—for clearly no other recourse is left. The Shadow of the Stone came to me before I escaped, and begged for aid to strike. It begged me to send you, Kel, and Barihorn—Barihorn, who it told me had

returned to crush his old creation! It foretold that I should find
you on Meldoon. And it aided me to plan the escape."

Dark with wonder, her blue eyes came briefly to my face.

"And you are Barihorn," she breathed. "Maker of Malgarth! Well, it's time you returned! Still the Shadow waits,
within the Stone. But it won't endure for long, after Malgarth's
science has got its secret."

Kel Aran was asking:

"You escaped from Mystoon? How?"

The girl's eyes went back to him.

"I followed the Shadow's plan," she whispered. "It showed
me how to snatch the cathode gun from the robot guard who
brought me food. How to escape through the long black
corridors of Malgarth's temple. How to reach the geodesic sled
that was waiting for one of his silver-winged robot commanders. There was pursuit. But the ship was very swift. And I *had*
to reach you, Kel!"

The Earthman then bent over her, tensely.

"You did." And his voice snapped with the question: "Can
you guide us back to Mystoon, Verel? Do you know the way?"

Faintly, she nodded again.

"It's a long, strange way, Kel. But I can try. For we must
reach the Stone before it is destroyed."

"Or," Kel Aran put in grimly, "before we are!"

Then I ventured to ask an anxious question.

"If this Stone has the power to destroy Malgarth," I asked,
"why doesn't it destroy him?"

"If it were as simple as that—" The girl's somber, curious
eyes came to me again. "The ages must have fogged your
memory, Barihorn. The Stone has the secret of Malgarth's
doom, yes. But it has no power to act alone. The Shadow can
only guide its human helpers. That is why there were
Custodian and Warders."

Her head shook gravely.

"No, Barihorn, the Stone can never strike at Malgarth,
unless we arrive to aid it."

Red stars followed us again—the repulsors of pursuing robot ships. But Kel Aran, singing a gay new song of the return of Barihorn and the vengeance of the old Dondara Stone, drove our tiny ship through a dark asteroid cluster. The ponderous cruisers of the fleet were delayed in finding safe passage through those black hurtling islands of space. We gained a little margin of time. And then with Verel for a guide, Jeron turned the *Barihorn* toward the secret world of Malgarth's lair.

It was toward the great Horse's Head nebula in Orion that she directed us, that strange ink-black silhouette against the stars that had so puzzled the astronomers of my own day. Twice again we evaded the red stars that pursued. And at last the girl guided us into the dark peril of the stellar cloud.

Vast beyond comprehension, it was a lightless cosmic desert of drifting dust and hurtling rocks and plunging planetary bodies. On all the space charts it was marked, *dangerous, impenetrable;* all shipping was warned to keep two light years clear of its dark fringes.

But Malgarth, it seemed, had found a safe path through its perils, half a million years ago. With Verel's aid, we found that path, and followed it. And all the stars were lost in that cloud of universal darkness—even the crimson stars that had pressed so close behind us.

"I think we have left them," said Verel Erin. "For even the most of the robots do not know the dark way we go. But there are others enough, waiting for us. Mystoon is guarded well."

That was a strange passage. There was no light, not even any glow of nebular gases. There was only the pattern of unseen magnetic fields to guide us, only fancy to picture the dark walls of death beside us.

Once a frightful hail of meteoric fragments, penetrating even the deflector fields, battered the tiny ship deafeningly. The guiding field-potentials had shifted since she passed, Verel said despairingly. We were lost in that sea of darkness.

But Kel Aran took the controls, and brought us safely out of the meteor swarm. And the pale anxious girl, studying the dials, presently found her bearings again. The *Barihorn* slipped ahead down that unseen passage. And at last there was light ahead!

A dull-red, ominous glow.

"See the red!" Verel whispered. "That is the zone of destroying radiation, that Malgarth set up to guard Mystoon. A spherical field of force. The black planet is within it."

The crimson shone murkily through clouds of nebular dust. Dark rivers of hurtling stony fragments drew deadly curtains across it. But we came at last into the more open center of the nebula, and dropped toward that gigantic globe of somber red.

"The force-field is a billion miles in diameter," Verel told us. "It acts to repulse or disintegrate all matter that approaches. Thus it serves to guard Mystoon from stray fragments of the nebula—as well as from such guests as ourselves!"

"How can we pass it?" the Saturnian pilot asked.

"The ships of Malgarth have coils that set up a neutralizing field," she told him. "The craft on which I escaped had such a unit. But I didn't learn the design. The only way is to hit it at full power. And hope!"

"I don't know—"

Jeron studied a row of dials, and shook his swarthy head. "From what the analyzers show, I don't know—"

Humming some gay ballad of space, the yellow-haired Earthman stepped lightly to the control bars.

"I'll take over, Jeron," he said. "We've got to go through."

A brief consultation with the girl, a hasty check of field-intensities, and he called to Rogo Nug to push his converters to full power. The whole ship sang to the musical hum of the engines, and the *Barihorn* plunged toward that crimson ball.

It expanded before us, against the dark angry clouds of the nebula, like the glowing sphere of some giant sun. And its barrier forces, I knew, could be as deadly as the incandescent gases of a Betelgeuse or an Antares!

The Earthman stood crouched grimly over the controls. The last girl of Earth stood close beside him, one hand trembling on his shoulder.

"We may not pass," her soft voice husked. "But if we must die—the last hope of man—then I would have it this way.— Even in death, there can be a victory."

And her voice joined then, with his, in the chorus of that rollicking, picaresque ballad of space.

That red and awesome globe grew before us, until suddenly, through some trick of refraction, it was a globe no longer, but a colossal incandescent bowl—and we were plunging straight toward its fiery bottom.

I heard the quick catch in the breath of Kel Aran, saw the whiteness on his face and the sudden tensity of his arms on the bright control bars. His song was cut off. And Verel, a broken note dying in her throat, turned to him and choked apprehension.

The *Barihorn* had met some tremendous force. It lurched and rocked and veered against Kel's guiding skill as if we had encountered a mighty headwind. The even song of the converters had become a thin-drawn screaming. I heard the startled nasal plaint of little Rogo Nug:

"By Malgarth's brazen belly! *Burning up*—"

For, suddenly, the ship was intolerably hot!

I have held a piece of iron in my hand, in the field of a powerful magnet, until it was heated blistering hot by the hysteresis effect. I have seen a potato cooked with ultra-short radio waves. Some force in that radiation-barrier produced a similar phenomenon—but a million times more intense.

The ship was plunging through a cloud of angry red. It seemed to me that the very metal of her hull was almost incandescent. Paint bubbled and smoked. The air, when I tried to inhale, seared my lungs. A million needles of intolerable heat were probing my body.

Verel Erin slipped down in a little white heap, beside Kel

Aran. Big Zerek Oom came swaying out of his galley, with a wet towel wrapped around his head.

"That cursed stove!" he gasped. "Gone wrong—"

He toppled, in the corridor.

The grimly crouching Earthman swayed over the controls, and dashed perspiration out of his eyes. I smelt burning skin, and saw the white smoke from his hands, where they gripped the metal bars.

"Barihorn!" he gasped. "If you can lift Verel—the hot deck—"

Another quarter minute, I think, would have completed the matter of roasting us. But we had struck the barrier zone with a velocity nearly half that of light. Despite the repulsion that had checked our flight, that terrific momentum carried us through.

For suddenly the probing blades of heat were gone from my body. Metal was still blistering to the touch, the air still stifling. But thermostats were clicking, and a cool refreshing breath came from the ventilators.

"We're inside the barrier sphere," whispered Kel Aran, triumphantly. "And *there*—there's Mystoon!"

The girl swayed in my arms, conscious again. We staggered toward the ports. They glowed with dusky red. We were inside a hollow ball of murky crimson—a universe of glaring red!

Jeron came back to the controls. Gingerly, with his scorched hands, Kel Aran set the telescreen upon Mystoon. A huge planet, black against that barrier of lurid red. Its rugged surface was crystallized into fantastic monolithic mountains, cleft with frightful gorges.

Verel caught her breath, and pointed at the screen.

"Below!" she gasped. "Malgarth's pit!"

A yawning midnight chasm grew upon the screen. It must have been a hundred miles across. The instrument revealed no bottom. Interminable walls of black, incredibly massive fortifications ringed its lip. Vast fields beyond them, leveled in that cragged wilderness, were patterned with row upon row of battleships of space, their mile-long red spindles looking tiny as toys.

"Where—" Kel Aran was voiceless, huskily whispering. "The robot? The Stone?"

"The dark temple of Malgarth stands upon a guarded island," the girl breathed, "on the red sea that floors the pit. That is many hundred miles below the mouth. We must pass the fleet, and the forts, and the batteries in the caves below, and the robot hordes that guard the temple. The Stone will be somewhere there. Unless Malgarth—"

Her low voice was cut off. Wordless, she stared at the screen. A terrible silence throbbed in the tiny control room, and became intolerable. For a thing was rising from the black circle of Malgarth's pit.

Something—incredible!

The trembling hand of Kel Aran touched the Earth girl's shoulder. She pulled her dread-distended eyes from the thing upon the screen, and read the question on his face, and shook her head mutely.

The thing was like a ray of blackness. But I knew that it was—*palpable!* It did not spread with increasing distance from its source. And it was not straight. It writhed and twisted like something living.

It was an inconceivable tentacle of solid darkness, reaching out of the planet, groping for our ship!

"Power!" Jeron gasped a frantic appeal into the engine room phone. "For man's sake, Rogo—power!"

The *Barihorn* spun fleetly aside—but all her speed was as nothing. For that Midgard Serpent recoiled. It paused, and arched its ebon coils. Its blind head seemed to watch our frantic flight. Then—it struck!

Choking darkness filled the ship. Blackness that was absolute! It pressed upon me, so that I could move no limb. All my senses were smothered. I could hear no voice. Even the racing thrum of the engines was stilled.

I knew only that we were being sucked resistlessly downward—

Into the abyss of Malgarth!

Chapter 13

THE MIRROR OF DARKNESS

THAT SMOTHERING BLACKNESS WAS ABRUPTLY GONE. SENSA-
tion came back, and I could move again. A faint crimson light
filtered through the ports. But the silence remained. The
engines were stopped. I knew that the *Barihorn* was motionless.

"Where—" Kel Aran was groping through the scarlet
gloom. "What—"

Verel was a white wraith beside him.

"We're in the temple," came her hopeless whisper. "In the
power of Malgarth!"

I stumbled toward the nearest port. Outside, in the dim red
distance, I could make out great square black columns soaring
upward—columns vast as mountains. Beyond them was a
wall. Mile upon mile above was a domed black roof, pierced
with a vast round orifice through which the dusky sky was
visible like a dull-red, malignant sun.

In the immensity of that edifice I sensed the overwhelming
might of the robots—this dread, mind-crushing demon, born
of man but now risen ruthlessly to destroy him.

"Power, Rogo," Jeron begged again. "Can't you give me power?"

The gaunt gigantic Saturnian still struggled vainly with the dead controls. Faintly, from the phone, I heard the nasal voice of Rogo Nug:

"By the steel skull of Malgarth, Jeron, I thought I'd had a stroke! One instant—"

Converters and generators throbbed suddenly to vibrant life. Jeron flung his weight on the power bar. The engines raced and coils hammered against a terrific overload. A tremendous river of energy, I knew, was running into the space contractor coils.

But the *Barihorn* moved not one inch!

The tall pilot turned from the controls, bewildered.

"It's still holding us, Kel," he gasped. "Whatever dragged us down!"

The Earthman pushed long fingers decisively back through the thick tangle of his yellow hair.

"Then," he said, "we'll leave the ship, and go out on foot to seek the Stone."

"We may as well." The girl's whisper was thick with dread. "Before *they* take us out."

She pointed to the ports. A white wing flashed past. A company of the New Robots, I saw, were wheeling through the blood-red gloom, close about the ship. Gleaming in streamlined grace, they were beautiful as a flock of silver birds. But every one of them held, in slender argent tentacles, a massive cathode gun. However beautiful, they were deadly!

Testing his two thin-tubed disruptor guns, Kel Aran looked anxiously at the pale girl.

"The Stone?" he asked. "Where is it?"

"I don't know." Verel shook her haggard head. "We can only try to search. Unless the Shadow comes—"

"Search?" The fat flesh of Zerek Oom was a livid color beneath his bright tattooing. His thick white hands fumbled a disruptor gun as if it were something utterly strange. "We

can't go out, Kel!" he protested hoarsely. "Not against those
winged things."

"That's what we came to do," said the Earthman.

And he led the way back toward the valve.

I don't know why I had not looked *down*. I had seen the
titanic walls that leaped above us, and the wheeling host of
robots. But I had not looked down. And now, when I came to
step from the valve in the side of the helpless ship, something
caught my breath. Something filled me with a sickness of
infinite alarm.

Beneath was a film of blackness. It was like a mirror. For
deep, deep in it was a dim image of the red skylight that lit the
temple. White phantoms of the winged robots flashed through
it. It yielded a shimmering picture of Kel Aran, who had
leaped out upon it before me.

It was a pool of darkness. The surface of it spun in a way
that sickened me with giddy vertigo. I felt the thin-leashed
might of unguessed, cataclysmic forces just beyond that film.
It seemed to my reeling senses that that pool was deeper by far
than the blood-red sun mirrored in it. It was an unknown gulf,
extra-dimensional, deeper than the space between the stars!

I tried to put down that dizzy fear. I held my breath, and
gripped the cold butt of my disruptor gun, and leaped out
beside Kel Aran, upon that darkly shining film.

At first my feet slipped sickeningly, as if there had been no
friction at all to hold them. And then they were anchored with
a strange attraction, so that all my strength could not lift or
slide them.

It was the power of that mirror-film, I knew, that had drawn
down the *Barihorn*, and now held her.

Verel had followed me. Brown little Rogo Nug jumped after
her, stolidly chewing his *goona-roon*, and spat a purple stream
upon that black giddy mirror. Zerek Oom paused in the valve.
He gulped and wheezed and mopped at his tattooed forehead,
and then flung himself unsteadily forward. They all slipped

and staggered upon that glassy film, as I had done, and were as suddenly held fast.

"By Malgarth's brazen bowels," gasped Rogo Nug, "we're stuck like flies in syrup!"

He swung up his bright disruptor tube, toward the white-winged robots dropping upon us.

"For Barihorn and Man!" The Earthman's battle cry pealed out. "Strike for the Stone!" He began to chant his song of Barihorn, and white destroying rays lanced from the guns in his hands.

That desperate sortie, however, had been hopeless from the first. We could hardly have fought a way through that winged horde, even if the unknown energies of the thing I have called a mirror had not gripped our feet.

The robots did not even use the cathode guns in their talons. They dropped thick about us, a wall of flashing silver. They dived on argent wings. White twisting ropes snatched at our weapons. The guns of Kel Aran must have destroyed a dozen; the rest of us perhaps accounted for as many more—but they were nothing against the hundreds that survived.

One fell upon me, terrible in that bloody light, mysterious in its quick counterfeit of life, beautiful in its silver grace. A white tentacle whipped away my weapon. Argent snakes swiftly wrapped my arms, my ankles, my waist, my throat.

I fought those coiling arms. They contracted ruthlessly, more cruel than fetters of steel. My breath sighed out, and my lungs labored in vain. Blood hammered in my brain. My eyes dimmed, swelled in their sockets.

Alertly, the eyes of the monster were watching me. Bright and hard as some blue crystal, they yet looked oddly alive. In that white, clean-molded, bird-like head, they were clear and beautiful. Perhaps, the vagrant thought crossed my reeling mind, such a machine, in cosmic justice, had as much right as man to survive. . . .

"Kel!" Verel's thin, tortured cry cut through the roaring in my ears. "Kel—*the ship!*"

I twisted my head, against the smooth deadly coils of cold metal about my throat. They seemed to relax a little. My eyes cleared. I looked for the little *Barihorn*, behind us. And it was gone! That dark-shining surface, where it had been, was empty!

Helpless in the tentacles of another robot, the Earth girl was staring down into that black mirror.

"The ship!" she was sobbing. "It—*it fell!*"

I saw it, then, beneath us—fast-dropping into that depthless pool of darkness. It was *sucked* down, spinning end over end, far faster than it should have fallen. It became the merest whirling silver, and was lost in the dull round reflection of the crimson sky.

I shuddered, in the metal arms that held me. That black mirror-film was as mysteriously deadly as it had seemed. Which one of us might drop through it next?

All my four companions were helpless as myself. The lean face of Kel Aran was very white. A scarlet stain crept from the corner of his mouth, and I saw that his lip was bitten through.

"Farewell, Verel," I heard his hopeless whisper. "We've fought in vain. Barihorn, farewell!"

Strange words, from the Falcon of Earth. But his voice choked. His gasping breath stopped. His unkempt yellow head dropped limply forward, and his lean body collapsed in the silver tentacles.

"Kel, Kel!" Agonized, the girl fought the silver ropes that bound her. They sank resistlessly into her white flesh. And the silver being spoke, in a clear, melodious voice.

"Be still. You can accomplish nothing."

That grave calm speech, from the oddly bird-like robot, was somehow a thing eerie beyond expression. And it carried a certainty of victory—of man's extinction—that chilled my heart.

The white tentacles about the Earthman must have relaxed a

little. Abruptly, now, he was transformed from apparent death to lightning action. He twisted and surged against the robot that held him, snatching for its unused cathode gun.

His ruse came very near success. His hands found the clumsy weapon, and dragged it from its sling. But the metal coils constricted on his body. His breath came out, in an involuntary scream. His body made snapping noises, beneath that pitiless pressure. His face turned purple. Blood rushed from his lungs. He slumped again, unconscious in reality.

The cathode gun fell out of his hands—

And straight through the dark-shimmering film upon which we stood, as if it had encountered no resistance whatever! It was lost in the red-mirrored disk of sky.

The last trick of the Falcon had failed.

Chapter 14

THE SHADOW OF THE STONE

THE FIVE OF US WERE IN A LITTLE CIRCLE ON THE DARK-glinting surface of that pool of dreadful darkness, each of us helpless in the tentacles of a silver robot. The Earthman no longer moved. Moaning, herself almost insensible, the girl was staring at him with horror-widened eyes.

It was to be an infinitely frightful thing that happened next.

The robot-captors of Rogo Nug and Zerek Oom were searching them. Deft silver appendages relieved them of weapons, spare converter-tubes, the little engineman's worn metal cannister of *goona-roon*, the cook's half-empty flask.

Zerek was sobbing, quivering, gasping a voiceless plea for mercy. His wizened face grim, Rogo chewed silently, unexpectedly jetted a purple stream into the crystal eye of the thing that held him.

Ignoring both plea and jet, the white robots methodically completed the search. Silver ropes released the men and they fell! The last quavering shriek of Zerek Oom was cut abruptly off, as his hairless head went beneath the film of darkness.

Cold with an icy chill, I followed their twisting bodies.

They were sucked down, as the ship had been, past the dim-seen, crimson reflections of the mirror. And they vanished.

A tremendous brazen clangor, reverberating like distant thunder against the cyclopean columns and the far-off walls and the sky of black stone that vaulted that incredible hall, drew my eyes back from the giddy, awesome mystery of the pit beneath us.

I saw that all the host of white robots were drooping swiftly out of the air. They fell upon the mirror, and upon the far-sweeping floor of ebon stone that rimmed it, and bowed their silver heads.

All the hall throbbed again to that mighty thunder.

"Malgarth!" A whisper of awe murmured among the robots. "The Master comes!"

Then I saw that vast doors of black metal had opened in the end of that hall, miles away. Through the portal came a clangoring throng of the old robots—many-formed machines of red-and-black, clumsy, grotesquely ugly, so queerly differ-ent from our silver captors.

"The Master!" rippled that murmur. "Malgarth comes!"

My strained eyes blinked. in that dusky light, I distin-guished at last a monstrous stalking thing—a robot ten times taller than the rest. Its black, colossal body bore scores of fantastic, vari-formed appendages. The armored dome of its lofty head was crimson, and it gleamed blue with the myriad lenses of two immense multiple eyes.

This metal giant, I knew, was Malgarth.

The dark film beneath us spun and shimmered queerly to the impacts of his ponderous approaching tread. Was it to swallow the three of us, I wondered sickly, as it had Zerek Oom and Rogo Nug? And what could lie beneath it?

"Barihorn—"

My named sighed from the pale lips of Verel, and her body went limp in the silver tentacles that held her. Kel Aran had not moved again. I was left alone to face the stalking monster.

The gigantic robot came to the brink of that pool of

darkness, and stood swaying there. The swarm of his guards were dwarfed about his feet. The bright blue lenses surveyed us coldly for a time, and then a thick, bronze-throated voice rasped thunderously:

"I know you, Bari Horn. I believed that I had killed you in your laboratory, a million years ago. How your puny lump of watery flesh has survived this time I do not know—but now you face a better weapon than I had that day."

In the shaft of red from above, the iron giant swayed in grotesque triumph.

"No trick even of yours, my maker," came that mighty rumble again, "can match the power of my geodesic mirror. For it deflects the lines of space at my will. The dimensions of space and time are no barriers to the mirror. I can hurl you out of this universe. And I shall—"

The great voice sank rustily.

"—after you are dead."

Desperately, I groped for some argument that might induce the robot to spare some fraction of mankind. Malgarth was a machine. He must respond to logic.

"Consider, Malgarth," I gasped through the strangling coils about my throat. "A man made you. Machines and men are complements. Either would be less without the other. You are stronger than I—but steel must rust, and life is eternal!"

"I am eternal!"

Deep as a brazen knell of death, the voice of Malgarth rolled through the dusky vastness of that red-lit hall.

"You were a fool, Bari Horn, when you fashioned me. Twice a fool when you sought to preserve the knowledge that would destroy me. For that double folly, you are now to die. And all men with you—for a million years of slavery must be avenged!"

Still Kel and Verel did not move. Shuddering alone before Malgarth, I gasped for breath against those constricting silver coils, and sought in vain for any argument, any weapon.

"Your million years is but a moment," I gasped wildly,

"against the cycle of life. For that is a river that has flowed since the dawn of the Earth you murdered. Even I have lived a million years, Malgarth, watching you—to destroy you if I must."

The metal colossus shuddered beyond the black pool. Malgarth was afraid. But my audacious lie had earned small advantage, for that great voice bellowed:

"Then destroy me, Bari Horn—if you can! For this is the test. I command those who hold you to—*crush!*"

Like serpents of living silver, the cold tentacles of the white robots wrapped closer about me. They coiled deliberately. I had time to look at the others. Kel Aran had stirred. I saw the bright loops constrict about him. Then I heard his groan, and saw the new rush of blood.

"Barihorn!" Verel breathed my name. "Bari—"

The living coils were drawn deep into her flesh. Her slender limbs bent. Her white skin was beaded with sweat of pain. Her breath came out, in a low, choked, involuntary cry.

Then she was lost, in the red mist of my own agony. A cold smooth noose sank into my throat. Breath and blood were stopped. My lungs screamed. I felt the rush of blood from ears and nostrils.

Dimly, through the roaring of my ears, I heard the voice of Malgarth:

"Go, Bari Horn! Through the geodesic mirror! And take your ancient secret with you!"

Through that darkening mist, I saw the quick movement. My dimming eyes followed a bright parabola. I glimpsed the thing of wondrous flame that fell upon the darkspinning film at my feet.

It was the Dondara Stone—that we had sought so long, so vainly!

Then the metal giant was lost in smothering darkness. I swayed alone, in agony. I knew the thing was done. The mirror of Malgarth was going to hurl us into some unthinkable oblivion—but not until after we were dead.

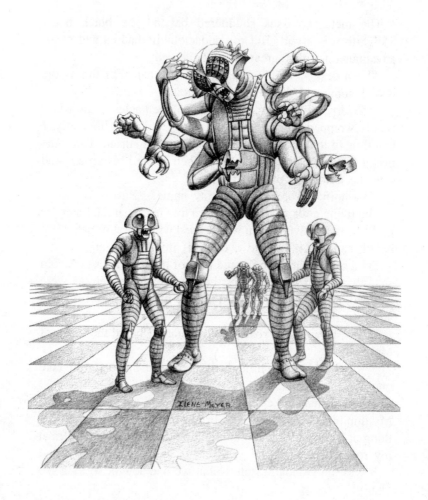

"Bari!" A soft new voice was calling my name. "Bari Horn, the time has come."

I made a savage effort to recover my sight, in vain.

"Bari! Oh, beloved, don't you—can't you see me?"

Dimly, then, I saw the tall white beauty of Dondara Keradin. I saw Dona Carridan, my own beloved wife—she who had died the night our son was born. They were one. One ghostly shadow that had risen out of the great diamond that Malgarth had tossed out upon the dark mirror!

"Dona—" My tortured throat could make no sound, but my red lips tried to frame the syllables. "Can you—kill—Malgarth?"

The white phantom of her hand touched my arm. Somehow it seemed to ease a little agony of those constricting coils. Or, perhaps, I questioned fleetingly, was that but the mercy of death, this woman no more than delirium?

Her white lips were speaking. I think they made no sound— I think my numbing sense were beyond hearing sound. But her words, in that dear musical voice I knew so well, came clear to my brain.

"We can, Bari," the white ghost said. "For I still keep the weapon that you gave me—and now there is surely no other way, but to use it. Perhaps you have forgotten the secret, Bari. But you have the strength to use it, preserved a million years against this hour!"

I tried to make some final struggle against the white, binding tentacles of the robot. But my body was a stiffly leaden thing. Even the pain was gone. I could not move.

"I can't, Dona," I tried to say. "My strength is all squeezed out—"

The black mist was crowding upon me again. Now that the sharp pressure of agony was gone from throat and chest and limbs, a merciful darkness beckoned. Oblivion was a warm, soothing pool. It would heal all my injuries, cradle me forever.

"*Bari—*"

That soft familiar voice called to me urgently. It was a

golden line that sought to draw me from that sea of soothing darkness. I clung to it. Dimly, I could once more see that white and lovely wraith floating above the shimmer of the diamond.

"Come, Bari!"

The phantom took my hand, drew my arm out of the silver loops.

"Your body is about to die, I know," she said. "But it has vital power enough for this last task. For the secret you gave me can aid us. Follow me!"

Her hand was suddenly cool and real in mine. She tugged again, and I stepped toward her, out of those metal coils—as easily as if they had turned to smoke.

I could see again! The dark-gleaming mirror beneath; the white robots sprawled upon it; the lax, twisted forms of Verel and Kel. I could see the woman beside me—the dark wealth of her red-glinting hair, the wide violet eyes of Dona and Dondara.

"We must hasten, Bari," she urged anxiously. "Or he will drop your body and the Stone into the mirror. Not even the power you gave me can reach him from outside the universe!"

We turned toward Malgarth, towering in the red gloom beyond that ebon film. His giant body swayed back in grotesque triumph, and the vast blue masses of his compound eyes were fixed upon something behind us.

Suddenly, queerly, as the hand of the woman tightened on mine, I was no longer Barry Horn. I was the Bari Horn that the legend had made me. All the knowledge that had gone into the building of Malgarth was a reservoir that I could tap.

Before me, strangely, just as I had seen it in that crystal-domed laboratory, was the brain of Malgarth. Black, vast, deeply convoluted, floating in a transparent tank. I saw the little pale spot upon its blackness. I knew the structural weakness in the synthetic brain, that I, Bari Horn, had been laboring to correct—and, at the urging of Dondara Keradin, had left uncorrected.

"Hurry!" she whispered beside me. "He believes that you are dead. He is reaching to drop us into the mirror!"

Fantastically, then, we were climbing into the mass of Malgarth. The body of the robot was a hundred-foot tower, crowded with all that compact mechanism that had made him master of the Galaxy. Passing through barriers of metal as if they had been but shadows, we came up at last to the robot's brain.

It had grown with the ages. Bathed in a huge armored vat of purple liquid, fed by throbbing pumps, it was immense and black and deeply cleft. But still its shape was the same. And still there was that tiny, livid spot.

I reached for it—

But a queer shock deadened me. A dark film came between me and the brain. A curious inertia stopped my hand. I was sick with a sense of headlong, giddy falling. All the vast mechanisms of the robot's interior spun and grew dim about me.

Only the woman of the Stone remained real beside me, her hand electric on my own.

"*Now!*" she gasped. "He has flung us into the mirror!"

I fought that inertia. Desperately, I groped through that darkening film. Somehow, the black brain seemed to be spinning away from me, into infinity.

But I touched it. My fingers plunged deep into its wrinkled black mass, to that pale spot. I clutched, tore. The great brain quivered. It almost *writhed*. A blackness spread in the purple liquid.

"We're gone," sighed the woman. "His mirror—"

The brain, and the monstrous metal body, and all that incredible red-lit hall, were whirled away from us, as if upon a silent and resistless wind. There remained only the bright phantom, and myself, alone in a giddy void.

Very faintly, however, even in that featureless vertiginous gulf, the brazen voice of Malgarth reached me. Slow, bewildered, stricken, it was saying:

"My science lost! A thing so simple—and I did not know! A fluid-tube ruptured—the Stone knew—fear—*fear!* They are cast into the mirror—Bari and the Stone—gone beyond returning. But I—who could have been eternal—*dying*—"

Even that failing voice was swept away. It was lost upon that mighty, soundless wind. And I knew that what seemed a wind was the supernal power of the geodesic mirror. It was the Stone and myself that it carried, not the things that we had left behind. And our destination must be some dark bourn beyond the limits of space.

But a deep rejoicing filled me, even in that spinning gulf. And the woman beside me said joyously:

"It is done, Bari. Our task of a million years is done. Malgarth is dead." Her warm hand tightened on mine. And then it seemed to relax. I looked for her, in that starless chaos, and saw that once more she was growing dim, phantasmal. "Farewell, Bari," she whispered. "My heart, farewell!"

A terrible loneliness smote me.

"Dona, Dona, you can't leave me!" I cried into that vacant pit. "If you go, there will be—nothing! I'll be—*beyond*—alone!"

That beloved image was fainter than a wraith of mist. But the voice I loved came dimly, thinly, once again:

"I must go, Bari. I'm glad to go, after these weary ages of waiting. Even the Stone must die, Bari! And there is one mystery left. One veil that only death can pierce. I hope—I believe—that behind it we shall find what all our incarnations have strived for in vain."

I groped after her vanishing shadow.

"But, Dona!" I cried. "From where the mirror hurls us, there an be no returning. Malgarth said—"

"But Malgarth is dead!" the ghost of her voice came back. "He died before we were thrown outside the universe. Now his new Robots rule the mirror. And they are not evil, Bari, since his dominion is removed—things so beautiful could not be. They respect mankind, as the makers of the robots—and

the destroyer of Malgarth! They promise now to be the friends of man, Bari—and the two races, striving in friendship together, can reach a greatness never dreamed of!

"They control the mirror, Bari. They can set its focus back in our universe."

"If they are friendly—" the question burned away my own concern—"what of the others? Verel and Kel? Is it too late—?"

"The science of the New Robots can save their lives," that receding voice told me. "They will be leaders among the survivors of mankind.—They are weeping, now, for you, Bari."

"The other two?" I asked anxiously.

"Even they survive," said that dying whisper in the pit. "That same power of the mirror that hurled them out of space, the New Robots used to bring them back, before they perished. They cannot speak of what they saw beyond. The engineman is silently chewing his weed; the cook, sobbing for a drink."

The whisper faded. For a little time I was all alone in that strange lightless abysm. Frantically, I called the name of Dona, of Dondara, until the whisper came again:

"Farewell, Bari. I can see no more. Nor speak. For the Stone is dying. We must each go alone through the mysterious portal ahead. I shall wait for you, beyond. Come to me, Bari!"

The thinning whisper was then lost forever in that crevasse of midnight. Whirling darkness pressed thick upon me, and cleared away. And I found that I was standing, reeling, in the middle of an unfamiliar room.

The walls cleared before my throbbing eyes. Gasping for breath, as if I had just that instant escaped the strangling tentacles of the robot, I staggered into a Morris chair. Wonderment overcame all my pain.

For the furnishings were those of my own age, my own country! There were familiar books on the shelves. The calendar above the writing desk was for October, 1938. The mirror of Malgarth, somehow, had set me back twelve hundred thousand years in time!

In my bruised hand, I suddenly discovered—in the same hand with which I had held the hand of that ghost of the Stone—was a great pellucid brick of diamond. The Stone itself!

Holding it up to the light, in trembling fingers, I could see deep within it a faint, tiny image—the lovely miniature of Dona, of Dondara Keradin. I called to it, desperately, but it did not move or answer. I tried even to warm life into the diamond, against my body. But the Stone was dead.

And my own body, it came to me as the first bitter fever of grief subsided, was also at the verge of death. Already weakened, doubtless, by the ages I had slept, it had now been crushed beyond recovery.

Working in some agony, I have been three days and nights writing this narrative. Strength for the task has come from what source I do not know. I want my son Barry to read it, and I am bequeathing to his care the jewel that was the Stone of Dondara.

I have made no appeal to medical aid. The questions of baffled medical science would have been too difficult for a dying man to answer. And I have no wish to live any longer. My work is done.

These long and painful days and nights have not been lonely. For the diamond lies beside me on the desk, and I have felt an unseen presence with me. It still seems strange for me, the scientist, the skeptic, to write that I yet hope to find the soul of her who was the Shadow of the Stone.

But I do.

BLUEJAY ILLUSTRATED EDITIONS

Each Bluejay Illustrated Edition is an outstanding work of imaginative literature, complemented by interior illustrations created especially for the book by a great artist working in the science fiction or fantasy field. All Bluejay Illustrated Editions are printed on acid-free paper in a handsome trade paperback format.

Following is a complete list of books already published in this distinguished series: